The Poet's Daughter

by

Konnie Ellis

Also by Konnie Ellis:
The Dharma of Duluth
The Ice Dancer

"The Poet's Daughter," by Konnie Ellis. ISBN 978-1-947532-26-7 (softcover): 978-1-947532-27-4 (eBook).

Library of Congress Control Number on file with the Publisher.

Cover photo by Lane Ellis

Published 2017 by Virtualbookworm.com Publishing Inc., P.O. Box 9949, College Station, TX 77842, US. ©2017, Konnie Ellis. All rights reserved. No part of this publication may be reproduced, stored in a retrieval system, or transmitted in any form or by any means, electronic, mechanical, recording or otherwise, without the prior written permission of Konnie Ellis.

For the immigrants

PART ONE – NORWAY

BERTHA

1891

Chapter 1

"YOUR MOTHER IS DEAD." I was six years old when I heard those words. After that pronouncement, everyone around me seemed to be speaking at once, yet I heard nothing but a blur of voices and the clinking of coffee cups. The room was strong with the smell of coffee, and I stood at the edge of a forest of black skirts and heavy shoes. I maneuvered myself to the back of the pantry where I could look out the low window to the green yard and our apple orchard and the fjord beyond. The gulls were circling out over the bay and back toward the dock, where they dipped down, snatching bits from the fish cleaning table. Nearby, the small green boat rocked in the water beside the dock. It was the boat my mother used to row me and my brothers down the fjord to the flat rock point for picnics.

"Berta, come here," someone called, and when I turned, I walked through flour on the pantry floor and watched my footprints appear as though made by a ghost. Aunt Inga led me to the parlor and settled me on the rocker that creaked, the one I didn't like. Before she returned to the kitchen she said it was all right about the flour. I didn't remember spilling flour and I said it was a ghost that did it. I felt the heat of guilt on my cheeks, as though I were to blame for of all the darkness in our house that day. I slipped down from the rocking chair and stood behind the drawn curtains of the parlor and felt the sun on my face. I closed my eyes and became invisible.

That same day I was put to bed on a cot with a heavy patchwork quilt in a back room where I had never slept before. It was still light out and my aunt's big yellow cat sat at the end of the bed, looking straight at me. I fell asleep, even though I tried to keep my eyes open. I didn't know if I was awake or dreaming as I relived the events of that day of my mother's death. My father had walked with me to her room where she was lying in bed with her hair down and shining like it had just been combed. She smiled at me and held my hand in hers, and I felt the burning warmth of her hand around mine. Her smile was just a little smile, but I knew it was just for me. Her face was pale and she looked very tired, but also beautiful. I knew that my mother was beautiful, even more so than anyone in our whole town. She didn't cough once the whole time I was in the room.

It was while I was in the kitchen having a glass of milk that she died. I knew this before anyone told me because I heard someone scream with the worst sorrow you could imagine. The scream started high and then dropped as low as a sorrow could go. I went to the bedroom door and looked in. I saw that my mother's face was empty and that she was dead. My whole body shivered and then I was gone. When I came to, the house was crowded with people and my aunt was sitting beside me.

From that day until I left by train, my little sister and I stayed with my aunt, who lived on the upper side of our house, just up the hillside from our house. Since my mother's illness, our baby sister, Aagot, had been staying with the Johnson family who owned the store down near the dock, so it was just little Mette and myself at home now, with Father, and our two big brothers, Konrad and Peter, up until the time Mother died. By then we had sometimes stayed at Aunt Inga's house overnight, so in some ways it didn't seem like a sudden move away from our own home. I think that since it was impossible to understand my life at that time, I just had to go along with whatever happened. At least that's what I tried to do. I mostly kept my feelings to myself during the day.

My sister, Mette, slept when they took my mother to the graveyard beside the church. Mette was only three years old and still took naps. I was not allowed to go to the church or the graveyard, but I watched the procession from my aunt's bedroom window. I was supposed to be napping too, but I was too old for that, and I watched my family and the minister and the school teacher and all the neighbors walk slowly toward the churchyard, everyone dressed in black. I remember it as if the people were walking a few inches above the road, like they were floating toward the graveyard. Although I could hear the clomping of horses' hooves, even the horses seemed to be hovering slightly above the road as they moved along. The wooden coffin was covered with white and yellow flowers, and appeared to wobble as the horses pulled the wagon along the old dirt road. My brothers followed close behind and I wanted to leave the house and run after them, but I knew that I couldn't. I had to stay with my sleeping sister.

I was old enough to know that my mother would be buried in the ground. I had been to the graveyard with my mother in the very recent spring to put flowers on great grandmother's grave. Mother had told me how it was done and that the spirit of the dead rose to a special place of peace and that the body remained in the ground, for the flowers, she said. And I knew the verse about "dust to dust." Still, I felt afraid. If she was gone, anyone could be gone. I didn't want it to be true. I lay down on my cot and hid my head beneath the pillow.

It was not long after the burial that my father received a letter from our relatives who lived on the Lofoten Islands, off the coast of northern Norway. Erling Johnson brought the letter to the house one sunny afternoon when I was in our yard folding clothing fresh off the clothes line. Aunt Inga would take down the items, and I would fold them carefully and place them in the basket. The whites were bleached white from the sun and the whole basketful smelled like summer.

I followed my aunt inside. My father sat down in the big chair and took his glasses out of the round table drawer and opened the letter. I folded my hands together tight because he looked serious. When he finished reading, he looked at me for what seemed like a long time, and then smiled a sad smile. He didn't say anything at first, so we just stood there waiting, with my aunt holding my dried yellow Sunday dress over her arm. That's when he told me I would be going to stay with my aunt and uncle on the Lofoten Islands. He said Uncle Albert Bratberg was Mother's brother. Father spoke directly to me and not to my aunt, saying that they were kind folks and that I would like them. Then he stood quickly and looked out the window.

My aunt and I finished with the clothes line as if nothing had happened, but we were both thinking very hard. When we finished our chores, my aunt said we would look at the map tonight and she would show me the Lofoten Islands. After supper, Aunt Inga unfolded a worn-looking map onto the kitchen table. She pointed to where we lived, which is on a fjord in the middle of Norway. She slid her finger from our location along the map up to the very top of Norway, to a group of tiny islands out in the ocean. She said it was very beautiful there. I asked if she had ever been there but she hadn't. She had heard about it from our relatives and had seen pictures in one of her school books. I asked if there were palm trees and tigers, like in Peter's picture book. She pursed her lips and said no, it was more like here; it wasn't a tropical place at all. There were lots of fish and mountains, and she said I might see whales and seals there too.

My sense of time was vague, but it was not long after the letter arrived that my travels began. Mette and I had been staying at Aunt Inga's house. It was very early one morning when my father came to Aunt Inga's to wake me. He said it was time to get up. It was the day we were to take the train and it was time to go. My brother, Konrad, was waiting for us in the dark kitchen, and I thought I saw a shadow of someone in the parlor, but it was just one of those odd glimpses you get when you're not quite awake. My father helped me into my winter coat, which surprised me, since it was still summertime.

Outside, the buggy was ready to go. While my dad tied the suitcase to the back of the buggy, I petted our horse, Flicka, before climbing up onto the high seat. I fell asleep almost as soon as I curled up under the blanket where I leaned against Konrad, who had grown tall that summer, though he was just ten years old.

The sun was up when we arrived at the train depot. My big surprise was that only my father and I would be taking the train. Konrad was staying behind. I knew, of course, that I was going to my aunt and uncle's house, even though I had never met them because they lived very far north. I tried not to cry when Konrad took my hand to say goodbye and handed me a little bag, for later, he said. My father settled me at a window seat and sat beside me. We watched Konrad wave as the train pulled away and I waved back like I was accustomed to taking the train and going far away from my own life. Father patted my hand.

The train was large and black and the whistle blew as we started to move. Konrad disappeared in the morning mist and black smoke from the train, and I strained to see where he had been waving, until my neck hurt. I sat back in my seat and played with the end of the envelope my father had pinned to my coat collar, probably bending its edges. Why did he have to pin an envelope to my coat like I was a tiny child? I knew how to read and I was smart. My father said it was to be sure, just to be safe.

We were a reading family, and we had a fine bookcase filled with wonderful books. We had more books than anyone in town and sometimes the school teacher even borrowed from us. It seemed like I had always known how to read. I used to sit next to Konrad when he read Hans Christian Andersen stories to me and Peter, and it wasn't long before I was reading for myself. I just figured it out, and asked Konrad or my mother about the words I didn't know. I had a special place where the sun shone onto the blue rug where I liked to curl up and lean back against my father's chair and disappear into a story. Mother told wonderful stories without books. They were about trolls, and flowers, and walks in the mossy woods. I loved closing my eyes and picturing the stories she told. She had a soft, true voice that brought you right into her story.

What would my aunt and uncle be like? Would they really be nice, like Father said? I felt like I was in the middle of my own story. And even though it was scary, it was kind of exciting to be on a train heading to the Lofoten Islands. I liked saying those words to myself. The Lofoten Islands. I might see whales and seals! How remarkable it seemed, that I was going to live on an island out in the great blue ocean. I had no sense of time as we traveled along. One minute I would be scared and sad and the next minute I was all excited. I was like two people in one. The train was noisy and crowded and part of the time I stared out the window trying not to think, just make-believing I was brave. I saw a white horse on a hillside that looked like Flicka and I rose out of my seat, but then I was old enough to know it wasn't our horse. How could it be? Still, it was horses that I watched for after that, until I dozed off again. Horses and mountains and dark places filled my dreams on that train going north.

Sometimes I startled myself upright when the steam engine whistled. When I did wake to a fully alert state, I was surprised to find a little grey pillow under my head and a plump woman sitting on the seat beside me. She was eating raisins, and her jaw moved with little jerks as if the raisins were too hot to eat, like when your potatoes are too hot and you should have let them cool before taking a bite. The lady said my papa would be right back. Then she put away her raisins without offering me any, stood up and bustled down the aisle of the train car to the door, and I watched as she stepped off the train. From the window, I saw her walking away with a woman in a green coat. They walked just the same and looked like two fluffy birds as they swayed away up the road.

The Poet's Daughter

My father came back with our bags, saying this was our stop. He was sorting our tickets and I told him about the women and how they walked and that I couldn't think of what kind of bird it was they walked like. I wasn't sure he was listening, but then he said that Mother walked like a sand piper. "So light she was," he said.

Just then a man in a uniform stopped beside my dad and he signed a paper. From here, he told us, we would be transferring to a buggy, and that would take us to the boat. We walked to the depot where Papa found a bathroom for me to use, and then we went around the front to a buggy which was pulled by two large horses, one white and one reddish brown. We sat in the backseat and our suitcases were tied to a rack in the back. Just opposite us sat an old man and a boy about Konrad's age, or maybe a little younger. The boy's name was Bjorne, but I couldn't understand his grandfather's name because I think he was speaking with chewing tobacco in his mouth, and so was my father. The men talked about the weather, and a tunnel that was to be built through the mountain. I was tired and barely listened. Then it was quiet, except for the boy's occasional humming, which I liked. The old man closed his eyes but I don't think he slept because the road was rutted and bumpy, at least at first. I closed my eyes and thought of Mother. I could almost see her crossing the yard, carrying a basket of buttercups. She loved wild flowers, especially buttercups. I opened my eyes again so I wouldn't cry. The boy was looking at me. He smiled and looked away.

The road followed the curves of the mountain and went up steep hills and past waterfalls. At the highest point we had a glimpse of blue water below, and we turned a corner and started down the mountain to where it leveled out and the horses snorted. I listened to the sound of the horse's hooves clomping along and I snapped the clasp of my little purse open and closed to their rhythm. The purse was my birthday present from just two weeks earlier. It was my mother's purse, the small lavender purse she kept inside her big purse. She would give me her big purse to hold when we went to the grocery store. She kept money in the little purse to pay for what we bought, which was usually flour and sugar and coffee, and maybe spices or tea. Sometimes she picked out material from long rolls kept under a table in the back with the thread and buttons. We had our own cows and summer garden, so there was little we needed to buy, but I had always admired both the big purse and the little one, and Papa said she wanted me to have the lavender coin purse.

The buggy passed more waterfalls and crossed wooden bridges and followed a road bordered by long expanses of green land with farms and red barns, much like at home. By the time we came to the sea's edge, I was glad to climb down from the hard seat of the buggy. The old man took the boy's hand and they walked off down the road toward a farm. The boy turned around and waved at me before they continued on like they were going home. It was good to be on plain ordinary land and smell the sea in the air. But I didn't see my aunt and uncle anywhere. Where were they? What would we do if they didn't come? How would we get to the Lofoten Islands? And just which of the islands would we go to? What if it gets dark? Papa said not to worry; soon I would meet Uncle Karl and Aunt Elvine and we would be crossing the water to Stamsund, my new home on the Lofoten Islands. We stood side by side looking at the distant islands and inhaled the salty breeze off the sea.

The Poet's Daughter

Then there they were, waving. They came rushing toward us in a kind of fast walk and my aunt scooped me up into a big, wiggling hug and it was like we had known each other our whole lives. My uncle had such a big smile that I started laughing, and he clapped his hands together and then picked up my suitcase. Aunt Elvine held my hand as we walked toward the dock, and I felt safe and knew that it was going to be okay. Father was calm, like always, and he and Uncle Karl walked along talking as if no time at all had passed since they had last seen one another.

We boarded a large fishing boat that would take us to their island and I sat beside my aunt, who put a wool blanket over our legs as we sat on a wooden bench. The sea was dark with bouncing waves and I liked it. The sun was bright, making many colors dance over the bubbly waves. Near the shore there were a lot of gulls hopeful for fish, but we left them behind as the boat was empty of fish as we made our passage across the strait.

My aunt asked me to tell her all about my train ride and I did. She was interested in everything I had to say, and so I was interested in her too and asked about their house on the island, and did they have a yard? Did they have an apple orchard, and what was their house like? "You'll see," she said. "It's your house now, too." We were quiet then, watching the sea as we swayed along with the waves toward my new home. Once out in the sea, I could spot the furthest mountains, which were white with snow; the nearer ones looked as green and smooth as the finest moss. We passed another fishing boat on its way toward the mainland. It was smaller than the one we were on, and we all waved at the fishermen. They didn't have their nets out, so they were moving pretty fast. Here on the sea I felt good. I'd had many boat rides in our little oar boat back home, but this was a big boat on the enormous sea and I liked its rhythm and sitting next to my aunt and watching the island as we came near. Although I wanted to get to the island, at the same time I wanted to stay on the boat like this forever, watching the waves. I kept thinking it was like the sea was breathing. I wasn't at all afraid, even though my shoes were getting wet from some of the waves. I was a born sea person.

It wasn't long before we could see the dock, and other fishing boats anchored partway out from shore. The houses on the hillside were mostly red, like in our village back home. To the left of the houses, a flock of sheep was grazing on what seemed way too steep a hill. My uncle shouted out toward shore and soon we were gliding in beside the dock. We had arrived at our Lofoten Island! My father helped me off the fishing boat and onto the dock, and he and Uncle Albert tied up the boat. Uncle carried my suitcase and Aunt Elvine held my hand. As we walked along, my uncle said, "Well, here we are. We'll have to get you some good boots on Saturday."

The rest of the day went by quickly. I saw all the rooms of the house and I met my cousins. They were quiet and formal toward me, but I had a curious feeling I would like them. We had a delicious supper of fish stew, rye bread and cheese, with berry juice to drink. I was so tired I must have seemed stupid to my new brothers and sister. I was told to think of them as my family rather than my cousins. As it was summer and still the time of the midnight sun, it was light out when I was settled in my new bed and I didn't really know what time it was. When my aunt shut the door to my room, I was ready to fall asleep and my eyes hurt from the sun and the sea and all of my traveling. I fell asleep to the sound of my father and aunt and uncle talking downstairs.

I awoke to the sound of squawking seagulls, a familiar sound. Except for listening to the gulls, my mind stayed empty for what seemed a long time and I wanted it to stay like that. I was thinking that I was like an empty boat, when I heard the door creak open and my aunt looked in. She came to sit on my bed and her hand smoothed over my cheek. The sun was shining on her hair and on her silky dress, which was covered with little red roses.

She helped me arrange my suitcase clothes in the wardrobe, and then I dressed for the day. We went downstairs together where my father and uncle were at the table having coffee. My father said he needed to start back home after I had my breakfast. It seems they had been waiting for me. I could hardly eat my oatmeal, my hands shook so. I hadn't known Papa would be leaving so soon.

Down at the dock with all the fishing boats and people loading nets and gear, I was distracted before I had time to realize what was happening. My father kissed me on top of my head and climbed into the boat that was to take him back to the mainland and off he went, leaving me alone with my aunt and uncle on the shore. I didn't want him to go. I was stubborn and I wouldn't leave the dock. My aunt stayed with me while the boat became smaller and smaller as it sailed away on the sea. It was a hard day.

From the house and whenever I was out in the yard that day, I watched the sea for my father. But he was nowhere to be seen. He was gone. That night I watched the sea from my window. Every day afterwards, whenever I had some time to myself, I watched the melancholy sea.

As time went on I forgot the details of the day my father left in the boat, but I knew when I was looking out to sea that I was looking toward my old home, and Peter and Konrad, Mette, and my baby sister, Aagot, and my mother in the graveyard under the Linden tree. In some part of my mind, my father was still in the boat on his way home, always at sea, rolling along with the waves.

The days flew by that summer on my Lofoten Island, and by August I hardly had time to think about my old life because I was so busy living the new one. The mornings were organized so that we all had our chores, from the moment we got up until the breakfast dishes were washed and put away in the cupboard. It was at breakfast that I got to know my brothers and my older sister, Astrid. Astrid was old enough to help my aunt with breakfast, and she made delicious blueberry pancakes. Magne was only three years old and very active and funny. Anton was ten years old. He was most like my brother Konrad.

I sat next to Magne at breakfast and Anton and Astrid were across from us, with uncle and aunt at the ends, unless my uncle was already out fishing. Often, Magne would start laughing for no reason at all. He might hold up a raspberry like it was something magical, and then pop it into his mouth, saying it was a fish. Or he would look at himself in the mirror of his spoon and then hold it out for me to look into. Anton would roll his eyes, considering himself too grown up for such foolishness. Astrid humored him and thought he was cute. Still, sometimes we all started laughing at the same time. You could feel when us children had that morning energy and just about anything could set us off. It was quite surprising, but I think that's how I settled into the family sooner that you might have thought one could, at least for a lot of the time. Except for my times looking out to sea.

I could tell Anton and Astrid had been told not to make a fuss over me, and to just act like I had always been a part of the family, and they did as they were told, pretty much. Still, sometimes I caught Anton looking at me with his deepest eyes. I pretended not to notice.

I was adapting to my new home. Every day I played by the docks or back on the big, flat expanse of rock behind the house. I came to know the neighborhood and the hills, the bushes and trees along the gravel street that wound all the way down to the dock. I liked the look of the sea in the morning after breakfast on a sunny day, and the orange of the evening sky when my uncle's fishing boat came in for the day.

In my room I had a shell collection along the windowsill, inspired by Anton's much larger collection. The table next to my bed held a small bowl of moss with a wooden rabbit in its center. The rabbit was a present from Konrad, which he must have carved with his pocket knife. I found it on the Sunday after my father left for home, which was the first time I had worn my winter coat since the train ride. I named the rabbit Hvit, and liked to hold it in my hands.

On days when Anton was off in the boat with my uncle, and Magne was taking his nap, I would sit up on the biggest rock behind the house and make up stories. They were often about my rabbit Hvit, and how we would sail through the sea of tall grass on a smooth piece of driftwood. Sometimes we would sail near Anton and Uncle Albert in the fishing bay; other times we would sail home to Father. In truth, I wanted to go back home and have everything as it had been before my mother died. At the same time, I wanted to grow up as soon as possible and go fishing with Anton and Uncle Albert.

For the first weeks at uncle and aunt's house I was rather quiet, and mostly listened to the others, but it wasn't long before that changed. I talk all the time now and make up stories when I am inside doing chores with my aunt. She likes my stories and has her own to tell, often about when she was little and growing up on a nearby island where she and her sister watched the seals come and go.

Big sister Astrid likes stories too, but she is seldom at home since starting to work full time at the dairy just outside of town. I miss seeing her smile at breakfast, which had made me feel good, even when she didn't say anything. She is nice, but at the age where she is finding her own life.

One day Anton heard me talking to myself outside and made fun of me, so I stopped that and just kept those stories going in my head, unless he wanted me to entertain him with my "wild tales of the sea," as he called them. I told of herds of bright blue whales that amazed everyone and how they came when you where least expecting them, such as when you were sitting in the yard with a glass of raspberry juice, just biding your time watching the white caps in the sea. Sometimes I didn't know if my stories were true, or if I had made them up.

In late August, Anton promised to take me to the end of the road after supper. We had potatoes and fish, and the last of the season's cloudberries with cream for dessert that evening. I pretended I wasn't excited and took my time with the berries. "Coming, aren't you?" Anton had to say to get me moving. I slipped on my sweater and we took off up the road, which curved at the upper part and from where I wasn't to go further by myself. From the top you could see far out to sea, where the mountains of the other islands were green as emeralds below their tall jagged peaks. As we started down the road where it heads back toward the sea, I saw a man with a limping dog. Anton said he was Old Man River. He turned off by the time we got down to the sea, and we walked along a nice beach with overturned driftwood in big clumps, like an old dead forest. He said we couldn't take off our shoes because of fish hooks and poisonous jellyfish, but I think he was making that up. We stopped to sit on a long, dry log where we could listen to the waves and see what there was to see.

I was thrilled just being there on that log with Anton. It was the best day. He was quiet and started to say something, but then he didn't. We kept listening to the sea and watching the waves. A big white bird flew past and landed out on a rock. It was bigger than a seagull and had extremely long legs that looked crooked. When it flew off, Anton got up and said it was time to get back, and then, like he had just thought of it, said he was very sorry that my mother had died. He held my hand as we started up the road, but let go when we got closer to the turnoff to Old Man River's place. My hand felt alive.

We took that same walk many times afterwards, and Anton became my best friend. I don't know if he thought that I could be a best friend, because mostly I talked and he listened, though most of the time we just walked without talking, usually picking wild berries along the side of the road and eating them as we walked along. At our beach we hunted for shells and interesting pieces of driftwood and looked for whatever had come in with the tide the day before.

Usually he acted grown up, but sometimes he would play like I did. He helped me make a sea monster from a special tree stump, which we covered with long strings of seaweed that we wound around its wooden arms and big lopsided head. We called our monster Hegge and pretended it came alive to tell us stories. I said that Hegge was friendly during the day, but at night he became an evil troll who ate every child who dared to come upon this very beach. Anton said Hegge threw the children's bones into the sea, where they turned into twisted clumps of driftwood. "See this?" he said, holding up a small, pointy stick. "That's a finger bone." Anton laughed and chased me down the beach, howling like a gruff old sea troll. I screamed like crazy and there was no one to hear, just the wind over the sea. It was the very best place to scream, and then you'd feel better ever after.

When I started school, Anton would pretty much ignore me during school hours, and then after school he was off with his friends. I had my own girl friends to walk home

The Poet's Daughter

with and more indoor chores and schoolwork to do. I loved school and reading and writing, and especially story time when our teacher would read to us in the late afternoon for half an hour before the school bell rang to end the day.

She has been reading a story about a little woman who lives in a miniature wooden house in the woods, with a roof covered with grass and flowers. Her two pet goats use a ladder to climb onto the roof, and she uses their fur to spin into yarn. One goat is as black as night, and the other is snowy white. She dyes their yarn into brilliant colors using flowers and leaves and secret potions that she cooks in a big pot out in her yard.

The brightly-colored yarn would hang on a branch of her apple tree until the moon was full, when she would take it down and begin to weave. Under the moonlight she wove magic shawls with designs of many colors. She wove red birds the color of sunsets and blue birds the color of mountains, and purple birds the color of spring violets. These shawls she traded to the wicked troll of the mountain so he would protect her chickens from the fox that lived by the river, and her goats that ate grass on her roof. We all loved to hear what happened next in the story, even though our teacher would stop reading just at an exciting place, like when the old troll poked his head out of a cave and you could smell its horrid breath, so we had to wait until the following day to hear what happened next. It drove us crazy.

There is a girl in my class who likes to draw and paint. Her name is Marget, which I find to be a friendly name. She brings her drawing book and little watercolor set with her everywhere, and she and I like to plunk down in the wild flower field near her house. While she paints buttercups and daisies, I make up stories. Sometimes I continue the story of the shawl weaver and the fox and the troll. Often Marget and I are silent, or we end up having philosophical discussions out in our field of flowers, like little adults, because Marget knows about death too, as her brother died of consumption during the winter before I came to the island. More often though, we talk about school, our teacher, and cute Bjorne Narvik who lives out by Old Man River's road. We have our serious days and our other days, when we end up giggling ourselves silly in the grass, holding our stomachs because we laugh so much it hurts.

I had just changed into my after school clothes and was thinking about the apples I could smell baking downstairs when my aunt called up to me. "Berta!" I hurried down to the kitchen, wondering at the excited tone of her voice. There was a letter from my father! I sat on the butter stool and Aunt Elvine sat on her kitchen chair and opened the letter. She read it aloud:

Dear Berta,

Everyone is fine here and we hope that you are fine too. Konrad has been helping with the haying at the neighbors, and last week Peter helped me dig up the potato patch, which produced an excellent crop this year. We have plenty of apples from the orchard, and a good supply of carrots, beets, and rutabagas, enough to last through the winter and enough to share with the neighbors.

The Poet's Daughter

Baby sister Aagot is living with the kind folks next to the grocery store, and Mette is still with Mrs. Johnson. We all send our warm greetings to you.

What are you learning in school? I hope you like your teacher.

I send my love to Uncle Karl and Aunt Elvine and to Astrid, Anton, Magne and my dear little Berta.

With a warm heart for you,

Your father

Indeed, this letter warmed my heart, and I think I have especially loved baked apples ever since that day of the first letter from home. My aunt read the letter to me several times that day and helped me follow the words written in the swirls of my father's cursive hand. I knew just where he sat when he wrote the letter. I pictured him seated at the small desk beside the window overlooking the fjord, pausing to look out over the water, just as I look out to the Lofoten Sea where he sailed away, leaving me here. With this letter in my hands, I was now confident that he was no longer at sea, but safely back home. I wasn't sure if this comforted me or not.

I had so much to say, so much to tell him and to tell my sisters and Konrad and Peter. I missed Mrs. Johnson and Aunt Inga too, and I wanted to thank her for finding the Lofoten Islands on the map. I wanted to see everyone back home. That was when I made a vow to myself that I would work harder at my lessons so I could read the next letter myself, and be able to write in cursive, and tell about my new life on this island in the sea. Yes, I will write soon. I will.

When I was alone in my room at the end of the day I held the letter close and thought of the sound of my father's calm voice. I suppose it was a coincidence, but when I looked out my window late that night, I saw the northern lights for the first time since arriving at Lofoten. The lights were whirling and flashing from red to purple and white, and I thought they were an echo of light from the cursive words of my father's letter.

I was a good student and became an even better one. I admit to being obsessed about learning to write well enough so I could write a good and proper letter. My early attempts at cursive writing were not at all successful. I practiced writing my own name, adding many loops and curls as I tried to duplicate the look of my father's elegant handwriting. My teacher was strict and insisted I stop adding unnecessary loops, and I improved my legibility considerably following her instructions.

After school and after chores, instead of joining Marget as before, I practiced my letters, making row after row of the letters of the alphabet in cursive. Using pencil for the first few days of my practice, I quickly made the change to pen and ink. I was careful not to drip ink and made small but precise letters so I wouldn't use up my writing notebook too quickly.

After working on single alphabet letters, I graduated to common short words, such as "look" and "boat," taking great pleasure in connecting the letters into whole flowing words. Following the easy words, I took up words I liked the look of, such as the word "Lofoten," my most challenging word, with its cursive letters connected with just the right amount of curves and circles and lofty letters. I also enjoyed the capital B of my own name - Berta. I can hear the soft "B" as pronounced by my little brother, Peter, as I write my own name. "Ber-ta."

Marget had not been happy with my student resolve, as I had abandoned our expeditions to the wildflower fields since concentrating on my cursive studies.

"Berta, you shouldn't ignore your friend," my aunt said. "She comes everyday looking for you and finds you always too busy. One day she'll stop coming by. You don't want to lose such a good friend, do you?"

I knew my aunt was right and I was aghast at the thought of losing Marget's company. I set aside my writing. On my walk to Marget's house, I scolded myself for ignoring our friendship. Would she forgive me? Would she be out exploring the hills with a new friend? But Marget was in her front yard playing her circling game around the flag pole. She just said "Hi" and laughed, and we were like we always were.

We walked up to our field, jabbering all the way. It was a warm fall afternoon, following several chilly days when frost covered the road and dock each morning. We were both energized and decided to continue on at the top of the meadow, turning onto the road Anton and I used to reach our secret beach. I didn't say I wasn't supposed to take this road alone, but then, Marget was with me. Still, we both knew we were doing something daring.

Many of the bushes beside the road were losing their leaves, while others were still the shining golds and reds of fall. We found a few late maturing berries here and there, still tasty enough for a snack. The sky was blue as we walked up the road. A wagon loaded with sweet-smelling hay passed us by and the driver waved. Marget thought he was in her sister's class at school, but she didn't know his name.

We continued on behind the hay wagon, which quickly drove out of sight, and by the time we rounded the bend, the sky had turned a pale orange. It was here where we first spotted Old Man River's dog, limping in our direction. He stopped right in front of us, looking up as if asking a question. We didn't know what to do. Why was he alone? Marget and I both got scared at the same time. We petted the dog and told him to go home, pointing where he should go, before we turned around, anxious to go home ourselves. We started out walking fast, and then faster, until we were nearly running, knowing something was wrong. By the time we reached the meadow, the hay wagon, now empty of hay, came up beside us.

"Trouble at Old Man River's," the young driver said, and told us to get right on home. The hay wagon continued on straight and we turned down the hill toward home and ran all the way. By the time I came in the door of the house, my legs felt shaky and I was breathing hard. I'm sure Marget ran all the way to her home as well.

It wasn't until after dinner that night when Uncle Albert and Anton came home late from fishing that we heard the news. Old Man River had been found dead out in back of

The Poet's Daughter

his house by the wood pile. "His heart gave out," Uncle Albert told us all.

I took it hard. So did Marget, though neither us had even met Old Man River. We took it upon ourselves to see about his dog, the old limper. We walked right out to the house a few days after the burial, and there was the dog, sitting beside the front door. He was lying down with his nose on his paws and he didn't get up as we walked closer to the house. The look in his old dog eyes told the story. We just stood there, dumb as a tree, until a woman opened the door, holding an old cloth in her hands like she was in the middle of something. Marget started crying right there in front of us, so the woman escorted us inside and poured us each a jelly glass of berry juice.

"There, there, *min stakkars lite jenta,*" she kept saying, patting each of us on the shoulder like we were little lambs. She was Old Man River's sister, she said, and was staying in the house to clean up. She said his name was actually Ole Roehmer. Wouldn't you know but that we helped her clean the house all that afternoon, and took in the wash from the line out back. His old trousers and shirts looked empty on that clothes line, and it felt odd to be touching them and folding them up in a make-shift laundry basket. That work settled us somehow, for when we started home late in the day we were both feeling more in charge of our world, and probably a bit older.

One day Marget and I met each other at the graveyard. She was coming in with a bouquet of wild flowers, just as I was on my way out after leaving some buttercups on Old Man River's grave. I waited for Marget at the entrance. Yes, she left flowers for Old Man River, and for her brother, who was buried nearby beside the birch forest at the end of the graveyard. We knew that soon the wild flowers would be gone for the year.

Marget and I walked home together without talking, something we were comfortable with on serious days or whenever we needed a quiet time, or just when we were listening to the birds. When we neared her house, I broke the silence and told her I knew how Old Man River got his name.

It seems he had once lived on the mainland and loved fishing a particular river that had a pool where the trout were big and tasty. But that part of the river was guarded by an old man who wouldn't let anyone else share his part of the river. He threw rocks at anyone who tried to fish in that pool. He was the one they called Old Man River. When he was one hundred years old, he disappeared. Some said he fell into the river and his body was never found.

It was around that time when it was noted how the big rocks on the far side of his beloved river took on an uncanny resemblance to the old man's face. It was said he had become a troll to continue to guard his section of the river. No one admitted to being afraid to fish there, yet nary a soul had dropped a fishing line into that infamous pool ever after—except for our Old Man River. It was then that they started calling him skinny Old Man River, to distinguish him from dead Old Man River. They say that's when he moved to Lofoten, because he didn't like being called "skinny." Some say he moved because of the troll. Once on Lofoten, he told everyone his name was simply "Old Man River." And so that's how he got his name, I said with a sigh.

The Poet's Daughter

Marget told me that was the best story I had ever made up, and started to laugh. We broke into one of our giggling fits and that was that. From then on, life went on pretty much as it had before, though we ended our secret trips to Old Man River's grave.

Before long, winter moved in and the world was beautiful and white with cold and the rivers froze up. Marget didn't like to go outside as I did, preferring to stay at home after school, so I mostly saw her when we walked to and from school together. My aunt was sleeping a lot during those early weeks of winter, usually resting when Magne took his naps, so I was free to play outside.

After the fishing slowed down, Anton had more free time and we became skating fanatics. My uncle rounded up a pair of skates for me that fit well enough with a thick pair of wool socks. I was anxious to skate on the river I had heard so much about. Anton explained that skating was just like walking, except you glide and move faster. He laced my skates and showed me how to do it for myself so the leather sides supported my ankles. I skated without falling on my first try and I loved it. Anton said I had a natural sense of balance and good stamina. Uncle Albert came with us on Fridays. He skated with great long strides, holding his hands behind his back as we three skated up the river as far as the ice had cleared, which was well over a kilometer.

When Anton and I were on our own, we liked to race. He nearly always won, but sometimes I would get to the marker rock before Anton. It never occurred to me that he might have let me win by slowing down, but that may have been the case, as I was younger and he was tall for his age.

When we met school friends on the river, we would become one big parade of skaters, laughing and acting foolish and falling onto the snow banks to make snow angels or sometimes, as winter moved along and it got dark early, we would lie in the snow and look up at the stars, truly millions of stars. Often on those skating nights, we glided along under the northern lights, which would flicker over the shiny ice and light us all up so that we felt electrified into the happiest kids on the planet.

The river was usually cleared of snow by the strong winds, but the wide opening of the river where it reached the bay often needed clearing by shoveling. This was done by groups of the older men of the village who were freed for a time of their fishing chores. Folks of all ages skated there on nice days, men and women skating hand in hand, or by themselves, circling the rink area again and again. We children darted about and stayed on the farthest side of the ice, though we preferred our more private river. One of the best things about the days on the bay rink was when one of the women took it upon herself to provide refreshments on the river dock. This meant cocoa and lefse, and hot mulled wine for the grownups. That didn't happen very often, but we swarmed like bees when it did. It was usually Mrs. Morkved or her sister, who lived with her and was known for her accordion playing and jovial manner. We loved to see either of them heading our way, though most often the sisters came together.

Aunt Elvine had a baby that winter, little Jenny. Her big sister, Astrid, came home from the dairy early each day to help with the baby, until my aunt's strength returned. We all got used to a new routine, which meant getting up earlier and getting used to waking in the middle of the night when baby Jenny cried. I liked how the whole house settled down in the night when Jenny stopped crying and was being fed. It felt cozy and warm in the house, and I would turn over and fall into a deep sleep. Often I had dreams of skating on an endless river, waking only when I was called to breakfast.

It was just after Jenny was born that Anton and I took our longest skating adventure on the river. None of the other kids wanted to continue beyond the high drifts of snow and cascading icicles covering the boulders of the rapids. Anton said if we went along the edge around the bend, the river would be clear again because the winds always blew away the snow up there.

You would think it was impossible to get past the river's ridge of ice, and it wasn't easy getting around the icy boulders while wearing skates. I had to take giant steps through deep snow when we got to the river's edge. Even so, I followed Anton along the river bank, which was rocky and steep. I kept up with Anton; I didn't want him to think I was a weakling, but I wanted to turn back. I slipped. Oh, it hurt, and I thought surely I had broken some bones. I definitely injured my shoulder, but I didn't cry out and said it was nothing and that we should go on. I even laughed, and that kept me from crying. Anton took my hand to pull me up out of a crevice and we moved slowly the rest of the way over the snow bank, until we slid down to the river like a couple of otters. Anton was right; the river here was clear and beautiful.

We were only able to skate a quarter of a kilometer before we were blocked again. Sitting on a fallen tree trunk to rest, Anton took two pieces of peppermint candy from his pocket. As I unwrapped my peppermint and popped it in my mouth, I thought the cool flavor a good surprise and reward for our dangerous passage and my sore shoulder. While we were sucking on our candy, an elk came out of the woods from the other side of the river. He stopped to stare at us and snorted. Maybe he smelled the peppermint. After a short time, he loped off and we started back. This time when we got to the barricade, we tried the other side of the river and that was a much easier passage. When we got home, I think both Anton and I felt we had gotten off easy, knowing we had been in dangerous territory. I know I felt relieved to step into our warm kitchen filled with the smell of soup.

I didn't start skiing until I was ten years old. By that time Anton and I had been skating together what seemed like our whole lives, and I had many friends who liked to skate on the rivers as well. That was the year that Bjorne took a fancy to me, and we sometimes skated almost all the way to the marker rock, holding hands as we skated. Of course, holding hands through wool mittens was not like holding hands in summer. I liked Bjorne because he made me laugh and he was always joking around. Plus he was so cute, with his blue eyes and rosy cheeks. He wore a checkered jacket so I could always see him coming from far away. He liked to bring me a cookie, fresh from his mother's oven, but half crumbled from his pocket and none too clean by the time he handed it to me. Who knew what a boy would have in his pocket besides a cookie? Still, I ate the crumbles. Anton scowled when I skated with Bjorne. I told Anton that was foolish, and that he and I were cousins and best skating friends besides.

The Poet's Daughter

Thankfully, Marget became a skier. I was most grateful to have my friend's company for more than just the summertime. I had received skis two years previous but hadn't been enthusiastic about skiing until Marget started skiing. We used a trail through the birch woods near her house, which was level for most of the way, with a few steeper hills to climb which made it all the more fun skiing down on our return trip. She thought the trail was a road to an old mill before the upper road was built, but now it was mainly a deer trail, and our ski route.

It came out at the beach where Anton and I had played the first year I moved to Lofoten. I could even make out the outline of our old Hegge monster down on the far end of the beach, now covered in snow and ice. I hadn't been to that beach at all the previous summer. I was quite athletic, but Marget was simply an amazing skier who could glide along like the wind. I always skied behind her, straining to keep up. Still, I liked skiing a lot. It makes you feel wildly alive after a fast ski on our trail, like you could do anything you ever wanted in the whole world.

We would end up at Marget's house, where I would leave my skis, and her mother would fix milk coffee and hard tack with cheese for our snack. She always said we had rosy cheeks when we came in from skiing. Marget's mother had a tall box decorated with rosemaling beside the fireplace. It had posts along two sides for hanging mittens and hats and socks. I always admired that box and liked how warm my mittens would be when I was ready to return home.

Konnie Ellis

I wasn't a grownup the year I turned twelve, but nearly so. It was the year Frida was born, Jenny turned three, and Magne started school. It was also the year that Anton would graduate from school. I was writing poetry and articles for our school paper that year and was devoted to my new role, which I considered that of a professional writer. I took my responsibilities seriously and wrote with the passion and precision that had dwelled within me for as long as I could remember.

I was sitting in class one cold winter day when a man came to our classroom and called the teacher into the hall. We couldn't hear what they were saying, but we knew that something serious was going on. Our teacher returned to the classroom alone and walked to Kjell's desk, putting her hand on his shoulder and saying something to him privately. He followed her into the hall and left with the man. From our desks, we could see just enough from the window to watch as they walked down the road. Our teacher said we would end school early that day and finish with the daily reading. We were not relaxed or excited about the reading at all and could hardly listen. Our teacher's voice was strained and tight. When we were dismissed for the day and as we put on our coats and boots and winter gear to leave the building, you could hear our breathing and the clinking of the buckles on our boots. Outside, we all wondered what was going on and hurried home to see if we could find out. Marget was holding back tears, which made me all the more emotional myself, but I was more accustomed to keeping my emotions inside.

The lower grades were still in school, so Magne wasn't yet home. Anton and I met just as we reached our front yard, each coming from a different road. He hadn't heard anything, except that something had happened but he didn't know what. My aunt didn't know either but said we'll all know soon enough. When dinner was ready, she said we should start without Father and that he would be along soon.

We had nearly finished dinner when we heard him at the door. I was relieved about that, so at least Uncle Albert was okay. He took his time hanging up his coat. Instead of changing from his fishing clothes, he came right to the table, put his hands on the back of Anton's chair, and said that Leif Olson had drowned. He and his brother couldn't get their boat out of storm's way. That was all he said. Leif was Kjell's father.

I looked at the sky for a long time before I fell asleep that night. Kjell was a nice boy, not too foolish, and very good at math. He sat in front of me in class, and sometimes when I was daydreaming, I would study the waves of his red hair. What must he be feeling tonight, at home in bed? What was to become of him? It was just he and his mother and the younger brother now. Where was Kjell's dead father on this cold night? Was he still in the cold, dark sea?

They found the body late the following day, washed up on the point where the storm had hit so hard. Anton told me about it. He had been near the dock with his friends after school when the men came in with the body. I was glad I hadn't been there.

The weather turned, and the day of Leif Olson's burial was a beautiful sunny day, unusually warm for winter. The sea was calm and ice had blown in and settled into big blue chunks along the shore. As Anton and my uncle and I walked past the dock toward the church yard, I didn't even want to look at the sea.

At the graveyard, the pastor's words were brief and the coffin was lowered into the ground, into one of those graves they prepare in the fall before the freeze. We listened in silence to the sound of snow and frozen dirt being shoveled onto the grave. I had never been to a burial in winter before. Kjell helped with the shoveling. He looked small holding that big shovel.

Afterwards, as everyone was leaving the graveyard, I heard more about the accident. Apparently Leif had been hauling in the fishing net when the waves were high, out by the outer edge of Black Island, and he was swept overboard and got caught on the net. His uncle tried to pull him up with the netting, but he slipped off and away as the boat rocked in the waves.

"Another victim of the sea," someone said. "They couldn't get around the point," another said.

"No use," were the last words I heard as we turned off toward our house.

At school the following day, Kjell was not in school. Before our lessons began, our teacher had us pray together for Kjell and his family. All we could notice was his empty desk. I kept thinking about the gravedigger who dug the graves in fall for winter's dead, hoping one wasn't to be his own. How could I write about Leif Olson's death for our monthly paper, as my teacher wanted me to do? My mind was a jumble of thoughts all that morning, and when I sat quietly later in the day with my paper and pen, posed to write the story, I wrote a poem instead.

Vestfjord so wondrous
We love and yet fear you.

The Poet's Daughter

Why, these icy graves
for those out searching
for their daily bread.

I took the long way home after school, so I could think. Walking helped. Words and phrases kept sifting through my mind – *fearsome, hidden in the waves, sea of night.* I muttered words to myself, half stumbling along and my mind so into itself, all filled with words waiting for the right place in a poem. At home I read over Anton's history book about how each winter the Gulf Stream and the Artic Ocean meet and form the spawning grounds for cod from the Barents Sea. I read about the tides and the unpredictability of storms, and types of whales, until I realized I was just distracting myself from the work at hand. I closed the book. No history book could explain Leif's death at sea.

I wrote many poems that year of Kjell's father's death, and at the end of the following school year, my teacher read my poem called "The Ocean King" to the whole school at the program that was always held on the last day of classes. I was proud to have my poem read aloud, and that occasion was one that encouraged me to continue writing and to always do my best. It is an honor to hear your poem read aloud in front of others. I learned that when you hear it spoken, it is added to the world and you just let it go on its own way from then on.

After school was out, I traveled to my first home back in Beitstad, Nord-Trondelag, for my confirmation in the

Beitstad church, the very church where I had been baptized. I had been to the confirmation of my friend Marget in May, right here in our Lofoten church, and I was ready for my own spiritual experience and looked forward to this Lutheran rite as part of growing up. My father wanted me confirmed in his parish, fulfilling a promise he made to my mother before she died. Letters had been exchanged to arrange the confirmation in Beitstad and before the week was out, I was on my way.

My father and his new wife, Anna, were there to meet me at the depot in their buggy. Anna kissed my cheek and I liked her immediately. It seemed as though I had seen my father just yesterday, though it was actually the summer before when he made a trip to Lofoten. He always made emotional times seem easy, or at least easier, because of his calm and patient ways. We stopped at the house where I changed into my white dress, and Anna smoothed out the lace collar and fastened the snap in the back, but there was barely time for more than a quick glance around the house, which seemed quiet and empty with the others already at the church. Apparently my train had been late, yet my father assured me that the pastor would wait for us. It had rained earlier in the day, and I was careful not to step in a puddle as we made our way down the street.

Once we arrived at the church, I was escorted to a room with four other girls who were also being confirmed. Nora was one of the girls and we recognized each other, even though we hadn't seen one another since I had moved to the Lofoten Islands. We had hardly known each other before, but I had always thought we would someday become friends. She was friendly, as were the other three, and as the outsider they tried to make me feel at home, even though they were as nervous as I was. When Father's new wife, Anna, came to pin a flower on my dress, I was grateful. She was kind and practical and had a relaxed way about her, much like Father, and she explained to all of us just what would happen and in what order. We still had a little time, because they were waiting for a woman who was going to sing the solo in a hymn. I was glad I wasn't the only one who was late.

Anna had us comb each other's hair and that calmed us all down, and I felt more a part of the group. Nora and I combed each other's hair and that made me feel happy. Finally it was time for us to walk down the aisle of the church. I felt light as a feather walking into the church, wearing the white dress I had made for myself and finished just last week. Listening to the sound of the floor creak as we five girls walked down the wooden aisle of the stone church, the sound seemed like some earthly sound meant to travel up to the rooftop and beyond. That beyond is what I kept thinking about as I made my way to the front of the church. I stood solemnly before the pastor and received Jesus Christ into my heart.

The sun had come out when we stepped out of the church. The land was ever so green and fresh in Nord-Trondelag. The hills and mountains were smooth to the eye, not as high and jagged as back on the Lofoten Islands. I was in a bit of a daze seeing my brothers and sisters and cousins. After many years of our contact being no more than letters, it was like going back in time to see them all at this important event in my life. In just one day we all had to leap over the many years that had changed us. You would expect this to be impossible, that the mind could so adjust, but that was how it happened. Of course, I had seen my father several times over the years when he had been to visit me at Stamsund, though those visits were always brief.

Back at the house, we had a lovely meal together and I answered lots of questions and asked my share as well. I tried to see the children I remembered in the faces of my brothers, now all grown up. Even baby Aagot was growing up. After our meal, young Aagot had to leave with the Johnsons, the family she had grown up with after Mother died, and they had moved to a nearby town some years past. I could tell Aagot wasn't at all ready to climb into the Johnsons' big buggy and simply stood at my side, looking up at me. "You are my big sister, aren't you?" she said. She knew I was but needed reassurance. I gave her a good hug and told her we would always be sisters and someday we would get to know each other better. "Yes, we will," she said, sounding sure of herself and happy enough so that she could leave. After one soulful look, she laughed and ran outside to the waiting buggy.

After our meal, my sister Mette and I sat beside each other on the couch and held hands, like long ago, and I liked that. I was tired and leaned back against the sofa pillow. The trip from Lofoten had gone well, and I especially liked the train ride, though I had too many concerns to enjoy it properly, as I expected I would upon my return trip. I had five days before I left.

I slept well my first night at my old home. Even though school was out for the summer, Anna and I were the only ones in the house after breakfast. My father was busy at work all day down the fjord on a boat building project, and Conrad and Peter were working at a neighbor's farm for the summer, coming home for a late dinner at the end of each day. Mette was babysitting for a neighbor, and Aagot had gone home to her village with the Johnsons.

I found it pleasant to work in the kitchen and around the house with Anna, and I helped weed in the garden. Anna seemed healthy and well, but she was actually quite delicate and needed a long rest each day after we had our lunch. She encouraged me to enjoy the village and to visit some of the girls I had been confirmed with.

I had wanted to see Nora, but she had gone to Trondheim the day after our confirmation. I did visit with Julie one afternoon, but she seemed so much younger than me that I wasn't entirely comfortable. I felt like I was her babysitter and she kept asking me what we should do. Still, she was sweet and we did have an enjoyable time sitting out on the porch making dolls out of hollyhock flowers, something I had learned many years in the past.

Mostly I walked along the beautiful green hills and along the fjord in the afternoons. At the end of each day I invariable found myself at the graveyard where my mother was buried, and there I liked to sit and daydream. One day the pastor's wife crossed the graveyard and introduced herself, telling how she had known my mother and what a lovely person she had been. I think I gravitated to my mother's grave by some rule of nature, and waited for something to happen. I didn't speak to my mother, as I've seen others do at gravestones; I just waited. It was peaceful, but nothing happened. It wasn't until my last day that I received something I had been seeking. The day was especially beautiful, with not a cloud in the sky, and only a soft breeze as I strolled across the graveyard. The Linden tree was in bloom and the aroma of its flowers welcomed me. The quiet and beauty and something I could not name came into me, and I knew this nameless peace would always be there for me, wherever I was, no matter what happened in my life ever after.

I was ready to go home to the Lofoten Islands. Along with my father and Anna, and Mette and Conrad and Peter, we had a good last meal with more reminiscing and talk of getting together soon, though I knew it would be some time before I saw them all again. And as much as I liked my father's new wife, Anna, who was so kind and pretty, it still made me sad to be in the old house without my mother, and in a way, I was glad when it was time to leave. It was a whirlwind of a trip, even though I had five whole days in Beitstad. Early the next morning I was on my way back to Stamsund and my Lofoten home.

Here in Lofoten's fairyland strand
my heart ever beats
to the never ending rhythm
of the sea

Do you know what it's like to be sixteen years old? I am sixteen years old and my cousin Anton is in love with me. We are a problem to everyone except ourselves. I am both happy and confused. Anton is so dear, as he has been from the beginning. My uncle has been writing to the minister in Utvik to arrange a job for me. I am to become the house helper to the schoolmaster and his family as soon as I graduate from school. That seems far off, yet it is only a matter of weeks.

Anton and I leave the house at different times but often meet at our secret beach. It is springtime and I am happy.

The Poet's Daughter

On Saturdays I walk along the lane past the apple orchard, thick with blossoms, each tree as white as a perfect cloud. By the time I arrive at the beach, Anton is pacing up and down over the rocks and sand. He waves wildly and I run to him. We kiss. We lie on the beach and tussle for a while before I push him away. It's our routine and we laugh and pretend it is just a game. We end up roving the beach, picking up shells and interesting pieces of wood. Anton has a book on shells and we each have our favorites. Sometimes we make a face on the sand out of shells and stones and watch the waves wash over the visage. It makes us sad, but we do it every time we come to the beach now. Before we leave, we sit on our special rock and watch the clouds float by.

The sea is as blue and deep as Anton's eyes. How can I be without Anton? But we are first cousins, we must simply be friends, yes, Aunt Elvine keeps telling me so. Deep down I know Anton is not the one for me, so why do I think of him the moment I awake? Surely this spring I am happiest when we are together, even when we simply hike in the mountains, talk little and just exist under the sun. Sitting on top of the mountain and looking down on the green land and the blue sea, you would think there could be no place on earth as beautiful. And everywhere the spring flowers are blooming. It is so good, yet perplexing. Anton speaks of the United States and how we could move to America. He is learning English. He wants to study architecture and engineering. I think I am too young to figure out what to do. Last night I heard Anton and his father arguing out in the yard. It scares me.

Marget is moving to Oslo when she graduates. She is going to work with her aunt's friend, who knows someone in the state theater who knows someone who paints scenery. She is going to be an assistant and learn scene painting. She is ecstatic and jittery and can hardly wait. Oh, how I want to go to Oslo with her. We could share lodging and I could look for a job at a newspaper, or go to the university! I dream of this but cannot think of a way to make it work. And how can I say goodbye to Anton? We must always be friends. Marget and Anton must always be my friends, no matter how long we live or where we live.

At night I think about saving the money I earn at the schoolmaster's home and how long it would take to save for a future. I dream of floating above the ocean on a feather bed of money with a pillow case filled with lots of blank notebooks to be filled with poems and poems and poems. I fall asleep looking out the window at the stars.

Goodbye, Lofoten. So long, dear family and friends. Goodbye, Anton. I know I will see you again someday, in America, perhaps. Goodbye, Marget. Let us meet again in Oslo. My life has been rich in friendship, both with my new family and Lofoten friends, and with the family of my early days. Letters have passed back and forth over the years to my father, my brothers Peter and Konrad, to Mette, and to young Aagot. Soon I will see Aagot again, as the parish I am leaving for in the morning is near her village where she lives with the Johnsons. Goodbye, beloved mountains. How I will miss the flowers in the high summer meadows, and the skating and skiing in winter. I will always remember going to sea to fish with my uncle, and the sound of the waves and the splashing of fish. The sea is forever in my blood and the mountains are in my bones. I am a Lofoten Norwegian.

The Poet's Daughter

I am also a writer. What began as an obsession to learn to write letters to my father, turned me into a poet. I was eight years old when I wrote my first poem. It was about the sea. I had so much to say about the sea, about the sky, the mountains, my friends, about everything. Writing was my secret life. I wrote about my oatmeal breakfast, the petals on buttercups, Anton's eyes, the endless dark night skies.

I wrote about the time my aunt called me to dinner and I ran so fast down the hill that I almost slid into the neighbor's pig sty. Oh, woe was me. Again and again I wrote of the sea where my father sailed away when I first arrived at the island. I wrote about the seasons, and the waterfalls of spring, about the aurora borealis that I saw night after night from my bedroom window, about nights of skating on the shining frozen bay and enticing rivers. I wrote of the midnight sun and bonfires on midsummer night's eve. I wrote secrets. I wrote my life.

Oh Vestfjord, where my heart ever beats
to the never ending rhythm
of the sea

Chapter 2:
On the mainland again in Utvik

WHERE AM I? It's so early in the dark that no birds are singing, and I am curled up beneath my feather bed. Only as my eyes adjust do I see that the lace curtains are not those from my Lofoten window, but are the bird lace curtains in my upstairs room in Schoolmaster Benum's house, here at Utvik. I have been here for two years now, yet I still have these mornings of confusion when I first awake. This time in bed before the day officially begins is the time when I let my thoughts drift where they may.

I still think of Anton. I hope he doesn't still miss me. After I left, the first month I was here with the Benums, I missed him a lot. It helped that I was so busy those first weeks. One evening not long after I had moved in, as I came down the back stairs, I saw Mr. Benum burning what looked like letters in the fireplace. I tiptoed back up the stairs. I just knew they must be from Anton. The following morning I made a point of being the first one up, and once downstairs, I slipped over to the fireplace to look over the ashes. I found everything burned to a black crisp. But then I spotted a bit of paper, still mostly smoky black, stuck to the side of the fireplace. I picked it up gingerly, afraid it would fall into tiny bits, and indeed most of it did disintegrate and float down into indecipherable nothings.

The Poet's Daughter

All except for the corner of the envelope, and sure enough, I could read Anton's name as the sender.

As time went on, I settled into the days without my Lofoten family, and without Anton, and day by day they all slipped further into my past. Life in the schoolmaster's house has been good, as the Benums are kind and warm folks.

Mrs. Benum introduced me to Pastor and Mrs. Narvik shortly after I arrived at Utvik. As the Narviks were getting on in years, they were in need of assistance with church chores, and I offered to take on some of those duties. Their church was right next door to the Benums. It is an old stone church with nearly five-foot deep walls where church services have been held on Sunday morning for hundreds of years. I often touch the stones of the doorway when I enter as a way of thanking the stone craftsman of yesteryear and making some meager connection to the past. I think those old-timers must have been hardy folk. Pastor Narvik loves to show the church to visitors and tell of its history. He always mentions how it is ever cool and pleasant on hot summer Sundays, and in winter, the building retains the heat of a fire. When the church bell rings in the outer yard, it can be heard all the way down to the sea and even out to the farms at the edge of the parish. How many people have heard that bell over the years?

I have enjoyed keeping the churchyard graves trimmed of grass, and moss off the stones so you can read the names and dates. Working around the graves is of course peaceful, and I sometimes talk to myself as I work. There is one grave where I like to imagine I am tending my mother's grave as I weed around the flowers planted by that tombstone, which is one of the prettiest, having a small angel engraved above the dates. From the graveyard you can see the fjord and all the green fields of the surrounding area. This is rich farm country and the summers are mild, with pleasant breezes off the fjord. Lofoten was of a different and more rugged kind of beauty, with all of its sharp mountain peaks and thunderous storms.

So my time here in Utvik is divided between my work for Pastor and Mrs. Narvik, where I prepare the church's hymnal board, make wreaths for funerals, and keep the graveyard tidy. My live-in duties at Schoolmaster Benum's house consist of helping Mrs. Benum in the kitchen, caring for the chickens, and best of all, taking care of the children, Vermund, Olav, and little Gudlaug, who have been such fun to care for. I love them dearly, and they remind me of the little ones on Lofoten, though soon even the youngest of the Benums will be in school. When I am not too tired, I write poetry late at night.

Today will be another busy day. There is a wreath to finish and deliver to Pastor Narvik by noon, and if the white daisies are blooming behind the chicken house, I can add them this morning so they'll be fresh for the ceremony this afternoon.

Last week, sister Aagot walked all the way here just to visit, which was on a Sunday. She is now almost thirteen years old. After church, Mrs. Benum and I prepared a chicken dinner with potatoes and carrots, and Aagot arrived just in time. She was dusty and tired, but after a wash up, she revived, as she is very hardy. After dinner, she laughed when she told us about the wolf she saw by the side of the road in the woods, about two kilometers outside of Beitstad. She said it watched her as she walked along and she tried to keep calm and continued to walk normally, as if there were no wolf there at all. Her eyes gave away that she was shaken by the experience, and Mr. Benum said some of those wolves are aggressive at this time of year and assured her that he would escort her home himself in the morning. I knew he would take his hunting rifle along, so I hoped the wolf would be deep in the woods by then. I was glad I was soon to be living at Aagot's house with her adopted family, and she would no longer take that long and dangerous walk.

Yes, I haven't been here for so very long, yet soon I will be off to my new position at the dairy near Aagot's house, some seven kilometers from here. Although Aagot is not quite a teenager, she is wise and thoughtful for her years. She grew up with a fine family after Mother died, distant relations Mother had always liked. Since living with the schoolmaster and his family, I have visited with Aagot's family on three occasions and they have encouraged me to move in with them when I begin my new job at the dairy, as they have an extra room since their son, Olaf, immigrated to America. Mrs. Johnson is a warm and friendly person, and Mr. Johnson is a man of few words, but seems kind enough.

The rooster is crowing and the sky is lightening up. Time to get up. It looks to be a sunny day, which is always nice on a funeral day. As I dress, I recite my morning prayer, one I learned from Pastor Narvik. I heard him reciting this prayer in the empty church one day when I had finished watering some flowers on a grave. He is a true man of God. His one flaw is that he sings loudly and out of tune when he leads the hymns. Mrs. Narvik and I have discussed this numerous times. She cannot find a polite way of telling him to sing more quietly, or to have someone else lead the hymns. She never wants to hurt anyone's feelings.

On the stairs I walk lightly and slip out the side door and into the chicken coop with the basket. I'll miss collecting the eggs and talking my chicken-talk to the pretty birds; mostly reds, they are. They cock their heads and look at you. They're good listeners. I wonder what they would say if they could actually talk. Probably they would be very repetitious and silly, or maybe not. They are not the most brilliant of birds, yet being chickens next door to the pastor's yard, they might have little prayers and bits of wisdom, such as "Gather your corn kernels while you may." I'm afraid I let my imagine run wild when I'm in the chicken yard, but then a bit of levity is not a bad thing.

Actually I'm a little afraid of the chickens, the one I call Fat Red in particular. I have to reach beneath her while she's still lying on her nest, and I feel the warm feathers of her body against my hand as I gather an egg or two. She's never pecked my hand, but just sits there in her aloof chicken manner. I'm glad Mrs. Benum has never made me wring their necks when it was time for a chicken dinner because I know I could not have done it. I don't mind plucking the feathers, though, because the spirit has flown off once the head is gone.

Out back, there are plenty of daisies for the funeral wreath. I lay them on top of the eggs and head to the house. Since no one is yet up, I settle down on the porch to finish the wreath. It's kind of an honor to create something of beauty as a remembrance for the deceased and their family. The wreath I'm working on is heart-shaped, for an old man who died in bed. Pastor Narvik said he was a potato farmer who never failed to share a good crop in a hard winter. I'm tucking just one weedy-looking potato vine into his wreath, which will look much better with an adornment of daisies. No one may notice the potato vine at all, but I feel good about adding it, for the old man's sake.

    I learned to weave vines and flowers into circles and hearts. I can even do a cross. With several consumptives dying within a six-week period, just after I arrived at Utvik, I learned very quickly. I was an assistant to Mrs. Olson, the official funeral wreath maker, before she herself died. Mrs. Olson was elderly, so her passing was no great surprise to anyone. She had told me the day before she died that now she could leave in peace, because I was doing such a good job. I had just enough time to learn the basics before she died. She was kind and I can still hear her guiding voice and recall her knotted old hands patiently tucking in small twigs and flowers. She would like how well these daisies look, woven in with the purple clover.

    I wrote a poem for her. I wrote it on the very day she died. Pastor Narvik put the poem in her coffin. After that he requested I do poems for the deceased, and I met many interesting people that way, friends or relatives of the deceased, in order to find out about the person I was to write about. Pastor said my poems helped him with his eulogies. He was a good writer himself and often came over to use Schoolmaster Benum's thick dictionary, kept on a tall oak stand in the hallway. Oddly enough, Pastor Narvik and I used the dictionary way more often than Schoolmaster Benum. Pastor Narvik would stop on his way to or from church to tell me when he particularly liked a word I used in a poem, and often I would hear him use that same word in his sermon the following Sunday. And I would pick up on one of his biblical phrases now and again.

We had a pleasant writer's camaraderie, something I had never experienced before.

When I leave, there will be no one to do the poems for the dead. Mrs. Narvik will make the wreaths. She helped with the wreath for the last funeral. Unfortunately, she has clumsy fingers. Still, she'll do okay, and this is a small community so a funeral does not occur as often as during those days of consumption after I first arrived. Now I'll just tuck in these last few daisies beside the red clover, and that seems to be just about right to finish the wreath.

"Berta, that's beautiful." I almost jumped off my work bench; Mrs. Benum came up behind me so quietly. She put her hands on my shoulders and I started to cry. We would surely miss each other. "My dear, my dear, let's get the coffee going," she said, and that was how my last Sunday at Schoolmaster's house began.

Chapter 3

THE MOVE TO RORA WENT SMOOTHLY and I am all settled into life at the Johnsons' home with Aagot, who no longer needs to take that long walk through the forest of the wolves. Aagot's room is across the hall from mine, and she helped me settle in just fine. We are truly sisters again.

I spend much of my time at Bjerkan's Creamery where I work in the store. The dairy is just past the hill by Aagot's house, and the land is green and as beautiful as one could ever wish. It is truly wonderful. I don't know if I love the dairy because of the lowing herd of cows beside the dairy with their tinkling cowbells, or because of that young man, Haldor, who has begun stopping by to visit whenever he comes to the dairy for milk and cream. Like most people, he brings his own pail, and we supply the bottle for the cream. I suspect he really doesn't need all of that milk and cream. He does have a way about him. He is quiet and calm and sometimes makes me laugh, like yesterday when he made a joke about the church bells being like cow bells. It wasn't even funny, but the way he raised his eyebrows made it so. And, oh, I do like his eyes. They're the color of the sea on a day when the waves are sparkling under the sun. He walks like he knows exactly where he's going. I never feel confused by Haldor; he seems just right. I want to go for a walk with him, I surely do. For the past three days we sat for a time on the bench across the road from the dairy and ate our lunches.

He works with his father, who is a boat builder and a sailor. Haldor looks like he was born knowing how to do things, like build boats. He is also a sailor, and sometimes accompanies his father on excursions. Haldor definitely exudes confidence, but not in a show-off kind of way. As I said, he's just right. He knows more about me than I know about him, and that's because he is such a good listener. I need to stop talking so much and listen to him tell me about his life.

I can hardly wait to get to the dairy. I hope Haldor comes again today because I'm wearing a blue ribbon in my hair, one of the ribbons Aagot gave me as a present when I first moved in. Today, like most days, I'm scheduled to work in the store where they sell milk and cream, all in glass bottles as sparkling and clean as you could wish. We also sell brown goat's milk cheese, or gjetost, which is delicious on hardtack, and I often have that for lunch.

I asked if I could learn to milk the cows, and now on Mondays I leave home early in order to help with the milking before the creamery opens. The light is soft and pink on the sandy gravel road to the dairy, and I swing my lunch basket to and fro as I stride along. The birds sing in their usual cheery manner, much as they did when I was a child walking down the road with my mother, many years ago. I slow down just as a red fox crosses the road. It pauses to look at me before trotting across the meadow.

By the time I arrive at the dairy, I have begun to come out of my reverie and I hear the cows before I see them.

The Poet's Daughter

They have been down from the high summer meadow for a few weeks now, and as the weather is still good, we milk them right in the small pasture beside the dairy. It's just a matter of coming out of the barn with a pail and stool and calling out "Yoo hoo," and they come right over to you. It's like they have decided ahead of time who goes first, and it's always the same order.

I certainly had a surprise the first day I walked over to the cows and saw Nora standing there smiling, ready to teach me how to milk cows! She is so much fun. We take our places so we can talk or sing while we milk the cows, and the owner's son, Ingebrit Bjerkan, sometimes helps, especially if the weather looks threatening.

I don't like some of the cows' given names and rename them after characters in books, or the name of a flower. Bluebell is my favorite. I only milk three of the cows, as that's all I have time for before I leave for the store. They smell sweet and have a grassy breath as they come close. Today Bluebell nods her head toward my shoulder in a kind of cow greeting. She has never done this before. I pet her warm fur, as Nora recommends, before starting to milk and that helps her relax and makes the milking easy. When I finish, my cows saunter out into the center of the meadow and continue their business of eating grass. I watch them in their cow elegance before I say goodbye to Nora and walk over to the creamery. The cows seem to like their routine, just as I am getting accustomed to my own.

I'm glad it didn't rain today. If it's raining, Nora milks in the barn and I go on to the store. Even though Ingebrit cleans the stalls and puts down fresh hay, it's messy in the barn. I don't look forward to winter coming on, because my days of milking the cows will end. Nora thinks it's funny that I have been helping with the milking just for the fun of it and for learning's sake, but to me it is an interesting adventure, and besides, I enjoy visiting with Nora.

That evening, Aagot and I picked chokecherries for jelly. The glossy black berries were heavy on the trees, and we quickly filled our baskets. We each ate a few of the berries, laughing at how they make our mouths pucker with their sour taste, but that was part of the fun of eating chokecherries.

Why hadn't Haldor stopped by today? The blue ribbon in my hair seemed wasted; the cows didn't care. Oh well, it was still a good day, and here I am picking berries with my sister, enjoying what we were never able to do as a family. I remember so little about Aagot when she was a baby, but I do remember her eyes, large and inquisitive, the same now as back then.

Just where was Haldor today? I wish I could talk to Aagot about him, but she's only thirteen. Still, I don't really want to talk about him to anyone. Not even Nora. He's my secret.

Haldor has not come all week and now it is another Monday. I am still hopeful, but I walk to the dairy with heavy steps, my head down. Nora has already started milking when I pick up my pail from the barn. If I were alone, I would tell my concerns to the cows. Nora greets me cheerfully with a big smile. She is always happy and laughs at most everything. She laughs even when her cow flicks its tail after the flies. I believe it is because she and Ingebrit have fallen in love, and it is sweet to see them together after work, leaning against the fence, standing close to one another. I can well imagine a wedding in their future.

Alas, he doesn't come and he doesn't come. Oh, woe is me. If I were a chicken I would repeat these words over and over again in chicken-talk, but as a poet I can express my sorrow in hundreds of ways. At the end of each day I write and I write. I am at the prime of my life in energy and feelings, and here I am alone. Each day at the dairy I see Nora and Ingebrit and their strong and joyous love, and I feel forlorn, although I am truly happy for them. I write a sentence and cross it out. I write seven words, and cross them all out and substitute one word. I wake in the middle of the night with a perfect rhyming word, or the words to describe the golden glow on grasses in the high mountain meadow. Many nights I scribble in my notebook. I write about cows. I write of the summer rain. I write of the moon shining down on us all. I write about the night. My passion for words grows with every poem I write.

I become so engrossed in my writing that I forget Haldor, even when I am writing about him! Is it the poetry that I love? Is this true? I begin to write about my mother. I remember what I had long forgotten. As I write I remember more, and this new home with Aagot, far from Lofoten, brings to mind those early days as if from a forgotten well. I write stories as well as poems. There is much to tell. I am always buying new notebooks. Two weeks go by.

Marget has written to me several times from Oslo. She is mixing her own pigments, staining her hands, her clothes, as excited about her scene painting apprenticeship as I am about poetry. Her last letter is a response to mine asking where I should send my poems. Holding her letter close to the kerosene lantern, I review the list of publishers and newspapers and journals. Is my life as a writer to begin with one of the publications on this list, or am I only dreaming?

Moving to the floor with my stack of poems and a small pile of stories, I carefully position the lamp. Where to begin? The poems. With the reading of just a line or two, they begin to fall into categories. I sort them into piles on the pine floor. Poems about the Lofoten Islands and poems of family. Next, poems of night and poems about the moon. It's a toss up whether the poems about death are smaller or larger than the stack of poems about love. The nature pile is half Lofoten and half love. I make another pile of all of my copies of the poems for those who died when I was in Utvik. Poems of weather. Poems of the sea. Poems too complicated to categorize. And bad poems that need more work.

Sighing, surrounded by my poems, it is very late and I have to be at the creamery in the morning. At random I choose one poem from the top of five piles, and the rest I scoop up and place in my bottom dresser drawer, along with the stories. I spend the next hour copying the poems I have chosen. When I awake to the crowing of the neighborhood rooster, I am still in my day clothing and my fingers are stained with ink.

The brown laundry soap gets out most of the ink. In the cooling room at the back of the store is a jar of lemon

The Poet's Daughter

hand cream, which should finish the job except for my nails. Wouldn't it be just the day Haldor comes to the dairy, when my nails are ink stained and I haven't a fresh ribbon in my hair. For once, I hope he doesn't come.

It is only Nora and I milking in the morning, and she rushes over to me, bursting with a secret she must tell. Yes, she and Ingebrit are in love, which of course I know, as does anyone who sees them together, but her news is that they are getting married in the fall. "Before the snow comes," she says, tears of joy streaming down her cheeks. We hold each other and pat one another on our shoulders in a little musical dance. The cows moo and we both laugh and get back to our milking. We sing together until we have finished with the milking, surprising each other with our harmonies. We hadn't known the sound of our combined voices could be so beautiful. The cows added a few lower tones as well, and even seemed to be well in tune.

I was in an upbeat frame of mind by the time I got to the store. As usual, I washed up well and began filling the cream bottles, lining them up along the back wall, enough for the day. Some of the cream and most of the milk stays in the low cool room, where there is always a sweet and earthy smell and where it remains permanently chilly, even on the warmest summer days. It is much like a cave, as it was partially built into the hillside on the north side of the building.

The morning flew by and I paused to rest at the front door. There he is! I spot Haldor walking down the road, walking fast. I ran my fingers through my hair, and I believe I could actually hear my heart beating in my chest. I stepped behind the counter and slipped on a fresh apron. Stay calm, I told myself, but I was far from that as he opened the screen door. This was to be the day that changed my life.

I took my lunch a bit early, and Haldor and I headed to what we considered "our" bench. The sun was high and so were our spirits. For once, I was quiet and eager to hear what Haldor had been doing that had kept him away for so long. His face was tanned and ruddy, making his eyes bluer than ever, leaving me near speechless as I listened. He told how his father, Stefanias Sem Buan, owned a shipping vessel for hauling goods up and down the coast of Norway, and Haldor had been along on this latest trip, which went as far north as to the edge of the Russian border. Their cargo was lumber and potatoes, and various other goods which they either delivered or picked up along the way. He spoke of the various ins and outs of the fjords and how he was learning where to enter particular fjords to avoid hidden rocks and shallows. He was already familiar with sailing the middle and southern routes, but the north was new to him.

I listened to his story with fascination, of how they made their way to safety from a day-long storm up near Bodo. I listened as if my life depended on his words. He told of how they docked and spent the night, and how it felt to see the stars after the storm had passed on. It was that morning as they continued sailing north that they saw the largest herd of whales you could ever imagine. Haldor was then quiet for a moment, looking off into the sky before he took my hand in his and looked into my eyes, telling me that someday he wanted me to see what it was like to watch the first sunlight of day arise when you are out on the sea. He held my hand until he had finished describing the whales, how close they had come to their yacht, before turning to sail away to the west. Haldor smiled and bowed his head to kiss my hand. He took out his pocket watch and abruptly rose, saying he had some business to take care of, and that he would return by the time I finished at the creamery.

I had only another hour at the store and quickly finished my routine work without really thinking about my chores. I swept the floor, polished the counter top, hung up my apron and said good evening to Ingebrit's mother. I crossed the road and waited on the bench for Haldor's return.

I was both calm and fidgety. Most, but not all of the ink was gone from my hands, with the staining mainly on the undersides of my thumb and first finger. An edge of my thumb nail was still quite black, which I hadn't the time to have noticed earlier, but which was apparent now that I was sitting under the sun. Well, that's just how it is, I told myself, deciding to ignore the ink. It is nothing compared to whales. The sun felt marvelous and the buttercups beside the bench seemed brighter than regular buttercups. Across the road, the glass window of the dairy was a clean square of beauty. Just as I was pondering what a wonder glass actually is, Haldor came up beside me. I hadn't even seen or heard him coming up the road.

"Shall we go for a walk?" he asked, and I arose and took his outstretched hand and we walked off together like two lovers in a story. Indeed, that is what we became that day. He knew of a beautiful waterfall on the river off the Inderoy Bay, and it was on the grassy banks of that river that I came to know the love of my life.

Every day thereafter was beautiful, and I noticed the world as never before. We liked to lie on our backs and look at the clouds pass over, finding trolls and fish and boats in the sky above us. We felt like we were floating too. Had life ever been so fine? As you might expect, we spent many days beside the river that fall, until one morning when the first snow fell.

Winter settled in and a blanket of snow covered the land. The cows moved into the barn, and winter clothing came out of the storage trunks. Aagot was at the door with an armload of wood when I came home from Bjerkan's dairy one Friday afternoon. As I held the door for her, she said there was a letter for me. Mrs. Johnson was in the kitchen humming to herself, and the house smelled of baked apples and cinnamon. I helped Aagot with the wood and Mrs. Johnson handed me the letter from her apron pocket, saying it looked important. It was from Oslo, but not from Marget. It was from a publisher, the one I had chosen at random. I had sent them five poems.

I sat down by the fire to open the letter, first running my fingers over the beautiful script on the envelope. The handwriting was even more beautiful than my father's script, with the swirls and loops of my name as perfect a specimen of writing as one could ever imagine. I opened it as carefully as if it were alive. The letter inside was half a page long, on pale blue paper. The editor liked my poems, it said, but would not be publishing them "in their current form." He wanted me to shorten my poem about the Lofoten Islands and send it to him again. He thought it was a good poem, but too long and somewhat repetitious. He particularly liked the second stanza. The last sentence of the letter said that I had good promise as a writer.

The Poet's Daughter

My head was in a whirl. I read the letter aloud to Aagot and Mrs. Johnson. They didn't know quite what to make of it, but seemed happy, seeing that I was smiling and looking a bit dazed. As it was a special occasion, we all settled down at the table and had a nice bit of warm apple pudding, even though it had been intended for after dinner that night. I told Mrs. Johnson that it was the best apple pudding I had ever tasted, and truly it was.

That night was a long one. I had recently moved my dresser into the corner so my desk would rest next to the window's ledge, so I could look out at the sky. Facing the heavens was the place to be when I wrote. I wanted the stars and my creator as near as possible as I worked on my poems. What came to me that night was that I couldn't force the words into being; they would come naturally when the time was right. It was time to put my papers away for the night and get some rest.

I awoke early. It was not yet light out, but I stretched my arms and decided to get dressed. From the window I saw something moving in the yard. I stood still until my eyes could focus. Was it a deer? No, it was a moose between the apple trees. Watching it walk slowly across the yard and on up the road, I leaned as far as possible near the window until it was out of sight. This was the first moose I had seen since leaving Lofoten. Most likely it had smelled the last of the apples still clinging to the tree or hidden under the snow. Surely with that big nose, they must have a sharp sense of smell.

Before breakfast that morning I worked on the poem the editor wanted shortened. I took out two stanzas and changed a few lines to make for a smooth transition. It worked quite well. He was right; eliminating some of the repetitious lines made for a better poem. Still, I'll keep a copy of the first version. I have to admit I am excited about having a poem published in Oslo, although I was happy to have poems in my high school paper back at Lofoten. It's all about sharing thoughts about living, and it feels good knowing others can benefit in some small way from reading my poems.

It was after breakfast that I had to run outside, feeling sick to my stomach. This was unusual for me, as I tended to never get sick, and rarely ever had a cold. This happened again a few days later. That second time Mrs. Johnson was waiting for me at the side door, and suggested we sit in the kitchen for a chat. She was quiet at first, and so was I. Then she started talking about Haldor, whom I had mentioned many times, though I hadn't told her we were in love or anything about our times at the waterfall. "My dear, you may be expecting a child," she said, a question in her eyes as she looked at me.

I had been thinking this myself, but had pushed the thought to the back of my mind. Now everything seemed to be swelling up in my life, literally, as well as in quantities of love for Haldor, for poetry, for a whole new life ahead. Suddenly I kissed Mrs. Johnson on the cheek. "Yes," I said. "I believe a new life is growing." I told her that Haldor was at sea for another month, delivering goods to Trondheim, and he had business in that city that would keep him from returning as soon as he usually did.

From then on, Mrs. Johnson made sure that I had good portions of fish and vegetables each day and she insisted that I have eggs, as well as oatmeal for breakfast. I had an after-breakfast sickness only one time more, and then I was fine all the weeks that followed. We decided not to tell Aagot or Mr. Johnson until Haldor had returned.

Sometimes I knew things before they happened. Now and again throughout my life, that would be the case. I certainly had no way of knowing on which day Haldor would sail back home, but still on the day of his return, I was sure of it from the moment I awoke.

When I finished at the creamery that day, I lingered, taking extra time putting on my coat and scarf, mittens and boots. I was not surprised to see him come through the door. I surely did surprise both Ingebrit's mother, as well as Haldor, when I came right up to him and gave him a sweet kiss of welcome.

Walking over to our now snow-covered bench, he told me he had a surprise for me, and I told him I had one for him too. "You first," I said, and he brought a small package out from his pocket. Wrapped in tissue was a perfect tiny golden locket, which I held to my heart. He showed me how it opened and said I could place a picture inside. "Well, I'll need a picture of you then," I said. And that's when I told him I would also place a picture of our first child in the heart locket, and that would be in about five months time.

The expression on his face as the realization of our future dawned, I shall keep with me always. Although I am a poet, I would never have the words to tell of those few minutes on that cold winter bench, except to say we certainly did not feel the cold.

Chapter 4 (1905)

OUR MARRIAGE CELEBRATION WENT ON FOR THREE DAYS, as was the custom of the land. We were married at Beitstad, Nord-Trondelag, and friends and relatives came from afar to help us celebrate. Probably every extra bed in the entire neighborhood was filled with our guests. Haldor's mother, Ingeborg, was a great help, and together we did a great deal of cooking and baking on the days before the wedding, as did several of the neighbors whom I had an opportunity to get to know quite well as we coordinated our baking plans and figured out just where everyone was going to be staying. Ingeborg was a formal, yet lovely person who wanted everything just so and had a way of making the wedding preparations flow smoothly. Mrs. Johnson and Ingeborg rounded up enough white table cloths for the long tables the men set up outside, and I found it remarkable that so many beautiful dishes were already set out on the side board in the kitchen, ready to be arranged on the tables the next morning. There were blue and white plates, cups and saucers, glass stemware that glistened in the sun, pewter mugs for ale, and the best silver, already polished and ready for the wedding day.

The afternoon before the wedding, Aagot and I picked flowers for the tables, which we planned to arrange into three bouquets for each table, sure that our blue and white wild flowers would look elegant in Mrs. Johnson's cut glass vases. As we walked through the meadow with our armloads of flowers, we saw my Lofoten aunt and uncle, and Astrid, and the children coming up the road. They spotted us just as we saw them, and I nearly dropped the flowers I was carrying. Jenny and Frida came running toward us in their pretty frocks, and Magne was not far behind, dressed in his sailor suit. Only Anton was not along, but of course I knew by then that he had immigrated to America.

Shortly after my Lofoten family were all settled in and resting from their long trip, my father and his wife, Anna, came up the road from the fjord, along with my sister, Mette, and my brothers Peter and Conrad. It was a most joyous and nearly overwhelming day. I was thankful that Pastor and Mrs. Narvik and the Benum family were arriving the following day, as this day was quite filled to capacity.

Early the next morning there was a knock on my bedroom door. It was Marget, who had just arrived from Oslo, and Ingeborg was right behind her carrying a breakfast tray. We three had coffee and buttered waffles and went over the plans for the day. Marget hadn't been sure she would be able to come to the wedding, yet here she was! We ate every crumb of the delicious waffles, and Marget and I kept laughing and talking over each other, as we had so much to say. They helped me get into my wedding dress, and Ingeborg had pressed the apron with the Hardangar lace trim, which completed my costume with just the right touch. Looking out the window I could see that it was a beautiful day, and the long tables were already covered with white table cloths. I could see Pastor Narvik talking to people out near the big birch. There were so many people outside that I thought I must have overslept, but Ingeborg said everything was right on time. I sat down and Marget combed my hair so it shined, and then we all went downstairs, ready for the celebration to begin.

Haldor was standing by the fireplace, all dressed up. He did look fine indeed. He took my hand and we stepped outside into the sunny day. The ceremony itself and the entire morning passed by like in a dream. I talked to everyone and especially all the children. Haldor and I walked all the way down to the fjord and back with my father. I was quiet and let Haldor and my father do the talking. It was good simply seeing them together on this special day.

The tables were filled with food by the time we returned to the front yard. So many friends had helped with the food, enlisting their baking talents and ovens. Aagot had placed the wild flower bouquets on the tables, three to each one, just as we had planned. The tables were a fine sight to behold with delicious food of all kinds, including rye bread and raisin bread, limpa, flat bread and hardtack, ham, kjot roll, smoked salmon, pickled herring, rommegrot, lefse, gjetost and hard cheeses, rice pudding with raspberry sauce, apples and almonds, chokecherry wine, ale, silver pots of coffee, and a fine almond wedding cake on the center table. Everyone was wearing their best, with many of the women in traditional bunads. My father rang a bell to call everyone to the table. Glasses and cups were filled, and my father proclaimed a toast to our future happiness and glasses were raised by all. The celebration had begun.

The Poet's Daughter

I think I enjoyed the first day the most, and especially the dancing in the evening, when a second spread was set out with mostly bread, cheeses and ale, and berry juice and cookies for the children. Haldor was friends with one of the best fiddlers in the country, and he arrived in the late afternoon by boat with his fiddle and four musician friends. When they were tuning up you could feel the excitement in the air, and indeed, it did turn into a fun and lively time. I discovered that Haldor was an excellent dancer, as was his father, who didn't miss a dance all evening. Ingeborg was not a dancer and seemed a bit unsure whether all of the dancing was quote proper; nevertheless, I did see her tapping her toes to a lively national favorite performed by Haldor's friend Bjarne, with many people singing along. Haldor and I walked into the woods together, down to the ice house, where we sat and listened to the music coming through the birch forest. When we returned to the wedding party it was a fine scene before us, with our friends and relatives in their national costumes dancing and enjoying themselves, and the sky all aglow.

You would not think this revelry could go on for three days, but it certainly did, and every day was a new adventure, though similar to the day before. Old friends were able to catch up on one another's news, to marvel at how the children had grown, and make plans for future visits. Benches were scattered around the grounds and little groups formed and enjoyed themselves. The children played games and ran around the flag pole until they wore themselves out. Aagot and Astrid were in charge of taking the littlest ones inside for naps.

On the last evening we had several bonfires along the fjord's shore, where we ate lefse and sausages which we cooked in the fire. It was a sight to see those fires all along the fjord, reflected and sparkling on the water. There were so many fires because the entire village had come to celebrate with us and enjoy the beauty of the night. Our musicians played ballads that probably launched a romance or two among the crowd, and brought a few tears to others. For me the tears came when they played a song my mother used to sing to me, one I had not heard in all these many years. Still, how happy I was, though sleepy, sitting so cozily next to Haldor right beside the fire. It was late when I awoke, leaning heavily against Haldor, and only a few people were still at the fires, now burnt down to glowing embers.

Chapter 5

OUR LITTLE SOLVEIG LOOKS UP AT ME with her large blue eyes, the purest blue of innocence. This first year of her life has been filled with continual change, from her first tooth to her first step. I am letting her eat these wild strawberries in her own way. She looks at each berry before tasting it. The first two she squished between her fingers. She watched me eat several before she tried one. These are the first strawberries of her life, and we are sitting on a blanket at the edge of the field where the wild strawberries grow, up above the house. I like to sit here on this flat rock because I can watch the sea well from here. Haldor is away at sea for months at a time, and I feel connected to him looking out over the water. He sails with his father, the boat builder. They are basically a store in the form of a boat and deliver goods up and down the coast, picking up from one area and delivering to another. By next season Haldor expects to have his own boat. He already has his captain's papers.

We live with Haldor's parents, Sefenias and Ingeborg Buan, in that fine house just below this wild strawberry field. Sefenias's two younger sisters live with us as well: Karen and Martine, so Solveig does get a bit spoiled from all the attention. From here we can see the barn and several sheep out in the barnyard. Solveig isn't sure about the sheep, but she no longer cries when we pass them by. Last night she made a funny sheep bleat and laughed, pointing toward the barn.

There are still two upper windows of the house that need curtains. All the other windows have white lace curtains I have crocheted to fit, and I am glad that Ingeborg loves them so. She is good to me and I am glad I can make her happy with my handiwork. We are quite unlike one another, but we get along well. Both of us enjoy sewing and baking, and have a comfortable time together doing daily chores. She taught me how to use her sewing machine and made the dress Solveig is wearing today.

Solveig is falling asleep in my lap with her fingers stained with strawberries. I had intended to stop by to see the chickens on our return, but that can wait until tomorrow. She doesn't wake when I pick her up, and though she is heavy now, I enjoy her warmth against my shoulder as we head back down to the house. Ingeborg is out weeding in the garden as we pass by, and Peter, the farm helper, has just gone around the corner of the barn. He takes care of the cows and sheep, and general heavy work around the farm. Although he has only partial vision, he does well and knows the paths and layout of the farm, but prefers to walk near a building or use the widest road up to the house. Ingeborg always keeps his coffee cup on a hook below a kitchen shelf that is his alone.

Karen and Martine are shelling peas on the back steps and laughing about something. I put my fingers to my lips so they can see that Solveig is asleep and not to wake her as we step inside. I feel like sitting in the rocking chair with Solveig while she sleeps, but I settle her into her crib instead. This is the time of day when I can write.

The Poet's Daughter

I have been putting off writing to my editor in Oslo, as I am behind with a story he wants me to finish. Settling into the rocking chair with my notebook and pencil, I work quickly, as I had thought over how the story should end when I was in bed this morning. It is easy to finish, as it has already been written in my mind. I take the story to my desk and copy it onto good paper. I am brief with my letter and set it aside for the ink to dry. Although over an hour has gone by, Solveig is still sound asleep. From the upstairs hall window I watch Aunt Martine outside feeding the chickens. She has a way with them; I can tell by how she leans toward them when she scatters the feed that she likes them, probably more than I did when I took care of the chickens at the Benums' back in Utvik. Oh, I hope Haldor and his father sail home this week.

Downstairs again, I join Karen in the kitchen for a cup of coffee while I wait for Solveig to wake for her lunch. The kitchen smells of coffee, and soup simmering on the stove. The peas will be for dinner with creamed potatoes and fish. I always know what dinner will be, as Ingeborg is the most organized person you could imagine. The farm runs smoothly with her at the helm, though just as Haldor wants his own boat, I wish for my own home. Not to say it is not fine here, which it is; idyllic, really. It is just a natural longing to be on one's own.

After a week has passed and the sailors have not returned, we are getting anxious, as there have been heavy thunderstorms which let up only yesterday. The air is fresh and clear and Solveig is playing on the blanket beside us as I pick raspberries. Over the bushes, I spot the sails in the distance. We have time to return to the house with the berries, and I tell everyone they're coming in. There is excitement in the house and Ingeborg starts a fresh pot of coffee. Solveig and I are halfway to the dock by the time the men are anchoring out in the bay. I hurry us along so we will be on the dock when they row in on the small boat. Solveig is already calling out "Papa, Papa," and waving her little arm by the time we step onto the wooden boards of the dock and they are close enough that we hear the splash of their oars. Haldor hollers out his greeting. My, they look tired, and with that glad-to-be-home look too.

They tie up the boat and unload, and Solveig gets her share of kisses as we head up to the house, where we hear about last week's storm and yet what a successful trip they had, having received an excellent price for the load of lumber delivered to Bergen. After they settle in, Haldor comes to the kitchen with a present. He always brings some surprise from his travels. This time it is a small blue coffee pot with fancy cups edged in gold, with saucers to match. We marvel at how the set has survived intact, packed in a box filled simply with crushed newspaper around each piece.

The first day of their return is always a time for celebration, and that evening we have a dinner of ham and potatoes and carrots. We linger over a dessert of berries with fresh whipped cream, followed by coffee in the new cups, which Aunt Martine insists makes the coffee taste much better. Sipping the freshly ground coffee from my gold-edged cup, I know that she is absolutely right.

Haldor started sailing with Jonvick in May. He is from the island of Ytteroy and they sail a yacht between Levanger and Trondheim, delivering goods between the two towns, usually lumber. I'm very aware of the cargo, because the boat is large enough that Solveig and I are now sailors too. She is already quite grown up, even at five years of age. We joined Haldor on his sailing route in the middle of June. It is a wonder to be on the sea with Haldor on the "jekt." I now realize why he loves to sail and why he wants his own boat. Spending so much time outside under the sky, you see the changes in the sky as clouds pass by and I almost feel like a cloud sailing along on the sea, taking my good old time. We watch fish jump, and we see little towns and colorful houses, docks jutting out from land, small fishing boats, row boats, and white horses in green fields. Solveig likes to watch the animals and searches for waterfalls on the higher mountain slopes. We play a singing game where we reach our arms up high, so we nearly touch the sky. Life is sweet this summer.

I love watching the waves from the back of the boat, especially when the sun is first rising and the colors on the water keep changing. The colors are subtle, because these are the days of the midnight sun. The lack of darkness has disrupted Solveig's sleep, and yesterday she fell asleep in midmorning, beside me on the deck, her head resting on my lap, her clothespin doll in her lap. The sea carries us along smoothly and I feel safe for us all. Haldor and Jonvick are good sailors. So far, we haven't been to sea during a storm.

Between sailing times, Solveig and I stay in Trondheim with the Bernt and Aslaug Oien family. We all get along well and Solveig is enjoying her Oien cousins, as they are all quite close in age. Last week when Haldor was on land, we saw a picture show, which was our first ever. It was called "The General" with Charlie Chaplin. We all laughed until our sides ached. Partly I was laughing to hear everyone in the audience laughing so loudly, so that in a manner of laughing, we all joined into the adventure of the picture show. Charlie Chaplin has a way of walking which is a kind of side-to-side, hop-along walk with feet turned out. He moves like no one anyone has ever met.

After the movie, Solveig and her cousins had fun doing their version of the Charlie Chaplin walk out in the yard. I think we talked about Charlie Chaplin for the rest of that summer. I don't think a person could ever forget their first picture show.

On our last week of summer, we stayed on the island of Ytteroy with Jonvik's family. While the adults were having a day of relaxation, Solveig and Alfred Jonvik were off to explore the island. Alfred seemed a reliable young man, though a mere two years older than Solveig, so we thought it was fine for them to go farther than on previous days. Alfred wanted to show Solveig the ruins of a monastery from long ago. Before the reformation, there was a monastery on Ytteroy and this was their destination. Seeing the two of them walk off along the shore, I pictured myself at that age, following along behind Anton when we were off to play at our secret beach.

Solveig and Alfred were breathless when they returned, running into the house with sweet smelling twigs and a branch of red berries. They both spoke at once, telling about all the unusual plants that smelled nice, and berry bushes of a kind she and Alfred knew nothing about. The plants had not been in fruit when Alfred had been there before. They wanted to know what they were and wanted to go back with a pail to pick more berries. No one was familiar with the berries, but Jonvik said he would investigate. Haldor and I thought the aromatic plants were probably Mediterranean herbs that the monks grew, and we wanted to visit the ruins ourselves—as much for the ruins as for the flora—but time was running short, as we were to return home the next morning.

Chapter 6

SOLVEIG IS NOT QUITE OLD ENOUGH for school. We moved into a house owned by the Buck family when Haldor started working for Nicolai Buck, the owner of the limestone mine and factory in Hylla. He sails a vessel filled with lime to a processing plant in the Trondheim fjord and has a more predictable schedule than when he was sailing with his father, which I like.

This house is well made and beautifully finished, with fine details in the woodwork and brass knobs on all the doors. Solveig is fascinated with one of the ornate fringed window shades, which has a picture of a nattily dressed wanderer and his dog. She thinks the wanderer is a dancer and she likes to run around the house and twirl and dance on her toes. What a happy child she is, adjusting so well to the move from her grandparent's home.

This new home of ours has the most modern washroom I have ever encountered. The water flows through a pipe from a rain collection device outside the house, which fills a large water container in the washing room. A metal bin for a wood fire sits below the bin to heat the water, which then comes out through a faucet into a lovely round tub, which we use for both bathing and clothes washing. This arrangement is a huge improvement over carrying water heated on the kitchen stove. Before the snow comes, Haldor will close off the pipe to the rain source and we'll use the small hand pump that feeds from the well into another basin.

I have joined a group of neighbor women who gather for coffee and smorgasbord once a week. We each bring our handiwork along to work as we visit; most do knitting, though I prefer embroidery. This week I am embroidering a blue bird on Solveig's new dress. There is another child her age, daughter to one in the group, and they sit at our feet and play with their clothespin dolls or some other simple amusement. Some of the homes we meet in are nearly a kilometer apart; others are much closer, so I'm always glad when it's my turn to host the group.

Haldor bought me a sewing machine when we moved to the Buck house. It's a heavy metal machine with a wheel on the right side which I turn by hand. The metal is black with an ornate gold motif, like the rising of a new flower, and at the bottom are the gold letters of the machine maker. I sew Solveig's dresses and my own, and I plan to make curtains for the windows when I am able to find some nice blue material to match the kitchen table.

Working in my little backyard vegetable garden is a pleasurable chore, though lately it's been a time of melancholy. There is something about working in the soil that does that; it is like tending to the emotions, weeding around the radishes and carrots. Sometimes I sit on the bench beside the garden and watch Solveig open peapods, popping the fresh peas into her mouth while I daydream about the past and all the people I've known who are no longer alive. Mainly I am grieving for my sister, Mette, who died this year. I wish I had known her better.

I don't like to talk about her death, still so recent. We heard of it just after we moved to the Buck house. Poor Mette, only twenty-five years old, leaving Gundmund, three and a half, and Bjarne, just two years old. I expect her husband will remarry soon, a good person he is. Mette herself was three when our mother died. Alas.

We went to Beitstad for the funeral on a passenger boat, arriving just as darkness fell, and my uncle and aunt met us at the dock. We stayed with them that night and I slept little. The next day we brought Solveig to stay with Father's wife, Anna, during the funeral, and she was happy enough with a rag doll Anna gave her as a present. That rag doll reminds me of death, all limp and too much a reminder of that day of Mette's funeral.

After the funeral we took advantage of our time in Beitstad to visit my grandparents, now into their nineties. I never knew them well, having lived on the Lofoten Island for so many years in my youth, but I liked them. They always made me feel special and loved. Grandmother Svarte gave Solveig two little spoons from her cupboard, and Solveig was proud to have them. I found it a kind gesture on her part.

When we arrived home after the funeral, Grandfather Buan had big news. He had decided to sell his farm and buy a larger farm, a dairy farm, over near Stod. He wanted to buy the property for the house and land, and did not intend to work the dairy. Grandfather wanted Haldor to buy the old farm, and they reached a satisfactory agreement within the week. Haldor bought the farm, yet sold it not too much longer after buying it.

The Poet's Daughter

Goodbye, Buck house. After two years up on the hill in the Buck house above the city, we have moved down to the heart of Hylla, which is right next to the fjord. Haldor went up the road to watch the Buck house torn down. He wanted Solveig and me to come and watch, but I thought it would upset Solveig to see the beams and the roof of the house where we had lived for two years come crashing down. Nicolai Buck is building a new house above the old one, and thankfully he is saving much of the fine woodwork from the old house to incorporate into the new one. His new house will be much larger and even grander. I requested the fringed shade with the picture of the wanderer and his dog, as Solveig was most fond of it, and Mrs. Buck brought it over one afternoon. I hid it away for a surprise for Solveig.

I was feeling low when we had to leave the Buck house, until Haldor told me that the time was right for us to build our own house! The sale of the farm had gone through and everything was settled at the bank. I could hardly wait, yet I knew it would take some time and considerable organizing. There were plans to make, and lumber to buy, a foundation to dig, and it all took time. We were living in an apartment in the house of Beret and Bergitta, two sisters, and their father, Lars, in their large house in Hylla—a three-room apartment just right for us during this time of transition. The apartment had a kitchen and living room downstairs, and two bedrooms upstairs. Haldor had known Lars for several years, as he made herring nets and knew all the sailors.

I had seen Bergitta before, as one couldn't miss her. She wears brightly colored clothing and is extremely friendly and a bit nosy as well, according to Karen in my sewing group. Bergitta delivers goods and takes orders, and her sister, Bergit, is the quiet one. They say no one has ever seen Bergit wear any color other than black. She is as pale as ice and keeps her dark hair in a bun so tight that her eyebrows are pulled upward, making her look chronically surprised. Yet she is the fashion designer and a lovely person. The sisters make their living sewing and knitting, and are known well beyond Hylla for their skills.

Since we moved into the apartment in their house, they have been generous with their knowledge and I am picking up many useful sewing tips. Solveig is old enough to do a little simple sewing and adores playing with the scraps of material the sisters are in the habit of saving for her. At the moment, Solveig is sitting on the floor making paper dolls from an old-fashioned magazine Bergitta gave her last night.

Solveig is growing up and surprising me in many ways. She had been pestering me to teach her to knit with some bits of colored yarn from Bergitta, but she is not yet old enough for that. Knitting is a complicated craft, and so instead, together we worked on covering an old box with pretty material, a box just the right size to hold her collection of yarn for the day when she would be old enough to begin knitting. She was dismayed that I wouldn't teach her to knit right away, but after her initial disappointment was happy enough working on the box, with its promise of knitting some day in the future. We used flour and water paste, and the box turned out looking right smart with a gingham top and sides covered with a yellow floral print.

Our current accommodations have been a great convenience, as the Hylla dock is right across the road. The general store is literally next door, and just down the street is the town's bakery. It didn't take us long to get into the routine of enjoying fruit pastries or kringer on Sunday mornings. Mr. Johansson is a baker of the first rate.

While living here with the sewing sisters, we experienced a tidal wave that grounded a ship. Haldor knew some of the crew and had them stay at our place overnight. Unfortunately all we could offer was the floor and some bedding, and a warm supper, but they were grateful, as they were badly shaken. The storm raged through the night, and few of us really slept. The thunder was close and the flashing of lightening strikes kept lighting up the bedroom. Solveig had climbed into our bed and though the wind whistled around us, she finally fell asleep. It seemed the storm would never end, but finally a silence fell over the house and I fell asleep.

When I got up to make breakfast for everyone, Haldor was already up and had started a fire in the kitchen stove. I took one look out the window and turned to Haldor, who put his arms around me, and we stood by the stove to warm ourselves and ease our cares. I fixed oatmeal and eggs and a large pot of coffee.

After breakfast, we went out to survey the damage, which was extensive. Along the shore, a number of boat houses had been badly damaged, and one had totally washed away. Tree limbs and lumber were floating all over the harbor, and seaweed had washed up onto the streets, along with oranges that were scattered all along the street. Lars was walking along with a big basket picking up the oranges. A roof at the house next to the bakery had blown down, and up the hill, someone's chimney had toppled. Fish had been thrown up onto the road, along with fish netting, yet I saw no birds at all except for one dead gull by Austad's dock. We later heard about the sinking of a large ocean ship, the Titanic, and wondered if it had been part of the same storm that brought the destructive wave to our own fjord. Later, we read in the papers that it was an iceberg that sunk the Titanic.

Haldor was glad we hadn't started to build our house yet, as we might have incurred damage. There were a lot of boats hauling lumber for rebuilding after that storm, and we had by then decided on a location for our new house. Haldor felt the land just above the sisters and Lars's house was the perfect location. It was a good-sized plot of land with a fine view of the harbor, right next to the road and convenient in every way.

The house is going up according to schedule. Conveniently, Solveig started school just before a lot of the messy, muddy, and noisy work began, which made me feel better for her safety, as she is a child of strong curiosity. After school, when the day's work is winding down, I take her up the hill to see how the house is taking shape. There is a high pile of dirt behind the house and we always save that for last. Solveig stares at the dirt pile in such a solemn manner, and insists on seeing it before we head back home to prepare supper.

After dinner Solveig stays with the sewing sisters, and Haldor and I head up the hill so he can point out the new work on the upper story. We walk through the sawdust and I enjoy the aroma of the freshly-cut wooden beams.

The Poet's Daughter

Looking through the wood outline of what will be rooms, I see the sky turning a pale orange. I have never felt this way about a house before, seeing it from its beginnings and looking forward to the life we'll live in this house. It is like looking into one's own history that has yet to be lived.

The work on the house continued through the fall, when the exterior walls were completed. A roof was finished with the help of two of Haldor's friends, one who had roofed his own house the year before. We were mighty glad to have it finished when the first snow fell, as it was a heavy snow for early fall. Haldor worked all through the winter and then into the spring, and I could hardly wait for the last nail and board to be set into place.

Finally, in the late spring of 1914, we moved into our very own home! You would have thought no one had ever built a house before, the way we carried on, moving our furniture and trunks and dishes into the new house. Lars helped and we borrowed a wagon for most of the heavy items. Thankfully, the weather was mild on the day we moved most everything. We let Solveig help raise the flag to the top of our new flagpole, where our beautiful Norwegian flag of red, white and blue was to be raised on special occasions for all the years ahead, as far as we could imagine.

That first summer in our new house, the hour before sunrise was my favorite time of day, especially when Haldor was home. We would leave the window open so we could hear the waves in the harbor and the squawking of the gulls. By the time we were up and finished with breakfast, the steamship whistle of the *King Oscar* would sound, and I would walk with Solveig to where she met the other children who were going to school. They had a good ways to walk to their school and several of them walked together, the older ones looking out for the youngest. Solveig's school routine and the boats and gulls were our clocks, measuring the passage of each day. In the afternoon the passenger and post boats came to dock, and I was always there to see them come in, to visit with friends, and to take care of errands. Early each month I mailed poems, and sometimes a story, to my editor in Oslo, and often I had a letter going out to Marget.

On Saturdays, Solveig came along and we regularly stopped at the post office across the street from the bakery. I did our errands always in the same order, as I liked to stick to a routine. When we shopped at the general store, the owner, who was fond of Solveig and liked to make her laugh, always had a caramel for her. He would close his fists and hold them out for her to pick the hand with the caramel, and they would both be delighted when she choose correctly, which was every time. He never opened the hand she hadn't chosen, but slipped it into his pocket. He had wavy hair, and eyes so dark they seemed to have no pupils. I never knew quite how to look at him.

We are stopping at Margrethe's house today. She is a widow who lives next door to the sewing sisters. Margrethe's husband drowned one stormy autumn night, some years before we moved to Hylla. This is another of Solveig's favorite places to stop because she likes to look at all the animal knick knacks in the glass cabinet. Plus, Margrethe's yellow cat, Mons, is docile and lets Solveig sit and pet her and talk to her. I help Margrethe put up her freshly washed curtains, as I had promised her on Sunday, and afterwards we have coffee and kringler. I am sorry to see Margrethe getting so shaky. She didn't spill the coffee, but was near to doing so. I had to reprimand Solveig for trying to feed part of her kringler to the cat, but she now understands that such food is not good for cats. At least I think she does. She's developing a strong mind of her own, the more so since she started school.

The days go by quickly. It seems besides my own chores, there is always something to do for someone else. I still make wreaths and bouquets for special occasions, and there are those who never learned to write, or are too shaky to do so, and I enjoy writing their letters for them. Most of the letters are going to a relative in America. I feel a vague connection to Anton when I write a letter to America for someone here in Hylla, even when I don't know them at all. I have received precious few letters from Anton over the years but have responded to each one. We are for the most part formal in writing to one another, but I do wonder what we would say if we expressed our deepest feelings, after all these years. Anton has become an engineer. I am so proud of him, as I know his parents are as well. He is a smart and fine person.

Haldor, Bertha and Solveig Buan in Norway.

Solberg Church at Beitstad, Norway where Bertha Buan was confirmed.

Haldor Buan (center) with crew in the Melana on Trondheim Fjord.

Sefenias Buan, boat builder and organist who loved to dance.

View of Trondheim fjord from Hylla where the family watched for the sails of the Melana.

Chapter 7

HALDOR IS HOME. Just as it was when we lived in his parents' house, homecoming from the sea is an occasion to celebrate. He is in the habit of sending a telegram when he is leaving Trondheim so I can estimate pretty well just when we'll see his sails in the fjord. We are so near the telephone company that Julie, the telephone operator, always runs over when his telegrams come in. Solveig and I both dress in something bright and watch for him from the big rock behind the house. We recognize his green yacht from afar and head straight down to Austad's dock. Now that he has his own boat, named the *Malena*, we all feel a special pride as he sails in. We watch him sail into the bay and drop anchor. This is when he looks to shore for us and we wave madly, as always. By the time he gets to the dock in the small side boat, we are up and ready to help with packages. While he ties up the boat, I buy a rather large fish from Lars's cousin, whose boat pulled in just before Haldor reached the dock. We'll have a fine fish stew tonight, and berries with cream for dessert.

It was especially nice to have Haldor home for the August Music Festival this year. Aagot and her husband, Andreas, have joined us for their last day of a week-long visit. Musicians have come from the neighboring communities, and the weather is fair for the big day. The sisters made a folk costume for Solveig, and Haldor and I are wearing our dancing clothes for the day's folk dancing. Solveig and her school friends are beautiful and gay in their bright Norwegian dancing clothes. Haldor and I sit on a bench by the pine trees and watch the youngsters kick out their feet in rhythm to the music as they hold hands, going round and round in the circle dance. Some of the girls have flower wreaths in their hair, including Solveig. Haldor and I visit with friends and partake of the table spread with good bread and cheese, and have ourselves a few good dances before we gather Solveig to join us to walk with Aagot and Andreas to the train depot. We wave them off on the evening train, back to their home in Sunnan. It was a peaceful and lovely walk home, with a warm breeze and happiness in our hearts.

Just as we arrived home, Julie, from the telephone station rushed over to tell us that a wire from Trondheim had arrived with the news that war had broken out, and the Germans were marching into Belgium. It was the beginning of World War I.

Haldor is sailing and I am alone in the new house. Solveig is in school and it's snowing lightly. Walking around the rooms of the house, I survey each room. The new blue curtains are up, crisp and fresh here in the kitchen above the sink; in the living room, one set of crocheted curtains are hanging in the seaside window and I'm making slow but steady progress on the second set. The shade with the wanderer and his dog is in Solveig's room, on the side overlooking the new apple tree.

The Poet's Daughter

The living room stove has proved to be a good one, and attractive as well, with blue front tiles and silver edging. I'm still fiddling with my little treasures and seem to be moving them around every day. The special vase on top of the cabinet seems perfectly placed; that one I need move no further. It was when we were still living with Haldor's parents that he brought the vase back from a trip to Trondheim. He had forgotten it in the boat for a few days, so it was all the more of a welcome surprise because by then I wasn't expecting any new gift. The vase is a deep sea blue with white lily of the valley flowers circling the widest section. It is remarkable how one truly beautiful object can make an entire room shine. Yes, that is a perfect vase.

My favorite spot to sit and crochet is here beside the window where I have a view of the sky and trees, and so I settle down with a cup of coffee and my half-finished curtain. The curtain progresses row by row. I take many breaks to watch the snow fall. Between counting crochet stitches and watching the snow outside, I'm in a dreamy place, half thinking of nothing while still thinking of Haldor, wondering just where he is at this very minute, probably nearly to Trondheim by now.

One more day's work and the curtain will be finished. I refill my coffee cup in the kitchen and water the geranium above the sink. It has a flower bud, something to look forward to. Today I'll work at the kitchen table instead of at my desk. After spreading my papers onto the kitchen table, I decide to start a new poem about snow. It's funny how the words start to fill the page, almost falling like snow itself. Sometimes writing is easy like that, as if the words are just waiting for me to put them onto paper. This one I'll send to Oslo, just as it is. Well, maybe with one last perusal in the morning. That's my general rule, to see how it appears the next day. As usual, when I'm writing, the time flies. It's nearly time for Solveig's return from school.

"Mom, Mom, guess what!" Solveig rushes in all excited. She tells me about the wolves as I hang up her coat. They could hear them howling in the woods nearly all the way home from school and everybody moved fast and the little ones were scared and Bjorne was crying by the time they got to his house. It certainly was the year of the wolves. We have been hearing them nearly every evening from the Kjolen Mountain woods, but rarely during the day. The school children always walked in a group, with the older children looking after the youngest. I assured her that they were fine as long as they stayed together. A wolf pack never bothers a group of humans. I was glad Solveig was such a sensible child, for the most part, and her uneasiness was gone after a glass of milk and an apple that we shared.

This year with the beginning of the war, and now the winter wolves, has me uneasy. It's hard to know what to expect. So far we have not been affected. Haldor has been sailing cargo for the Buck Lime Company on his ship since September. People talk about the war and are beginning to stockpile more goods due to the uncertainty ahead. You feel a difference everywhere. The sisters say the orders for new dresses are way down compared to last year. The bakery is offering less variety of goods, which is unusual with Christmas not far off, and I was unable to buy raisins at Austad's store earlier this week.

The Poet's Daughter

Here we are on the train, chugging along on our way to Sunnan for our Christmas with the Buans. It takes two hours to get there and we'll soon be pulling into the station. I have always loved riding trains, even though my first train ride was the sad one after my mother died and I was off to Lofoten. Haldor and Solveig are leaning toward the window, watching to see when we pull into the station. Haldor loves visiting his parents, and of course his two sisters, Karen and Martine, who are still at home; now at their new home at the dairy, Shevloa, which is not a working dairy as they did not want the work of keeping cows. Solveig is totally excited and can hardly wait to see everyone. They are all so dear to her, having spent all of her earliest years with them before we moved to Hylla.

There's the train whistle. We gather up our coats and our Christmas packages. "Look, it's Grandpa!" Solveig is waving and smiling. Good old Blakken has pulled the sleigh to the station, and after all of our greetings, we load up and climb in. Cozy under a big sheepskin lap blanket, we head off to Shevloa through the snow, accompanied by the tinkling of the jingle bells on Blakken's harness. I am glad the new house is not so very far from the old homestead. We pass Lake Snasa, white and smooth, a reminder of earlier summer picnics on the lakeshore now covered with snow. The pines beyond the lake are thick and tall, and quiet as winter itself. This is where the Christmas tree was chosen each year, brought home pulled behind the sleigh. When Solveig was a baby and before she could walk, she would sit near the Christmas tree and reach up with a tiny hand, talking to the tree in her baby talk. "Oh, here we are!" Solveig leans so far out of the sleigh that Haldor has to pull her back. We round the bend in the now almost-darkness of evening and there is Shevloa, with lights in all the windows.

We bustle in with our packages with hellos all around, and the warmth in the house feels great after the chilly ride from the depot. While we are all talking at once, we take off our coats and hand over mittens and hats to Martine. The long table has already been set with Ingeborg's best china, the dishes with gold trim and floral swirls. The large matching tureen is set in the center, which undoubtedly is filled with the traditional risengrot rice pudding. I see a platter of ham and sausages, including sylte; there is lefsa and Christmas bread, a cheese board with several cheeses, a wooden bowl of apples, and another of nuts and little marzipan candies on a golden plate.

Solveig and her Aunt Martine are admiring the tree in the living room, so tall it nearly touches the ceiling. "Martine, there's the little tea cup ornament your dad gave you the first year we stayed with you," I mention, pointing to the fragile blue and white cup hanging level with my shoulders. She claps her hands together in delight, and we hug again. Oh, how good it is to be with loved ones at Christmas time. Solveig wants to know when we'll light the candles on the tree and Haldor comes up beside us and says we'll light them after dinner, and it's time to eat.

Haldor's dad, Sefenias, says grace and reads us the Christmas gospel, his voice clear and full of meaning as he reads. How fine it is to share this meal with those who love one another and can only be together once a year. Although we are together with great joy, sometimes at Christmas I feel the loss of my mother, a tug at my heart, and wonder if the others think of someone who is no longer here too. Somehow, the light of Christmas and the quiet of the snow outside fill a person with what they need. And this Christmas bread with gjetost doesn't hurt either. So good.

The Poet's Daughter

I had wondered if Sefenias had been sad after Haldor sold the farm so soon after buying it. Maybe he wanted us to be nearer than we now are, over in Hylla. But he and Ingeborg seem very happy today. They are adaptable and make the best of things. Oh, now Karen is the lucky one this year – she found the almond in the rice pudding! She looks so pretty across the table from me, with her blond curly hair and big smile.

After dinner, Ingeborg wants Solveig to go upstairs and wait. She runs up quickly because she has figured out that when she comes downstairs again, the candles on the Christmas tree will be lit. Martine and Karen light the candles, each taking a side of the tree. They work with both speed and caution, each finishing their side at the same time. I call Solveig as soon as they're all lit and she speeds down the stairs and we all stand before the tall green pine tree, all aglow with lighted candles from bottom to top. What a sight it is to see this tree from the forest transformed into our symbol of Christmas here in the living room.

After we settled down around the tree, Ingeborg handed out the presents, one by one. Solveig received a blue knitted sweater with the traditional snowflake pattern circling the top and the sleeves. She spun around to model it for us. I was just as delighted as she was, as it was just what she needed for her trips to and from school. We all received and gave presents to one another—all practical items of clothing, for the most part, as is the custom.

Still, there is something new in store. Sefenias has bought an organ, which we have been eyeing ever since we arrived. We set the presents aside and turn our chairs to hear Grandpa play the organ. How startling to hear this fine music in the living room! He plays very well. The first song he plays is "Silent Night," which calls us all to our feet to gather near the music. Standing around the organ for the first time, I am restless with excitement. When he plays "Oh Christmas Tree" and begins to sing, we all join in. Sefenias has a beautiful tenor voice and leads the singing as we go through all the Christmas songs we can think of. Grandpa and Martine exchange places, and although Martine says she is still just learning, she plays "Oh Holy Night" on the organ while Sefenias stands beside her and sings. The rest of us listen, enthralled.

I expect we all fell asleep into a night of peace at the end of that unforgettable Christmas Eve.

Chapter 8

I CAN HARDLY BELIEVE IT, but after all this time, Marget is getting married and I am in Oslo. Solveig and I sailed with Haldor as far as Trondheim, where she is staying with her cousin's family. I continued on to Oslo by train, traveling alone for the first time in many years.

Last night Marget and I talked on and on in her apartment, catching up with all the latest news. It was like old times on Lofoten. Marget is now well established as one of the foremost theater scene painters, and has become an accomplished set designer as well, leading the way for women in this field. Her fiancé is an actor, which was no surprise to me, though her letters of the previous year mentioned an interest in a different actor from the one she is marrying, and whom I will meet tomorrow. We were both surprised by the late hour when her grandfather's clock struck 1:00 a.m.

The wedding was small and picturesque, held in an old wooden church which Marget must have chosen for its theatrical beauty. I loved all the wood carving on the beams and the sound of the music under the lofty roof. Her theater friends were there and I liked them all, as they were friendly and more demonstrative than ordinary folk. It was a blessing to be with my dear friend on her wedding day and see her so happy. I immediately took to her husband, who seemed like an old friend in no time at all. It seemed a shame that Oslo was so far from my home, and though they spoke of putting on an Ibsen play sometime in Trondheim, I had only a small hope that this would happen.

We all walked the married couple to the nearby dock, where they went up the walkway to the ship that would be taking them to Copenhagen for a honeymoon excursion. Their timing was close, for it was only about fifteen minutes after we arrived before the gangplank was pulled up and the ship sounded its whistle. Everyone on shore waved to those waving back to us from the ship. It felt a bit like we were all taking part in a play, or a parade, which seemed just right for my theatrical friend Marget. Goodbye and best wishes, Marget.

After the boat left, I did some shopping and found a book for Solveig, and a nice, round wooden waterproof container for Haldor's chewing tobacco. I really didn't like his chewing habit, but after perusing a number of shops, I couldn't find anything else that seemed something he could use and would like.

The next order of business was to find the office of my editor, Thor, whom I knew only through our correspondence, now of some years. Though our letters have always been about my poetry and stories, for the most part, I still feel that I am on my way to meet a friend. I find his office half a block off the main street, next to a book store, and step into the outer hallway that leads to a tiny reception area. I am somewhat startled meeting Thor in person, this tall person with a grand smile and open manner. He doesn't look at all like the older man I had imagined, but has curly reddish-brown hair, and wears glasses which rest midway down his nose. He introduces me to his publisher, a round-faced man with an inquisitive and friendly expression. We three visit over coffee in a small dark office, until the publisher takes a phone call. Thor suggests we go for a walk as we talk, as the day is sunny and mild.

We discuss poetry all the way from his office up Karl Johan's Boulevard until we reach the palace. This is the first time I have had a friend to discuss poetry with since I lived at the schoolmaster's house, just after leaving Lofoten. There I had talked to Pastor Narvik a bit about my poems, and about words, and that was good. But this is a new experience, talking to Thor about not only my poems, but poems by other poets, other writers, and I must remember all of the writers' names he is mentioning.

Here we are on the beautiful grounds of the palace, looking down over the city, and Thor is reciting a line from one of my earliest poems:

> *Here in Lofoten's fairyland strand*
> *my heart ever beats*
> *to the never ending rhythm*
> *of the sea.*

Too soon, I am on the train again, heading to Trondheim. The smooth dark chestnut I found on the palace grounds is in my hand, and I relive the day as I run my fingers over its smooth surface as the train moves along. I have a new book to read: Ole Rolvaag's "On Forgotten Paths," a present from Thor, but I leave it sticking out of my bag, preferring to look out the window for the time being. In my suitcase I have a list of poets he recommends that I read. I didn't tell him I have no readily available library in Hylla, but since I do get to Trondheim on occasion, I can look into their resources. One must always find a way.

Solveig is glad to see me but tells me she has been having a wonderful time with her cousins. We take the *King Oscar* passenger boat back to Hylla, instead of sailing with Haldor, as he has some labor organizing business to take care of that he'll tell me about when he returns. He was quite secretive about it before I left for Oslo, and told me to keep his doings to myself. I think it has to do with getting better pay for the lime workers at the quarry.

Oh, how tired I was when we reached Hylla and walked up the hill to our house. It was good to be home. Solveig was full of energy and ran upstairs and down again, just because she could, apparently. I was standing with my hands on my hips looking out the window, thinking about what to fix for our supper, when I saw Julie from the telephone company coming up the lane. I hugged myself, hoping she would not be delivering bad news. It was too soon for a wire from Haldor about when he would be leaving Trondheim for home. But Julie had a basket under her arm and was walking slowly, so I calmed down and noticed how heavy she was getting, and how she waddled as she walked. She has brought us a fish stew for our first night back. I am so grateful, but she says it is the least she could do, as I brought her that loaf of raisin rye just last week after I had baked so many loaves. It all works out, she says, and indeed it does.

I was already yawning by the time Solveig and I finished the dishes, and dark had settled in. I was so tired that I thought Solveig must be sleepy also, but after changing into our night clothes, Solveig came into my bedroom in her nightgown and asked if she could start her new book. We agreed she could read for half an hour by the kerosene lantern and that was long enough. Tomorrow was a school day. It was hard to stay awake long enough to make sure she shut off the lantern and went to sleep on time.

The week after our return was a busy one, with errands, catching up on chores, and visiting with the neighbors, in addition to the story I've started, inspired by my trip to Oslo. In fact, I have been unusually tired for several weeks now. Yes, my clothes have been getting a little snug around the waist for some time. It's been ten years since Solveig was born. If all goes well, it looks like there will be a new baby in the spring.

It's snowing lightly. I hope the school children are all dressed warmly enough. Watching for their return and the sound of their skis is a marker of these days, and they all come at the same time, as sure as clockwork. There are a dozen of them who all go together, but just five children by the time they ski down the road past our house, where Solveig turns in. I watch for her return with more concern since the time of the wolves, and so far there have been no incidents of daytime howling this winter, thank heavens. Seeing the young skiers reminds me of my Lofoten days of skiing with Marget, and sometimes with Anton and the kids from our school, which was near enough that we all just walked to and from, back then. Solveig's school is one kilometer up the King's Road.

It's been cold outside and Solveig's cheeks are pink. I have coffee while she has her milk and snack, as is our afternoon custom, after which she reads and I write. We are a good match.

"Mom, you're making faces," she says after standing beside me for a while. I have to laugh at myself and explain that I've put my editor, Thor, in the story I'm working on and that I must be remembering the way he had of wiggling his glasses back up his long, straight nose when they slid down. Solveig tried to wiggle a pair of pretend glasses on her nose too, and we both ended up laughing.

"Are you going to put me in the story?" she asks. I remind her that she was in the story about the wolves, from last year. "Oh that's right," she says, recalling how she thought the story was too scary.

Chapter 9

HALDOR HAS RETURNED and the *Malena* is docked out in the harbor. We are sitting by the fire at the end of the day and I am wearing the brooch Haldor brought as a present. Solveig is sound asleep. Haldor looks tired, but relaxed, after telling me all about meeting with the men who are organizing the lime workers' union. I could tell he had been anxious about it, so now that some improvements have been made, he's glad that he took part in the negotiations. This seems as good a time as any to tell him my news.

"Pa, it looks like you'll need to start work on a cradle soon. For our new baby."

"Well, you don't say," he says, coming over to give me a kiss.

We named him Bjarne, and he was born on a beautiful spring day in May. He fell asleep beside me that first morning, and Haldor opened the window so we could listen to the robins sing. Solveig hadn't wanted to go to school as she was already so enthralled with her baby brother, still just a few hours old. Haldor told her that her best friend was waiting for her at the road, so she gave Bjarne a kiss on his forehead and left for school. She stopped briefly at the doorway to say, "I have a brother now," then off she ran.

Those early months were fine, though I was fraught with fatigue and needed my rest sorely and took advantage of Bjarne's naps. It was a mild summer that seemed longer than other summers and I spent many afternoons in the yard sitting on a blanket with Bjarne. When a bird would land in the yard, he would laugh so that his whole body seemed to be laughing.

By fall he could sit with his box of empty thread spools and pile them up as high as possible. He didn't laugh when they fell down; he just piled them up again more carefully, until they stayed upright. Then he would sigh, pleased with his results. Bjarne liked everyone and when I had company he would sit with whoever wanted to have a wiggly, but happy baby on their lap. At six months, he was a babbler, quiet only when he slept, and he certainly did get plenty of attention with his winning good-natured ways.

My father came to spend Christmas with us, as Anna had died and he wanted to be with us in his loneliness. He came on the train and brought presents for all, as well as fruit and nuts and candy. Solveig, with her sweet tooth, loved the curled and colorful hard candies, which I put in a bowl on the table. Bjarne was seven months old and crawling all over the place. He couldn't be alone for a second, so Solveig was a big help when I was preparing Christmas dinner. From Shevloa we received a wonderful box of their holiday specialties, including sylta, fattigman, and Grandma Ingeborg's famous flat bread.

The Poet's Daughter

Shortly after my father returned home, things took a turn for the worse. Solveig became ill. Dr. Wold examined her and said she had rheumatic fever and must stay in bed and out of school for as long as necessary. Those first weeks she was feverish and lost her appetite and had bad earaches that kept her awake at night. In the mornings I could get her to eat a little oatmeal and sip warmed raspberry juice. She might take a cup of soup later in the day, but otherwise she would turn away from any food, backing away as if from poison, and especially from anything heavy, like ham or sausage. She liked me to read to her in the afternoons but quickly fell asleep after a few pages. She slept day and night. Thank heavens Bjarne was taking longer naps those early weeks of her illness. In the mornings he would wear himself out crawling fast everywhere he could go to explore, and he was beginning to pull himself up to stand at Haldor's chair.

After one very bad night of earache and fever, Solveig seemed better. She said she felt fine. We had the doctor come again and he agreed she was doing well, but he decreed bed rest for another month. After that, her schoolmates brought her assignments, and she quickly caught up with her school work and was back to her reading. Her appetite came back, thankfully.

When Haldor returned from sailing, he was greatly relieved to see Solveig sitting up in bed and smiling. He brought her a golden locket, and one for me as well, as mine had been lost in one of our moves. They didn't have chains, but he said he would find us chains next time, and we could have pictures taken to put in the lockets. He took pride in showing us the clever opening mechanisms.

As delighted as I was with the locket, I was actually more pleased with the coffee and other items Haldor brought back. Ordinary items like sugar and coffee, foods we previously took for granted, were now in short supply due to the war raging throughout the coast. Haldor said that even though Norway was neutral, Great Britain, our best ally, induced us to stop shipping fish and minerals to Germany, and that's why our ships were being torpedoed by the German U-boats. Of course the big freighters stayed on the coast and we were inland, yet we were still on the fjord, here at its end. There was a fear of how far the Germans would come and what they would do. There was even talk of unexplained fires. Uncertainty kept many of us awake at night. Oh, how I dreaded each time Haldor left to sail again. Many times I watched Haldor sail off and return, as the war went on seemingly without end. Bjarne was a toddler, and by 1917 I was expecting another child.

The first rose of summer bloomed on the day Lilly was born. Haldor set it in a vase next to my bed and said there were more rosebuds by the side of the house, just waiting to open. Tomorrow I should be up to walking that far for a look. Maybe. At the moment, it is ten o'clock in the morning on June twenty-third and Bjarne is touching the soft hair on Lilly's head, and he is quiet for a change.

The sun is shining down on us and the room seems touched by a white light. I think we have given her the proper name, Lilly, after the flower, lily of the valley, and the great French actress Lillian Greuze. With what bright eyes she gazes at me. I see both innocence and curiosity in those blue eyes. Her tiny hand closes on my finger with surprising strength from such a dainty one. What will you do in your life, little one? Who will you be? And where will you go? Who will you love? All these thoughts float through my mind, looking at her eyes, so bright and ready. I sing a little song to my Lilly about roses on a sunny day. Yes. She falls asleep while I sing and I'm at the edge of sleep myself.

Bjarne leans onto my arm and puts his finger to his lips. "Shhh, she's sleeping now, Mama, isn't she," he says. Haldor tells him that I need to sleep now too, and they leave the room together.

Later in the day, Grandmother Ingeborg brought me a tray with a roll, strawberries and cream, and coffee. She sat at the edge of the bed, patting the blanket near Lilly, still deep in sleep. I'm so glad to have Ingeborg here for this whole week. She has been telling me about all the books she left out for Solveig to read at Shevloa as she recuperates from her operation, proud as any grandmother that Solveig is such a good and avid reader. After Solveig became so engrossed with Anna Karenina, Ingeborg knew Solveig could handle just about anything.

Solveig had her tonsils and adenoids removed at St. Elizabeth's Hospital in Trondheim in early May. I had been terribly worried for her, though I knew she was in good hands with Dr. Olsen, and the Oiens took care of her in Trondheim until Haldor could sail with her to Shevloa for a full rest. Everyone says she is healing very well, but I miss her so. She is going to love her new little sister, I'm sure of that.

I don't know what I would have done without Lisa, our neighbor's daughter, who has helped after school during these early months with Lilly. I have been terribly slow to gain my strength, but at last I am starting to feel my old healthy self, which is perfect timing, because Solveig returns today. Lisa picked up Solveig's favorite pastries from the bakery, and a fine dinner is simmering on the stove. I keep checking the window to look for the *Malena* to come sailing into the harbor, even though I know they won't be here for another hour or so. I've been telling Lilly all about her big sister, and she looks at me with her big eyes, taking it all in. In some ways, I expect I have spent a lot more time with Lilly because of my poor health, as we nap together often and have extra cuddling and singing time. Little Lilly coos like a bird when I sing her favorite song, the one that makes her laugh and clap her tiny hands and bounce against the pillow.

Finally, Haldor's sails are on the horizon and I am flying down the hill, leaving the shadow of my unwell self far behind. Lilly is bouncing in my arms and Bjarne is loping along beside us, singing "here comes Papa's boat" in his loudest voice with a trilling vibrato from his hop-along gait. On the dock, he says, "Mom, you're good again." I'm happy to agree with him. As Haldor and Solveig sail near, I note how tan Haldor has become this summer and how pale Solveig looks beside him, though she appears to have grown taller in these last few months since spring. After we have finished with our welcome-home greetings, Solveig insists on carrying Lilly back to the house. I trust her capability, though I am a bit taken aback by her maturity. I stay close by, as Solveig has so recently returned to good health.

Shortly after Solveig's return, there was a fire out on a neighbor's boat. Haldor and several others rescued as much of the cargo as they could, but the boat itself burned to oblivion despite the men working late into the night trying to put out the flames. I watched the fire in the dark harbor from the living room window, wringing my hands mightily. We never knew the cause of some of the fires, whether they started from the easily combustible lime cargo, or from the Germans. There were tales of boats being burned in the night as retaliation against Norway because we were supplying fish to the British and not to the Germans. These attacks were said to be mostly on the ocean, and we were supposedly safe here at our end of the fjord. One never knew exactly what was going on, and we went about our lives with our lack of up-to-date information as best we could.

Wouldn't you know, but the *Malena* was the next to catch fire. It was a Sunday morning and not at night, so there was no thought of German mischief. The weather was stormy and the waves high. The lime cargo ignited and flared up. The Hylla Volunteer Fire Department had the fire out in time to save the boat, but the cargo had to be thrown overboard. When the storm passed and the ship dried out, fresh lime was reloaded and the *Malena* was ready to sail again. I was thankful the ship was saved, but I knew Haldor would soon be involved in the union for the lime workers again, something he definitely kept to himself. I expected there would be more meetings for him in Trondheim.

The rest of the summer was idyllic, and the weather matched our happiness. Sitting here with my notebook, I have improved one line of a poem that had been puzzling me. With the book now closed on my lap, I take in the domestic scene around me: Bjarne is busy with his wooden boat, loading a cargo of old thread spools at one end of the couch and delivering it to the other end of the couch, talking a blue streak all the while. Haldor is reading the paper and Solveig has her nose in a book. Lilly is near me in the kitchen cradle, playing with her toes and babbling to herself, or to her toes.

There is definitely a change in the air with fall coming on, surprising us as it does every year. I am concerned for us all, and especially for Solveig, as she has started back to school. She seems completely well and happy, but influenza is popping up everywhere. People are put to bed and never get up again. The children and the elderly are bearing the brunt of it, I'm afraid, and death comes quickly. I have heard that Pastor Narvik is very busy over in Utvik.

On Haldor's recent long trip to Russia, he lost one of his crew. He would only shake his head when I asked him to tell me about it, so it wasn't until last night that he finally told me what actually happened. He had delivered goods to Russia numerous times before without incident, if you didn't include some rough weather. This time, they anchored the *Malena* in the harbor at St. Petersburg and took the small boat in, as in times past. As they neared the dock, they could see dead bodies all along the streets of the harbor.

Haldor sat shaking his head slowly at this point and I thought he wouldn't be able to go on. But he continued, telling how no one was around, only the seagulls and the dead. I listened in horror, imagining the sound of squawking gulls and waves slapping against the sides of the boat, and the sun setting over the horrid scene of death. "Terrible, just terrible," Haldor said. As they rowed back to the *Malena*, he decided the weather was unfavorable for night sailing and told his men they would sleep on the *Malena* and leave at first light of day. A few hours later, they were all feeling ill, and Hans was sweating with fever. Haldor poured a small cupful of kerosene out of the lamp and took a big draught of the stuff, forcing it down his throat, thinking it might protect him from the dreadful disease that had come upon the city. Hans would not do the same, and in the morning he was dead. Fortunately, his firsthand crewmate was okay, but not feeling totally well when they sailed away at first light. They had no choice but to have a burial at sea for Hans, Haldor's faithful crew member of several years. It was with a heavy heart that they sailed over the Baltic Sea and returned to Norway from that trip.

Winter came on, as it always does, and people were afraid to go to church, avoiding large groups of people for fear of contracting consumption. A girl in Solveig's class died. We sang our own songs on Sundays in the living room, and read from the Bible. Haldor wore a white shirt every Sunday and walked about singing songs he learned from his musical father. Sunday was still a special day.

I wrote several stories and poems that winter of 1918, as I was filled with many feelings and experiences needing expression. By springtime, we were all happy to be outside again. Haldor tilled the garden, and Solveig and Bjarne helped me plant the vegetables. Lilly was walking and loved the grass and flowers and every day I made clover wreaths for her hair. Solveig would give Lilly a pile of red clover flowers, which she tried to connect and set on her head, from where they would immediately fall off. Lilly was persistent and proud when she finally kept a few clover flowers on top of her head. Then she would laugh and the clover would fall off again. It was a happy spring. I called it "the wild strawberry spring," as the berries were excellent that year, and I found that I was pregnant again.

In November, Armistice Day was cause for great celebration, and we had a dinner to mark the end of The Great War. The timing came about at the end of the wave of consumption that had plagued our community, and near the end of my confinement. I had missed the marriage celebration of my sister-in-law, Karen, during the summer, as I was feeling unwell. My neighbor's daughter has been doing our laundry and preparing most of our evening meals since late summer, and I am ever so grateful. We pay her a fair amount for her services and she is saving up for her future. She has told Solveig that she really wants to go to America, but does not want to tell her parents.

Alf Haldor Buan was born on December 26, 1918. He was a healthy baby with bright blue eyes and a tuft of curly hair and a soulful expression. I, on the other hand, was in poor health and depleted of energy. Haldor brought out the extra quilt to warm me and I felt like I was buried in layers of blankets and quilts as I lay looking out the window at the snow blowing wildly in our yard. Alf was tucked into his cradle away from the draft, and I drifted into sleep with thoughts of his little face and the snow blowing outside while we were toasty warm inside.

I must have slept for a long time, for when I awoke, our neighbor, Lisa, was sitting beside me holding Alf, rocking him in her arms. When she felt sure I was going to be all right, she told me about the day so far. She said Haldor had come over to her house in the storm, requesting her help. He was in near panic mode and said the house was a mess and I was not well and the baby was here. When Lisa arrived at our house, she first looked in on me and saw that I was breathing and comfortable under my pile of blankets, one of which she peeled back. Alf was awake but then fell asleep when he turned to his side.

Lisa said the downstairs was indeed a mess. Haldor had confessed that he had slammed the door to the back hall too hard, and the large milk container flew off the shelf, splashing high and low. Solveig had gone off to get more milk from the dairy, and the spilt milk was partially cleaned up when Lisa arrived, but was still dripping and had pooled in the corner of the kitchen. Even the broom was soggy with milk.

The evidence of Haldor and Solveig's efforts at making pancakes for lunch was poking out of an old bucket, which included broken glass and blobs of batter and pork grease. Apparently the hot fat hit the bottom of a cold bowl, which then split into pieces. Luckily, there were no injuries, just a mess to deal with. After Lisa finished describing the kitchen, we both put our hands to our mouths at the same time, to stifle our laughs. Dear Lisa, I was so glad that she was going to stay and help out until my strength returned. She was such a kind and capable person, and has managed well after losing her husband to the Spanish flu less than a year previous.

Lisa brought her eight-year-old son Gustav along with her each day, and we would all have breakfast together. Julie at Telephone Central wanted Gustav to stay with her, as she had lost her only son and was lonely, so Gustav and our three-year-old Bjarne spent a lot of time at Julie's house. Bjarne was an active, happy child and liked playing with older Gustav, whom he admired. It worked out quite well, and Bjarne became independent and confident at an early age. Lilly and Solveig adored Lisa and we were one happy family, even if I was slow to return to health, and Haldor was off sailing a lot that year. Lisa stayed with us until June, when she left for a job in Trondheim, the city where she would later marry a brew master.

Solveig spent a lot of time with her friends that summer, and still helped a great deal around the house when she was home. Solveig became an excellent cook, leaving behind her day of pouring hot fat into a cold glass bowl as on the day of Alf's birth. She reminded me of myself as a teenager, happy and delighted with life. She and her two best friends did everything together, always laughing and off on some adventure around town. They called themselves the "Three S's" because all of their names began with an "S": our Solveig, Sigrid, and the other Solveig from the woodcutter's family. They were all three confirmed together and then each left when their families moved, one to Trondheim and the other to Oslo. I know Solveig missed them a lot, but she went on to enjoy the company of others her age. All the young people knew each other from school and from church.

Solveig's knitting basket sits on top of the dresser, always with a pair of slippers or mittens going. She knits extremely well and she's quick with it. She learned in school and took to it immediately, even mastering double knitting and complicated designs, which she can do without a pattern. She gets the most serene look on her face when she knits, usually in the evening after a busy day. I think her knitting time is her daydreaming time.

The Poet's Daughter

Lilly is waking from her nap. If she cries out, Alf wakes too. She likes to watch me feed Alf. She's a good little sister to him, but she wants him to hurry up and learn to walk and talk so they can play together outside. Her recent game is counting his toes, which makes him laugh. I think they are going to be great friends.

Chapter 10

ANOTHER LETTER HAS ARRIVED from Duluth, Minnesota, from my brother Peter. There have been more letters since the war ended, and the ships are no longer torpedoed, losing both mail and cargo. Peter is encouraging Haldor to leave Norway and move to Duluth. I am reluctant, as Haldor makes a good living here. He owns his own boat, the beautiful *Malena*, and we have a wonderful home on the hill, a fine garden and fruit trees, with a view of the fjord. And what would I do without my friends, to say nothing of the mountains, and how could our own handsome flag that blows in the wind on the flagpole in the front yard be exchanged for another? I do not know how I could make such a change.

I know Solveig would not want to move to America, as she is training for a good job at the telephone company, and I suspect she is falling in love with handsome Nils Austad, whose folks own the grocery store by the harbor. But many are immigrating to America, young people just starting out in life, and others who are ready to move on to something new, enticed with tales of opportunities and riches in America.

My cousin Anton was the first person I ever knew to move to America. I thought he was very brave to do so, and

The Poet's Daughter

it worked out well for him. He is married and has two young daughters. His letters are infrequent, alas. The last time I heard from him, he spoke of a project his company was involved with, and it was fun to read of his enthusiasm. I can always hear his voice when I read his letters slowly, as if he is reading them to me. It seems another lifetime ago, when we were young and living on our Lofoten Island; our island of paradise, I sometimes think. Being young is a kind of paradise, even though it is filled with difficulties and traumatic times and little opportunities for independence. Now I have an idea for a poem: how one's youth is like an island, and how that magic remains with you as you travel through life, ever surrounded by a great sea. Yes, odd that I haven't written about that before.

The children are playing down by the dock. I often stand here at the living room window and watch them at their play. They like the shore just after the tide goes out, leaving surprises behind. They collect things like corks and feathers. Now they're doing their stomping dance, and Lilly and Alf look like little blond elves. They love to pop the air pockets in the long strands of seaweed. Lilly says she likes the way it feels, and Alf likes the sound. Bjarne takes charge of the beach and likes to order them around and wants them to call him Captain Bjarne. Sometimes he scares them and chases them down the beach. As often as not, he is off playing with his older friends. If Lilly and Alf aren't on the beach, they are on their rocks just off the road. These are smooth boulders they play on for hours. They tell me the rocks are horses, and other times they are boats and they will take you wherever you want to go.

And where are we all going? Well, Haldor has made the decision for us all. We are indeed moving to America. I am being torn asunder. On Sunday we are going to tell the children. Alf and Lilly are too young to really understand, and I expect Bjarne will be excited, as it is his nature to be ready for new adventures. Solveig will hold back her tears until she is alone, much as I do. They will all have time to get used to the idea, as there is a good deal of planning, paperwork and documents to be mailed back and forth. I will need to decide what to take along, knowing most everything will be left behind. Truthfully, I wish Peter had never moved to Duluth, Minnesota. He is definitely the person who has persuaded Haldor to make this move.

Haldor's parents have seen the children of many of their friends immigrate to America, or Canada, and they fully realize what this means. Haldor's dad is still trying to stop us from making this "crazy reckless move." I could fight more to keep us here, but I know how stubborn Haldor is once he has made up his mind, and so I must go along on this one to maintain the harmony of our family. There is only a small part of me that is excited about the move; mostly I am sad.

I have packed a picnic lunch in the basket. It is a perfect day to row over to the beach at the end of the fjord with the children. They love the adventure and I plan to continue the tradition as long as possible. It is something we do occasionally when Haldor is sailing. Today is one of those perfect days, just mild enough with a blue sky, yet not too hot, and the bay is calm for rowing and I need to forget about America for a few hours. I ring the bell to call the children to the house and watch them race up the hill, hopping and skipping and twirling along, exuding such youthful energy like frisky young ponies. They can hardly

The Poet's Daughter

contain their enthusiasm when I tell them we're going on a picnic and to get their hats and sweaters, because I have the picnic basket all set to go. Bjarne runs to get the box out of the closet that we always use for things they find, shells and such. It seems such a special day, of a sudden, and I wish Solveig did not have a class today so she could come along.

When we first moved to Hylla, Haldor taught me to row a boat and bought this little row boat so Solveig and I could amuse ourselves like this when he was away. Right from the start, I loved to row. We sat side by side on the middle seat when he showed me how to row, taking deep slow strokes to go forward. He taught me how to use the oars to turn, and how to go backwards. I practiced by myself until I could sidle up to the dock as smooth and quiet as a fish. Today Bjarne is sitting by my side, helping with the right oar. We are all quiet, fully occupied with watching the water and listening to the oars swish through the sea. Lilly and Alf are sitting together on the back seat.

Rowing to the very end of the fjord where we pull in is just far enough to seem a great adventure, and my arms ache just a bit as we glide in to the beach to the right of the wide flat expanse of rock we call Picnic Point. I pull the boat up onto the sand and set out the anchor. The children are already taking off their shoes and socks so they can walk along the soft, sandy beach. They know they are only to get their feet wet and to never go into the deep. Children learn to mind well when they live on the fjord.

I arrange our picnic on a blanket while they run up and down the beach like sandpipers. By the time they are back to enjoy our lunch, they are happy and hungry. We eat silently, munching on cheese sandwiches and sipping the last of the berry juice drink Solveig and I made last fall from cloudberries she and her friends picked in their secret berry-picking place, though I'm quite sure I know exactly where this is.

    There is a lovely breeze today and I like running my fingers through the sand. Lilly has already found several clam shells for the treasure box Bjarne brought along for their discoveries. He and Alf have been searching for dried starfish and now have as many as they can carry in one trip. There is room in the box for it all. Behind us the bushes are green with gooseberries, not quite ripe. Will we have time for another trip to pick them, or will we miss out? I fear my days will quickly be filled with packing and hours of visiting friends and family before we leave for America.

Chapter 11 - 1923

THE HOUSE HAS BEEN SOLD. The boat has been sold. I feel like I am in a novel I do not want to be a part of. But here it is, the day of the sale of our goods. I have taken this moment to sit for a while on the bench under the flagpole in the backyard, this place where the children like to play their games. I know someone will be looking for me before long, but I need to collect myself, my thoughts, and gather them together here under our beautiful Norwegian flag. Buggies are parked all the way up to the fork in the road, people having come from afar to our sale. All of our furniture is sitting on the lawn in front of the house and our gardening tools and everything we own is set out, even the pretty carpets. Our dishes have already been sold, most of my favorites, even gifts Haldor brought back from his many trips in the *Malena*, though I am glad that his parents took several of those.

There goes a buggy up the road. I shouldn't have looked, as it has Haldor's rocking chair tied to the back, along with a big box of I don't want to know what. The sound of the horses clomping along the road has been going on all morning. It wasn't that long ago that King Harald and his entourage came along the road past our house, their fancy buggy pulled by four classy horses. The whole parish knew he was coming through our town, and I had the children all dressed up and waiting on the front steps. Alf and Bjarne wore their sailor hats, and I put a big white bow in Lilly's hair. Solveig was in school that day. The children sat waiting for the king and his entourage, even though they were restless when they didn't come right away, but finally we heard the horses and saw them come into view, fast enough to stir up the dust on the road. We all waved at King Harald and he waved at everyone along the way. What a day that was! Haldor arranged to have a photo of the children taken sitting on the porch, waiting for the king. That photo is packed away in our trunk of treasures to take to America. I am also taking my sewing machine, even though it is very heavy.

"Oh, Mama, here you are," Solveig says, coming to join me on the flag pole bench. "The Pedersens just bought my dresser and Papa is helping tie it down on their hay wagon. It's just too much," she laments. I hold her hand in mine. Just last night she came to sit on my bed and we talked about the move. Mostly I listened, which is what she needed. Her belief is that if she were only a year or two older she could stay here by herself, work at the telephone company where she has been in training, not have to leave her friends, and perhaps she and Nils could marry. Now, she doesn't know what the future will bring. She remembered her best friends, the other Solveig, and Sigrid, who moved away back during her year of confirmation and were so dear to her, yet she made other friends when they had gone away. She isn't sure if it will be like that with Nils. "Maybe he is truly the one for me," she had said, before bursting into tears. I made cocoa and we sipped from our cups as the evening turned dark, and just sitting together and being quiet seemed the right and only thing to do. When Solveig was leaving for her own bedroom, she stopped at the doorway and said: "And he plays the violin."

The Poet's Daughter

Now sitting with Solveig under the flag, wouldn't you know who comes around the corner of the house—none other than Nils Austad himself, tall and handsome. As they walk off together, I wonder what the future will bring for us all.

"Yes, Bjarne, you can sit in the front," Haldor tells him. The big car, and the only car in our town, is taking us to the train station today. I have all of our important papers in my purse and put them in order for probably the tenth time. The importance of riding in a car, rather than a boat, is keeping Lilly and Alf occupied. Solveig cannot stop crying as we pull away from our dear old house, our home of all these years. Now the tears come for me as well, and I put my arm around Solveig as we cry together. As we pass the Pedersens' hay wagon they wave, and we wave back, and for some reason we are able to pull ourselves together. In the front seat Bjarne is bouncing up and down next to Haldor, pointing to this and that and asking how the car can go so fast, and he pretends to drive using an imaginary steering wheel. The farms and hills flash past and the fjord is soon far behind us as we arrive at the train depot.

I have been on trains many times in my life, but this one reminds me of the trip I made as a little girl to the Lofoten Islands, except now I am the grown-up with a husband and family of four children, and we are on our way to board the boat to America. As back then, there was great sorrow, as well as a hint of excitement about what was to come. I think we all relaxed somewhat on the train and busied ourselves looking out the window at the landscape of green hills, apple trees in bloom, and horses and cows grazing in the fields. The first tunnel through the mountain surprised the children and Alf and Lilly pulled their knees up and huddled together, their eyes wide open, so thrilled and surprised by the sudden darkness. We chugged through many tunnels, through many mountains, until we finally reached Oslo, and by then it was dark.

We took a carriage to a hotel and had our luggage brought to our room. Our trunk was stashed in the room behind the clerk's desk on the first floor. The room appeared to be in order, but as I pulled back the blankets of the large bed it was clear we could not stay here. Bedbugs. They swarmed over the sheets to get away from their exposure to the light of the room. I beckoned Haldor over to see the pests and told him to take the children to the lobby, and quickly. Solveig stayed with the sleepy children in the lobby while we got our luggage and trunk together and arranged to move to a hotel down the street, which we were assured was bedbug-free and as clean as a whistle. Fortunately, this was true, and we all had a good night's rest. It had been a long day of travel.

In the morning it was onto the *Stavangerfjord* and off to America. What a beautiful boat the *Stavangerfjord* turned out to be, with a cream-colored exterior with two red stripes of trim around the smokestacks. We walked onto the boat with trepidation and excitement, watching the other passengers looking as eager and unsure as we were. The feel of being on the ocean was with one as soon as you stepped onto the deck, with the subtle movement of the sea and the fresh smell of the ocean in the air. We took the stairs and went down a long hallway past other rooms until we came to our rooms. We had two adjoining rooms, with bunk beds in each room. Haldor and Bjarne and most of our luggage went into one room, and the little ones and

Solveig and I were in the other room. Alf will sleep with me in the lower bunk tonight, and Solveig and Lilly can share the other bunk. We all looked out the porthole window and enjoyed the novelty of seeing the sea through a round window. The bathroom was clean and by the time we had settled in and washed up, we heard the boat whistle. The ship was ready to sail. We were up on deck just as she was pulling away from shore and everyone stood by the railings to wave goodbye to Norway and to those waving from the dock. We waved to everyone.

It was an odd feeling to be on such a huge ship moving out into the ocean and away from my beloved country. It was more than a person could take in, being tremendously thrilling even as a tear fell. The sky was blue and there was a soft breeze and the sea air was invigorating. Solveig took the children for a walk around the deck, and Haldor and I stood together watching the coast of Norway become smaller and the ocean more prominent. We held hands like newlyweds. There was so much to say that there was nothing we could say and the silence held us together. I don't know how long we stood there at the railing, but at one point Solveig came with the children and said it was lunch time because the bell had just rung.

The tables were set with white table cloths and we were served by waiters in elegant dress. Bjarne thought it was funny that some of the waiters held a white dish cloth over their arm, but he, as well as the rest of us, enjoyed our first meal on the boat immensely. We had ham, new potatoes and peas, our choice of an assortment of cheeses and breads, coffee for the adults and berry juice for the children, with apple pudding for dessert, topped with whipped cream.

Honestly, it seemed that we would just finish one meal and the bell would be ringing to announce the next meal of the day. We did eat well every day of our journey across the ocean. I would have enjoyed it much more if I hadn't been hit with sea sickness on my second morning out. Thank heavens I was the only one to endure this. Solveig stepped in to help with the children, as did Haldor. Solveig took Bjarne to the top deck each day where he met a friend who had a ball, and they played ball endlessly, according to Solveig, at least until the ball went over the side several days into the journey. They thought the captain should be able to get their ball back, but one of the crew members said "she's gone now, boys." They invented a game without a ball and Bjarne declared himself the captain of the game. Their game had something to do with sighting whales and keeping an eye out for stray red rubber balls.

Solveig discovered the ship's library, which she loved, as the shelves were crafted by fine artisans and fitted out with books for all ages. She read to Alf and Lilly and Bjarne after lunch each day before they took their afternoon rest period.

After a week on the ship, Haldor and Lilly came rushing into the cabin where I was resting with Alf and insisted we come up on deck, as we were soon to be passing the sister ship to our *Stavangerfjord*, the *Bergensfjord*, on its way to Norway from New York City. I brushed my hair and splashed water on my face and tried to put my sea-sickness out of mind as I climbed the one deck to the top. Solveig and Bjarne were already at the railing, and we were just in time, as the *Bergensfjord* was nearly even with our ship. To our surprise, a choir dressed in formal attire was beginning to sing. Someone said it was the famous Normanna Male Chorus. They first sang the Norwegian

National Anthem, and many people on our ship sang along and I was proud to hear Haldor's voice, clear and true among them. I was not well enough to sing. As the ships passed one another, they finished our anthem and started right up with the American National Anthem. I knew that the sound of such a fine chorus singing over the sea would stay with me forever. I hope the children will never forget this concert we were hearing in the middle of the ocean.

I felt a little better after the concert, but not well enough to be up for more than half an hour. I was glad that Haldor took Lilly everywhere with him, up on deck, and into the lounge where he liked to have a late afternoon nip. He said everyone brought children there and I suppose it was all right, as it was a vacation kind of situation. Lilly talked about the old men her papa sat with and the stories they told, all about sailing and storms and how one man always talked about potatoes—the best kinds of potatoes to plant in the new country, the best potatoes to eat, everything about potatoes. Lilly thought he was funny.

Alf stayed by my side, where he felt most safe, except when he went to the library with Solveig. I think the children had a wonderful time, which made me happy even while I was feeling awful with each roll of the sea. Haldor loved being rocked to sleep by the waves of the sea and spent much time watching the sea from the deck. I would join him to watch the sunsets each day, which was the time I seemed to feel best. The days went on and on and the ocean was a place like no other, as there was no land to be seen in any direction, only the ever-changing colors of the water.

One day Haldor and Lilly were walking the deck when he spotted a herd of whales. He and Lilly saw the whales spout water like waterfalls. The whales moved on quickly, but not before Bjarne and his friends caught sight of them from their position on the ship.

I was feeling better by the time of our last night on the *Stavangerfjord*, and Haldor and I went up on deck to watch the moon. He pointed out some of the constellations that we used to watch from our yard in Norway. The big dipper was always my favorite. Haldor liked the North Star, which he called his guiding light. I slept little that night, imagining everything that might be ahead for us. I woke the children early and we had a last breakfast before we went up on deck.

The outline of the city of New York was coming into view. We saw other ships and tugboats and everyone was talking about how we would soon be arriving at Ellis Island. Haldor spotted the Statue of Liberty first. "Welcome to America," he said, and surprised me with a kiss.

PART TWO - AMERICA

LILLY

1923

Lilly Buan in Norwegian costume on 17th of May celebration in Duluth, Minnesota.

Chapter 1

PAPA HELD ALF so he could see, and Bjarne and I pushed aside someone's coat so we could squish ourselves to the railing. We waved wildly to the Statue of Liberty. She was very beautiful and majestic and my, so tall! She was a copper color and shone like a sunset on the fjord. The ship moved past her and I kept waving until Solveig said we needed to get ready for Ellis Island. I wanted to stay and watch the statue as long as possible so I could memorize it for all time, but I left with Solveig when she tugged at my arm.

Down in our cabin, Solveig combed my hair and my mother brought out a big bow for the top of my head. The boys were wearing their sailor hats and we were all ready to go. My papa and another man tightened the straps on the luggage and then we all went up on deck and walked off the boat like a herd of people. There were so many of us getting off our boat, you wouldn't have thought we could have all fit on that one ship. It didn't seem like there were that many people when we were just sailing along on the boat like we were until today.

On Ellis Island we stood in a line and walked through a large door bigger than a boat house door. There were men in gray uniforms inside who directed everything and we all

The Poet's Daughter

walked along between rows of railings. A tall man with a thin moustache looked at Mama's papers and directed us to another line. Papa held my hand and Alf stayed with Mama, and Solveig and Bjarne were right behind, so we were all together because you wouldn't want to get lost in that big building. When we got through the next line, there was a man at a table who looked at the papers again and handed them to someone with a nose like a bubble and he hit the papers with a metal hammer that made some marks. I don't know what he said, but no doubt it was in English, and then he smiled before calling for those next in line.

Next was the health line, where an officer was looking into everyone's mouth. Papa said since we had already been examined by a doctor in Norway and we had our papers, this wouldn't take long. He said we still had to go through the line. They were checking to see if people had a disease. The examiner looked me in the eye, examined my hair and ears, and that was all. None of us had a disease, so we could go on. Some people had a disease and were sent to another part of the building. Those people looked tired and sad and were wearing too many layers of clothing and many of them carried large woven baskets. One woman threw her arms out and looked to the ceiling and cried out in a language I did not understand. That's when I started crying too, but Papa said they would be all right and be given medicine. I was still scared for them, but then all of sudden we were outside again and boarding a ferry to go back to the dock.

Our next destination was the Union Station train depot. This depot had the highest ceilings in the world, I'm sure of it. Bjarne wanted to know how they got up that high to build the ceiling and the roof and Mama said her cousin Anton would know, but that when we get to Duluth,

Minnesota, we would go to a library and find a book about large buildings. She thought they probably used a series of tall connecting ladders, as they used for the stave churches in Norway. Papa said a building is like a large boat, only upside down, and in Duluth he would build a model of his *Malena*, and we would learn about construction.

Just when we were talking about boats and ceilings, a man with a cart filled with fruits and vegetables wheeled by. Papa went after him and came back with an apple. It was red and perfect looking with an unfamiliarly smooth skin. When Papa cut into it with his pocket knife, juice came drizzling out. Still, as odd as that was, Papa tasted it. "That's no apple," he said, spitting it out. He threw it into the waste basket. We were all puzzled, but then it was time to board the train so we more or less forgot about the weird apple.

We had comfortable seats on the train and we all thought the train seemed quite new, and Mama and Solveig approved of how clean it was. I do like riding on a train. I like looking out the window. When we started out it was daytime, and we passed forests and fields where farmers were plowing. The fields went on for a long time. We started to see rivers and small lakes. We didn't see any mountains. We stopped in many small towns to drop off passengers or pick up others. The conductor called out the names of the towns and some of the names sounded funny and made us laugh. The parts of the towns we saw were dark with old-looking buildings. Papa said we were seeing the backside of the towns.

The Poet's Daughter

I was sleepy by the time the sun began to set and we were seeing low green hills and red barns and white farm houses. Cows walked in lines heading to their barns for milking, with a dog following behind, just like back home. I liked watching it all and it was sort of like seeing a movie, but not funny like the only movie I had ever seen, the Charlie Chaplin film Papa took me to when we went to Trondheim. That day Papa bought me a bag of cherries. Just thinking of those tasty cherries made me hungry, as it was getting late in the day. I leaned close to the window with my cheek on the glass, watching red streaks of cloud in the sky above the fields. Alf was sound asleep leaning against Mama. I was still awake when it turned into dark night and each time we pulled into a train depot for passengers, or to pick up mail, it was dark and spooky. The tracks glistened under the lanterns and men ran across the tracks and disappeared. We saw so many railroad tracks and trains and brick walls, all barely visible in the dark. There are a lot of trains in America. I certainly hope they all stay on their own tracks and don't get mixed up.

We didn't get off the train until we got to Chicago, where we were to board a different train. The Chicago depot was large and the sound of voices bounced around like in a barn. People were sitting on the long depot chairs and some were sleeping, even lying down as if they were in their own bedroom. Mama said we would be resting here too, as we had several hours before it would be time to board the train to Duluth. Mama and Solveig and I went to a very long bathroom with rows of sinks where Solveig washed a few items, including my socks because I had gotten into something gooey when I took my shoes off on the train. She wrung everything out thoroughly and wrapped it all in a towel to dry. She said my socks would dry in no time. We all washed our hair in the sink and took sponge baths in the little separate washing rooms. I felt good and refreshed and not at all tired, but I didn't like the feel of my shoes without socks, and Mama said we couldn't open the luggage with the clean clothes until we got to Duluth.

Alf was asleep next to Papa when we returned to the long chairs, and Bjarne was marching around the open area with another boy about his age. Papa said it was okay for him to play as long as he could see him from where he was sitting. Solveig went to get sandwiches for us and she was gone so long that I got really hungry, because I was thinking about food and hoped she would bring good bread and cheese. I wished she would bring some cherries too.

Solveig came with an odd type of long roll with sausages inside. It was pretty good, even though the meat was lumpy. I think I must have fallen asleep after that, because when I woke up my socks were back on my feet and everyone was getting organized to get on the train to Duluth. It was still dark, but nearly morning when we found our places on the train. Papa talked to someone on our train car who spoke Norwegian and then he hurried back to us as the train started out.

I was used to the sound of the train by now and settled back in my seat to enjoy the ride. I liked the sound of the train chugging along. The conductor called out the name of each town before we stopped and each name was spelled out in large letters at its depot, so it was clear where we were. I was glad for the map Mama bought in Chicago because it was fun to follow our route on the way to Duluth as she pointed out where we were.

The Poet's Daughter

Even if you knew English, I don't think you could understand what the conductor was saying when he announced the town stops. It sounded more like an auction call, or as if he were calling the names of many people and running the names together, all in a loud over-the-mountain voice. We learned "All Aboard" and Bjarne kept saying that along with the conductor, making his voice low like an adult.

Solveig took me to the bathroom. I waited until I couldn't wait any longer because I didn't like the metal toilets and the shaking of the train as we stepped from our car to the next car, where the toilet was located. There was hardly room for both Solveig and me in the tiny bathroom, but we were glad it was clean and shiny, because with bathrooms on trains I was finding, you never knew what to expect.

I sure was tired of sitting by the time we arrived in Duluth. It was dark by then, so we couldn't even see where we were after all this time of looking forward to seeing Duluth.

Uncle Pete and Aunt Rose were there to meet us when we got off the train. Mama was very happy to see her brother after not seeing him for many years. He had a friendly round face and shiny dark hair, smoothed straight back, and Aunt Rose seemed much bigger than Uncle Pete, but mainly she was that kind of lady who seems to be bursting out of her clothes, as there was so much of her. They fussed over us and laughed good-heartedly and we followed along to a taxi, with the men carrying the luggage and a porter hauling the big trunk on a wheeled cart. We waited until the trunk was tied securely to the top of the taxi, and then the lights came on and we were on our way.

Papa said we were going to a temporary place that Uncle Pete had found for us, until we could move into a house. The temporary place was on Fourth Street. It was the upstairs of a commercial place that smelled like beer. At least, that is what I thought when we went into the entryway that led to the stairs. At the top of the stairs we went down a long dark hallway that smelled like oranges and Uncle Pete unlocked a door and we went inside. Even when he turned on the overhead light, it seemed dark inside. There was dark furniture and dark wallpaper and dark wood floors without carpets. Our luggage and the trunk were brought up, and Alf asked, "When can we go home?" That's when Mama turned aside, but not before I saw that she was crying.

Aunt Rose was already in the kitchen heating up a pot of soup with dumplings she had made for the occasion, as they didn't know just when we would be arriving because trains were often off schedule. Otherwise, she said, she would have made a good hot roast with mashed potatoes for us, and she would do that soon, too. We crowded around the kitchen table for our soup dinner with rolls. It was delicious, and I was happy that Aunt Rose was such a good cook. Before I put on my nightgown, Solveig took me to the bathroom in the hallway and I discovered why the hallway smelled of oranges. The toilet paper was those little papers they wrap oranges in, and that was the only thing I liked about Duluth so far. I was dead tired after that, and I remember climbing into a dark bed that smelled like mothballs. The adults were talking and I fell asleep in about ten seconds.

Chapter 2

I WAS GLAD TO LEAVE the temporary Fourth Street apartment, that's for sure. We have moved to a house at the top of the entire city. Now you can see Duluth! You can see sky and blue water stretching so far it makes you want to reach out your arms. Lake Superior is almost as big as an ocean. It is truly huge. This morning I noticed that you breathe bigger up here on top of the city. The air is definitely American air; at least that is what I believe. Bjarne and I have been debating whether it is American air or not. He says the air is good, but that what I am noticing is the lack of salt, because Lake Superior is a salt-free lake, unlike our fjord back home.

The hill up to our house is too steep for a regular train, so they use a car connected to cables. It's called the Incline and is both scary and fun to ride. Yesterday as we rode up the hill we watched a ship out on the lake, and Bjarne was excited seeing a tugboat and several sail boats as well. We passed purple lilacs blooming as we moved up the hill, and Solveig pointed out apple trees thick with white flowers. Mama was quiet and deep in thought, until she spotted a huge bush of white lilacs. Oh, she was so excited about that.

Papa and Uncle Pete have been working on the house, getting everything in order. You wouldn't believe what they did on Tuesday. Really. They carried a heavy iron stove up the stairs that run along side the Incline. The Incline won't take furniture, only passengers, so they actually carried that heavy stove all the way up to our house. It was the only way it could be done, and they did it. They joked about needing a mule, but they were sweating after they got it into the house, so I knew it was no joke. They also carried up chairs and a table. Some furniture was already in the house, so that was good. The linoleum rug in the kitchen was very nice, and my mother and Solveig have cleaned and put up curtains to make it feel homey. Solveig went out to look for lilacs to put in our blue vase, the one we took along from Norway.

I loved riding the Incline and rode many times that summer. We learned a few English words riding the Incline: "East Car Clear. West Car Clear." You heard that all the time before they started out. The drivers had to check with each other before one car could begin, in order that the car on each side balanced out the other car. There were three other stops besides the one at the top, and the last one down on Superior Street. Sometimes Uncle Pete took us for rides on the Incline just for fun, and he would buy us ice cream cones at the little store at the bottom where you got off. The cones were vanilla, delicious and creamy, and something we never had in Norway. America was a pretty good place, even though Alf was always asking Mama, "When are we going home?" He was just so young that it was hard for him to understand that we lived here in Duluth now.

The Poet's Daughter

I took Alf with me to pick wild strawberries in the field behind our house. We used old coffee cans for pails and if we picked it half full, there was still room so they wouldn't fall out. We ate some, of course, as they were mighty tasty and sweet. Sometimes we would just plop ourselves down in the middle of the field and feel the sunshine. There were buttercups, and red clover, just like we knew before. I didn't even use the word "Norway" when Alf and I were out playing or picking berries, because he would start in again about going home, asking, "When are we going to play down at the fjord?" or "When is Mama going to row us to starfish beach?" or "Why doesn't Papa sail his boat anymore?" I didn't want to hear any of that.

Sometimes I daydream about Papa's boat and pretend that he didn't sell the *Malena*, but that we all sailed to Duluth on his boat and now he was the captain of his boat again and we could watch for his sails out on Lake Superior. According to my daydream plan, I would watch for the sails of the *Malena* with Uncle Pete's binoculars. I asked Solveig why we didn't just sail to Duluth, and she said Papa's boat was a one-mast schooner and not big enough for sailing all that way over the Atlantic Ocean. She reminded me of the stormy days on the Stavangerfjord and said Papa would never have taken a chance with our lives.

I haven't learned very much English yet. The most I can say is hello, thank you, ice cream cone, east car clear, west car clear, and all aboard. Mama says we'll all learn English when we start school in September and she is looking into where we will be going and how we will get there. There are many schools in Duluth, and Mama's friend Mrs. Bjerkan, from back home, is investigating the school situation for us and they are going to meet this week for a plan. She and her husband moved to Duluth about a year after Uncle Pete moved here and they have a dairy. Mama had a postcard from her with a picture of the Incline that she kept by her desk back in Norway. At the time, I had no idea what an Incline was so I didn't pay much attention to the picture, but Bjarne recognized the Incline here from the postcard the first time we rode to the top. Mrs. Bjerkan's first name is Nora and her husband's first name is Ingebrit, which I find to be an odd name, but I like it. I've seen them at the Bethesda Lutheran Church twice. He is tall and has dark hair and eyes, and Mrs. Bjerkan is short and seems to be moving even when she's not. You might say she is animated. I like her because she laughs so much. Also, she gave me a beautiful doll with a porcelain head and hands as smooth as the inside of a tea cup.

The church on Sixth Avenue is very pretty; at least it was the last time I was there. The first time was a foggy day and it was dark inside, but if it's sunny, the windows are glorious with many colors. The services are held in Norwegian and I like hearing my native language spoken, including before and after the services when the grownups stand around and talk and us kids wait. That's when Mrs. Bjerkan's daughter, Dagny, and I fool around. We have silly name games we play while we're waiting. Usually my brothers and I stay home with Solveig, because the service is mainly for adults.

I like to go to Mrs. Bjerkan's with Mama so I can play with Dagny. When they have coffee, Dagny and I race around in their woods across the street from the barn, or in the woods down South Road. There are lots of maple and birch trees and a big flat rock where we have seen garter snakes. Sometimes Dagny has to get the cows from the pasture and I go along. She shoos them toward the road and across and down the lane to the barn. I am afraid of cows because they're too big and you never know if they'll come running out of line. Dagny says that a bobcat lives in the woods of South Road. I don't know if she's making that up about the bobcat or not, and I only half believe her. She likes to scare me but I just laugh, pretending I'm not afraid.

The last time I went along with Mama to Bjerkan's, one of the barn cats had died, and Dagny and I buried the dead cat and had a funeral. We stole the Bible from its shelf and Dagny read a verse. We baptized the cat and name it Noah. We knew we were doing something the grownups would not approve of, yet in another way we felt we were doing the right thing. It would be hard to explain to a grownup. Luckily, Dagny was able to slide the Bible back into its place before our mothers noticed.

I'm in bed and supposed to be asleep but I'm actually all ears, listening to the adults through these thin walls. Mama is mad. She is mad because we have to move again. We are too far from any of the schools and Peter and Rose should have known that before they rented this house on top of the hill for us and now what are we going to do and after they moved that heavy stove and have settled in, it is wrong, wrong, wrong, and why did her brother Peter ever leave Norway and she misses her old home and her friends and her beautiful little town and fjord and she had to give up her dishes and everything! Then it was very quiet and I knew Papa was holding Mama in his arms and it was probably going to be okay. I noticed that Bjarne was sitting up in his bed, listening too. He got out of bed and came to whisper to me. He said we were going to move to be closer to a school and we should be good about it and not pout or fuss. I whispered back that I knew that, but wouldn't it be nice to go back to Norway? He just touched my head and went back to bed. I went to sleep and I didn't cry.

All of a sudden I awoke into the blackest of night with the rain pouring hard on the roof. I listened for a while and then: Oh no, my doll. I left her outside; she'll be ruined! I slipped on my socks and snuck past Bjarne and Alf, sound asleep. In the living room I watched the rain and didn't know what to do. Where had I left her? By the front stairs or the back stairs? The big door was too hard to open at night when it was shut all the way. I stood looking out at the pouring rain until tears were pouring down my cheeks. I slumped down in the big chair and didn't know what to do.

That's when my parents must have heard my sobs, and Papa was there patting my shoulder and Mother was in the doorway. What is it, Lilly? *Min stakkars lille Li.* What's the matter? I was shaking so I could hardly talk. My words came out one at a time, each one like a shaky gulp. Papa put on his coat and went outside. It seemed like he was gone for a long time, but then there he was, dripping wet with my doll. Thank heavens, she was all right. Mother brought a towel and wrapped her up and tucked us both into bed. With my doll safely wrapped up in a towel next to me on the pillow, I fell right to sleep. I have the best mama and papa in the whole world, that's for sure.

In the morning I went downtown on the Incline with Mama, and from Superior Street we took the street car called the Dinky to Mrs. Bjerkan's for coffee. It's still a ways to walk after you get off the Dinky. Dagny wasn't home, so I sat with the adults. Of course I was only allowed to dip a sugar lump in the coffee and suck on that, but still, it was delicious. Mrs. Bjerkan had papers for us to look at spread all over the kitchen table. The school Bjarne and I would be going to is called Grant School, and it is located on Eighth Avenue. It is a brand new school, made of red brick and named after a famous American named Ulysses S. Grant. Mama and Mrs. Bjerkan filled out a form for Bjarne and me to start in September. Bjarne had already gone to school for two years in Norway, but because we didn't know English, Bjarne and I were both going to be in the same class, which is Level One A.

They finished the papers and Mama folded them up and tucked them into her purse, and then we had chicken stew for lunch. It had a lot of carrots in it and not very many potatoes, which is my favorite part of stew. Anyway, it was tasty enough, and I liked Mrs. Bjerkan's yellow bowls. I asked if Dagny would be in my class at school, but she was going to a different school, in Kenwood. That was too bad. After lunch we said goodbye to Mrs. Bjerkan, and Mama and I walked to the Dinky and then walked to Grant School. It was considerably bigger than the school where Solveig and Bjarne had gone in Norway. We went inside and up to an office on the second floor, and Mama gave the lady her papers. We waited in the office while she went to get the janitor, whose name was Hallberg. He spoke Swedish and could understand us, even though Swedish isn't quite Norwegian.

The office lady and Janitor Hallberg gave us a tour of the school, which was being cleaned for the start of classes in September. The wood floors were shiny and looked new. We walked past three drinking fountains, all in a row against the wall. There was a short one, a middle-sized one, and an adult-sized one. The lowest one was perfect for me and I tried it out. The water wasn't cold but it tasted good. Hallberg said it was the best water in the world, right out of Lake Superior, and that it gets nice and cold if you let it run a little before you take a sip. On our way downstairs I held onto the railing and when we got to the first floor, we saw the classroom where Bjarne and I would be. It had rows of wooden desks with chairs and one wall was all tall windows. The front wall was an enormous blackboard on one half, with a map on the other side that made me quite curious. Janitor Hallberg was very nice and said there was another janitor whose name was Beckman and he spoke Swedish too, and our teachers could come and get either of them for help before we learned to speak English. He told us that the first grade teacher's name was Miss Fisk and he was sure I would like her. Fisk means fish in Norwegian, so I thought her name was hilarious and could hardly wait to tell Bjarne. Mama looked at me with a look that meant be dignified and don't laugh, but I could tell Hallberg thought it was a funny name too.

What? Mama is waking us all up in the middle of the night. What's going on? The last time we all got up in the dark was in Norway when we watched a boat burn out on the fjord, and Papa and the other men went out in small boats to put out the fire. If I were an artist I would paint that scene of a boat on fire in the fjord in the middle of the night, when you can hardly make out anything except flames and the outline of the boat and some dark figures moving around in smaller boats. Now we are rubbing our eyes to wake up and follow Mama. We're going out to see the sky, she said, and to just slip into our shoes and come along. Papa and Solveig were already outside. Oh, it is the Northern Lights across the whole sky! This is the first time we have seen them since we left Norway, and it is feathering its light back and forth across the sky and over us in all the colors, not just green but blue and purple and even red. We all stood there quiet like we were in church.

In the morning it was a normal day and it was like we had dreamt seeing the sky in the middle of the night. After breakfast, Mama was busy at her writing desk, so Alf and I went outside to play because we had to be quiet when she was writing and we weren't very good at whispering. Papa had already left for the day for his new job and Bjarne was out exploring.

Papa has a job working for the street car company. You don't need to know English on this job, but it is a hard job laying tracks for cable cars going west. He has been working at this for one week and he takes his lunch with him in a metal bucket. He looks tired when he gets home.

He and Uncle Pete have already found a new house for us to move to that is two blocks from Grant School, so it will be easy for us to walk to school, and Papa will take the cable car that starts on Eighth Avenue to and from work after we move there, instead of the Incline like he does now. We will be living at Sixth Avenue East and Tenth Street and we have already started to pack for the move. It's actually kind of exciting, but I'm nervous too, wondering what living in our new house and neighborhood will be like, and then school will start right away.

Alf and I have our special rocks up here on top of the city, just like we had our rocks by the fjord in Norway. Here the rocks are large flat rocks that you can walk on like they are actual floors. They have moss in some places and the ones we like best are next to where the pin cherries grow. You can almost see through those red pin cherries when the sun is shining, and they taste good. I pull the branch down so we can eat a few, and then Alf and I watch the boats on the lake for a long time, until Alf wanders around and finds a red ant hill. We watch the ants crawl around for a while, but not for long, and we don't get too close because they bite. Still, we like to watch them carry things. I'm pretty sure those white things they carry are eggs. Sometimes they carry a dead bug into their underground tunnels.

We take some pin cherries home to Mama and she's pleased. Alf and I both have toothaches, so we go to Bjarne's bed, which is against the wall where we can stand on our heads with our legs against the wall to help us balance. Pretty soon our toothaches are better. We don't know why that works, but Alf discovered it and it really works for even the worst toothaches.

Chapter 3

IT'S THE FIRST DAY OF SCHOOL at Grant School and here we are. Bjarne's desk is two desks over from mine, but we're in the same row. Back in Norway I watched Bjarne and Solveig leave for school every morning and I was too young to go, but now I'm old enough and here I am sitting at my very own desk. The wood feels nice and smooth and I like the ink well in the corner, though there is an ink spot like a tiny eye right next to it. Under the desk is a drawer with paper, a pencil, and a ruler. The teacher is very pretty and I don't know what she is saying, but I like how it sounds. The girl next to me has red hair and she keeps rocking back and forth in her seat. I think the boy behind me just touched my braid, but I'm not going to turn around.

All morning I paid attention and listened carefully. We took turns going to the front of the room to the teacher's desk to pick up our first school book, and our teacher said "Welcome to Grant School" and I understood what she said. The word welcome is very similar to Norwegian. Then she said more and I didn't understand, but knew to say "thank you" before I went to sit down with my book.

It went on like that all morning, being in the dark about most everything, but I did get that we were supposed to be learning to read. Our book had a few big words on each page and some were easy to remember. I think the first English word I learned was "look" and the second word was "dog." *Dog* was easy because there was a picture of a dog, and *look* I learned because of the two round letters, and of how the teacher pointed to show that the word *look* meant to look at something. I had already learned to read an easy Norwegian book at church school, so I had the gist of it and was ready to go. The Norwegian I had learned was all about a cat. Reading was fun and I wanted to learn all the words right away. Teacher read to us, and I turned my page when the other students turned theirs. I could count the words on each page to match with what she said, and I knew I was going to learn to read very fast.

We took a break to use the bathrooms and I was glad to know where they were and that they were clean and had private doors. After that we were to go outside to play. The teacher kept saying *recess*. I thought it meant get your coat, but I think it meant time to go outside. At the back of the room there was a long enclosed hall with hooks for our jackets, and my clothes hook was right next to the red-headed girl's who had the desk next to mine. We each put on our sweaters and she said something and laughed and I followed her. In the hallway everyone was lining up at the drinking fountains and we joined the line for the smallest fountain, which was the longest line. Most of the children were in our line, with just a few who were taller than the rest in the next line. When it was my turn, the water was cold and refreshing.

Outside, my new friend and I took turns pushing each other on the swing. She didn't understand my Norwegian and I didn't understand her English, but we had fun anyway and laughed a lot before someone blew a whistle to announce that it was time to go back inside. Bjarne was running around with some boys near the door and it felt kind of loud and normal. We all filed in and when we were going down the hall to our first floor room, I saw Janitor Hallberg walking along with a pail. He waved to me and asked how it was all going, in Norwegian of course, which made my friend stop in her tracks to listen to us. She shrugged her shoulders and we went on into our classroom where the teacher read to us from a regular book, not a beginning reader. I listened to her melodic voice until a bell rang.

Bjarne and I went home for lunch and compared notes. He didn't like being in the same class with me because he had already done two years of school in Norway. He thought it was unfair. But he looked me right in the eye and said that by the end of the year we would both be reading and writing in English and we were going to learn fast. I agreed with him, but secretly I thought I was going to learn faster than him. He said the boys at recess were friendly but kept saying, "What's your name? What's your name?" and he didn't know what they meant. Mama didn't know either. We ate our soup and then went back to school for the afternoon session. Now we knew where to find our classroom and our own desks.

In the afternoon we learned to write our first words on soft paper with rows of lines. Each sheet had rows of two thick lines with a dotted line between each set. We wrote our names and copied what teacher wrote on the blackboard. I loved doing this. I didn't even want to leave school when the bell rang at the end of the day. I walked home for one block with the red-headed girl. Now I knew her name was Reba, and she knew I was Lilly. Bjarne stayed to play marbles with a tall boy who lived across the street from our new house. We had seen him before but hadn't known he would be going to our school.

I was peeling potatoes with Mama when Bjarne came running inside. He said he knew what "What's your name?" means and told us all. Bjarne's new friend, who spoke English and Norwegian, had told him. Now we could answer when people asked. The new friend lived right across the street from us and his name was Leonard Sather. We kept asking each other "What's your name?" and laughing, and Alf asked Mama and she said "Mother." I decided right then that I would call Mama "Mother" from then on.

She had been learning some English too, from Mrs. Bjerkan. Still, Reba and I learned each other's name just by ourselves.

Mother and Papa signed up to take a class in English. Papa was going to go to the evening class, and Mama would go in the afternoon. Mother was going to work too. I didn't understand just what she was doing, but it was for a Norwegian-American newspaper and she was going to make sure everything in Norwegian was spelled right and punctuated correctly and things like that. It wasn't an all-day job like Papa's job. The company was called Furh Publishing and the man who owned it had died, and Mother's friend, Anna Furh, had become the editor. She had already been to visit us and I liked her because she was so friendly and nice.

As time went on, both Bjarne and I learned to read and write and speak English. Mother wanted us to speak

English at home and we did. Papa and Mother were learning fast, but when they were alone and I was in the next room, I would hear them speaking Norwegian, and whenever their friends came to visit, they spoke Norwegian. Alf was picking up English faster than any of us. Papa said that was because he was so young.

One night I had a dream and I was speaking English in the dream. I was showing everyone some important papers and telling them about the trip we took on a ship crossing the ocean, and how a bell was always ringing to tell us to go to the dining room with the white table cloths where we were going to have ham and potatoes and cream cakes one-foot tall with strawberries. After my dream, which I told my mother, she said maybe I would be a poet like she was because I liked to describe things. I said maybe, but I might be an artist too, and I can be whatever I want in America. She just smiled and it made me feel good.

It was that week that I went home with Reba after school and we played paper dolls for a long time. We had the best time, as she had way more paper dolls than I had and so many clothes, including the most fashionable. Even hats. I really hadn't noticed that it was getting dark out, but when her mother said it was dinner time and asked if my parents knew where I was, I realized I should go home. I was putting on my sweater and wondering if it would be hard to find my way. Even though it was just a few blocks to my house, I wasn't quite sure, as it looked quite different when I looked out the door. I had a funny feeling. I was scared of the dark but didn't want to tell anyone.

Luckily for me, that's when Papa and Bjarne came up the walk right to Reba's door. Papa took my hand and we walked home. He said they were all out looking for me and finally someone knew that I had gone home with Reba and pointed out her house. Even though it was dark out, I could feel my face blushing red. Bjarne helped me feel better by talking about something else. He told me that he had been selected by Miss Fisk to be an eraser clapper next week. This was an honor he was proud to have. He and one other boy would have a turn taking the erasers to the basement to clap the erasers hard together to get rid of the chalk. They would do this each day after school for a week. I was happy for him but glad I didn't have to do that; just the boys did that. I wouldn't want to breathe all that chalk dust.

No one got mad at me at home, but I knew after that not to scare my parents again. The next day was Saturday and I was the first one up. I went back to bed because it was still cold in the house. Soon I heard Papa starting the stove in the kitchen. I got up when I thought it would be warm enough, and by then Papa and Mother were already having their coffee at the kitchen table. I played with my meager set of paper dolls in the living room and listened in on their conversation.

Papa's boss had asked the crew if anyone knew how to use explosives, and Papa had said he did. Actually he didn't, but he had seen dynamite used at the lime quarry in Norway and thought he could manage to light a fuse and get away before an explosion. Mama was glad that he told her after the fact, she said. They were blasting away a rock cliff in order to lay more rail track on the line going to the west end of town. They had been blasting for the past three days, and no more blasting would be required. Mama wasn't happy, but Papa said the line to the rock had been long enough to make it a safe procedure. Sure, she said, not believing a word of that, I could tell. Oh my, I thought,

The Poet's Daughter

surely one of those blasting days must have ended when he had to hunt for me at Reba's house.

Chapter 4

IT DOES SEEM THAT SCARY days come in batches. You wouldn't expect Alf to be the next one in a curious situation, but he was. He liked exploring in the dump by the school, which was rather a nice dump, as dumps go. Since everyone burned their garbage in their wooden stoves, the dump was just old cans and stuff and ashes that were always smoking. Mostly it was ashes dumped from wherever ashes came from. The smoky smell was pleasant and the dark look of the ground seemed like a place where mysteries hid. It was a whole half-block of black, smoking embers with an occasional interesting what-not sticking up. Everyone liked it, at least the kids did. You could find an old wheel or some little bottle that looked kind of magical, like it might have belonged to a pirate. You had to almost tiptoe if you were in your school clothes and wanted to walk straight through the dump.

Anyway, one day after supper Alf came in the side door to the kitchen where we were all sitting around with Papa reading the Duluth Herald and Mother reading the Duluth Scandinav. Alf raised a gun and pointed it at Papa and said *Bang*. Papa moved mighty fast and took the gun in hand. It was real. A real handgun. Alf said he found it in the dump. No one had guns that we knew of, except for a few friends who hunted with rifles for deer, or if they lived up in

Kenwood or near the trap woods, sometimes for bear. But this was a hand gun like criminals used. Bjarne said a crook must have thrown it away in the dump to hide the evidence. That night I expect it took each of us longer than usual to get to sleep.

Elsie Ora Nordahl, Elsie Ora Nordahl, Elsie Ora Nordahl. This was our new jump rope chant. Reba and I took turns jumping, and Reba's little sister was just tall enough to hold one end of the rope so we could use the long rope and jump in the center. Reba's sister couldn't say Elsie Ora Nordahl like we did, and instead said Nora Nora Nora. Elsie Ora Nordahl had been our first grade classmate and we liked saying her name over and over, and considered it totally poetic. We never told her that we did this, as she was more serious than we were and considerably taller. Someone said she had moved to Duluth from Chicago. With the start of the new school year, she was now in Level Two B, as was Bjarne. I was mad about that. I did not see why Bjarne should be promoted to Level Two B when I was only in Level Two A. I was just as smart as Bjarne. Mother said it was because Bjarne was two years older. Still, it did not seem fair. I jumped as if my life depended on it, landing hard against the sidewalk so I would fly up high in my jumps. My consolation was that Reba and I were still in the same class.

Reba is going to her grandparents on Saturday. I guess that means that Alf and I will have to be in Bjarne's army tomorrow. Bjarne is General Pershing and we are privates in the army and have to salute him and do exactly what he orders, for the good of our country. He sends us off on spy missions. Last week we had to go all the way up to the boulevard and hunt for a piece of black coal. He emphasized that it had to be black coal, as if all coal wasn't black. We do rather like the game, even if Bjarne is terribly bossy.

On my way back home from jumping rope with Reba, I took the route from Ninth Street that goes past the dump. It was getting dark, but still not dark enough for me to be late for dinner. I had time. No one was in the dump and the whole place was smoking low out of the ashes. The smoke came in slow winding whiffs that you could watch and wonder about, rather like the whole dump was trying to come alive. It was a solemn and ghostly place. I don't know why I liked to stand there and watch the embers burn and smoke like that, all dark and bluish until nighttime when you could see the red-orange of hidden fire. Hard to say how long I watched the smoking dump, but I felt good when I left. I tried to whistle on my way home but I can't do it right and just make airy whispering sounds. Bjarne can whistle as loud as a real police whistle.

Papa has a job on the Montauk, which is a very beautiful paddleboat. On Saturday we all climbed aboard and went up the St. Louis River with the Andersons, the Kjelseths, and of course, the Bjerkans. Alf and I stood at the back of the boat and watched the water churn and bubble so hard it looked like it was boiling. This was our first time on a paddleboat and I liked the sound the paddle wheel made as it moved us through the water, taking us all the way to Fond du Lac, where we had a picnic.

We found a good long picnic table, and first thing, Mrs. Anderson cut a watermelon open and that was something new to us. We had a good time spitting the black seeds around and slurping up the juicy red melon. And her potato salad was the best. We ran all over the place after we ate, as Fond du Lac was a formal park with huge open areas and we ending up joining in on a baseball game. I was an outfielder, close to the picnic tables where I saw the women laughing and looking relaxed and happy. The men were tossing horseshoes. I liked the clattering of the horseshoes as they flew against the metal posts. After the ballgame, Alf and I stood on a bench to watch the horseshoes for a while. Papa could throw a horseshoe and land it on the target most of the time. They were all pretty good at it, and Bjarne took a turn too. That clinking of the horseshoes went on all afternoon, so by the time the Montauk took us back along the river to downtown, it was late in the day and the sky was a beautiful orange. Alf and I moved to the back of the boat to watch the water change from the color of the root beer we had at lunch, into a midnight blue.

It's Sunday morning and Papa is back into his old routine as in Norway. He puts on a white shirt and walks all around the house singing his favorite songs. Oh, he does have a fine voice. Solveig says his voice is good like his father's. I don't remember my grandfather's voice, but Solveig does, and says he even played the organ. Solveig is only home on Sundays since starting work at the Northland Country Club. It is a fancy place where she wears a uniform and has her own cabin that she shares with another girl. She gives Mother part of the money she makes from her job. She was sitting on her bed this morning, looking at a picture of Nils. She must miss him a lot, as he is so far away back in Norway. Mother said he has taken a job on a boat to make enough money to come to America.

Solveig likes to hear all about what I'm doing and she listens really carefully. I told her about jumping rope with Reba, and then I told her about what General Pershing made Alf and I do yesterday and how he ordered us to go all the way to Chester Bowl to look for a branch in the shape of a perfect 'Y' because it was necessary for the war. Alf and I were both worn out when we got back. Solveig thinks it is funny that we have to salute Bjarne, but mostly I think she's sad. Mother says she's homesick.

I also told Solveig about the school program that's coming up and how our class will be part of it in the school gymnasium, and she wishes she could come to see me dance in the show. All of us girls are fairies and we have wings to wear over our shoulders. The boys are elves and toadstools. They wear either green hats, or hold cardboard cutouts of red toadstools with white dots. They like to use the toadstools like shields and poke at each other when we line up in the hall before we go into the gymnasium and climb up the stairs to the stage. I think the program is going to be wonderful, with us girls dancing around on our toes, after which we stand in a line and the boys go in and out between us and we end up in two lines and that is when we sing our song. Reba and I have good voices so we stand right in the middle of our line, and Henry stands behind us but steps forward between us for his solo. All the girls are in love with Henry. He has dark curly hair and reads better than anyone, including me. Reba says he smells like garlic, whatever that is. She says it is an exotic herb. Well, Friday is the big day for the program, and that is not far off. Solveig says they use garlic at the country club when they cook steak and that it looks like a small tulip bulb that comes apart in sections, and each part is called a clove of garlic.

The Poet's Daughter

The day has come, the day of our class program, and we're getting into our costumes. The skirts are filmy like curtains and you can see through them. I burst into tears. Teacher keeps asking me what is that matter, but I can't say. I just can't think of what to say in English. Finally she sends someone to get Janitor Hallberg from the furnace room. He comes to the back of the room where I am so upset and leans down. I explain to him that I have to go home and change and I use the word that I don't know in English. He says the English word is *slip*. He explains to the teacher and she sends me off and says please hurry back, a puzzled look on her face.

It has started to snow outside and I rush home through the falling snow. Mother is surprised to see me come in the door, and so is Alf. I tell Mother that my gray home-knit slip shows through the filmy costume. She brings my good silk Sunday slip and in no time I am ready. Off I go into the snow again, and even though it is snowing harder now, it is not sticking to the sidewalk so I can run, and run I do. I race back to school and up the stairs and see everyone lined up and set to go. In the coat room teacher helps me out of my regular skirt and into the fairy skirt and I raise my arms and on come my wings. I join the line of girls. I made it! The show is perfect. It is the best show I have ever seen or been in. Well, it is also the only one. There is nothing like happiness after a scare. Papa has a saying in Norwegian like that, which he would surely say to me if he were here at school.

Bjarne has a paper route. He wears a cap which he wears crooked and he seems pretty grown up. He makes some good money when he can sell all of his papers, but it takes a long time since he's just started and doesn't have a good corner yet. He's saving for skis. He says he is working out a plan to get a better corner so he can sell more papers and faster. When it's really cold, he says he has to hop around and wave his arms, and that helps him sell papers and warms him up as well. His face is always red when he gets home at supper time and he stands by the stove to thaw out. Sometimes he sits right on top of the Heatrola.

Mother has been writing more than usual. She is at her desk when I get up and when I get home from school. We kids have to be quiet when she's writing, and we do try. Her poems have been in the newspaper where she edits, and even in the Chicago Scandinav. I like when she reads one of her poems aloud to us after dinner on Sundays. I like the ones that are about Duluth, and also the new one about sailing on a boat to Norway. That one is called "My Christmas Boat."

When she is writing lyrics for a song, the house is lively with music. The person who is writing the song is called the composer. He comes to our house and sings the tune while Mother works on the words. They go over the sections many times. Mother and I both want to get a piano. We almost had a piano, but then that didn't work out. I had won a raffle at school and received a coupon for a piano. Papa and I walked downtown on a Saturday with the coupon, already overjoyed with excitement as we entered the piano store, only to find that the coupon was not for an entire piano but only good for a down payment, so we could not afford a piano after all. There were some sorry faces around our house when we got home with the bad news. Some day we will have a piano, I'm sure of it.

    I truly hate bad news. I had a hard week after not getting the piano. Then at school, a girl who is always mean to me and makes fun of my clothes because they are homemade, pushed me hard when I was at the drinking fountain, and broke off my front tooth. It sure hurt. I didn't let Mother or Papa see what had happened until the next week. I was supposed to be in a play but I didn't want to be in it with my missing tooth.

Chapter 5

HAVE YOU EVER NOTICED how sorrow appears at night? I had an uneasy feeling one evening in early February. Papa had come home from his current job at the fish warehouse and the cold air poured in near where I was playing with my paper dolls. When he had changed into his home clothes and hung his work clothes out on the back porch, we were all called to dinner, which was fish stew. Bjarne sat at his chair with his paperboy cap at that jaunty angle, and Mother made him hang it up where it belonged. He just shrugged and did as she asked. Alf and I stirred our spoons around in our bowls, digging for fish eyes, which we both loved, don't ask me why, as they're disgusting if you think about it. But I liked their texture and Alf wanted to see underwater like a fish. Solveig was sleeping and Mother said she would bring her a bowl later. She had been home all week with her tiny new baby. Both Solveig and the baby slept and slept.

After dinner Papa worked on his model of the *Malena*, while Bjarne and Alf looked on. He was working on the sails, and he explained the sails and which line went to each one. I wanted to help paint the boat, but it needed some sanding and he didn't have the green paint yet. I moved my paper dolls to the rug in the warmer part of the living room and fastened a yellow dress on my favorite paper doll. The dolls were my Christmas present from Solveig. There was a new doll and outfit for each month from Pictorial Review Magazine, which she subscribed to when she started working. She had been cutting them out and saving them for me for almost an entire year. I had never had so many paper dolls before and the collection was my prized present.

It was a normal evening and my uneasy feeling was almost gone when I fell asleep that night. It was the scream that woke me so suddenly. It was Solveig's scream. I sat up straight and started shaking. I could hear Mama and Papa moving around and quiet talk and soft crying. Then, they were saying the Lord's Prayer in Norwegian. I pulled my knees up to my chin and didn't know what to do, but I found myself getting up and putting on my socks. I tiptoed to Solveig's doorway and my mother came and walked me back to bed. She sat with me and caressed my hair and said to go back to sleep and she would talk to me in the morning. I said "Solveig is sad, isn't she," and she said "yes."

I couldn't sleep, and before long the sky was lightening up and I heard people coming and going. I got myself dressed. Mrs. Bjerkan was there, and Mrs. Fuhr from my mother's newspaper office, and a man dressed in black, like a minister or a doctor. He walked back and forth with his hands behind his back. Mother took my hand and told me that the baby had died. We walked together to the room, where the baby was lying on the bed wrapped in a blanket. Mother said I should say goodbye to the baby. I stood close to the bed. He was extremely tiny with the littlest fingers and it looked like he was sleeping, but he was too still. I kissed his forehead and said a silent goodbye to him and went back to Mother. She said I did it just right. I knew that Solveig was in bed in Mother's room.

The afternoon the baby was buried at Park Hill Cemetery. I wasn't to go along because I was too young, that's what they said. Reba's mother and Reba came over to stay with us, and then Bjarne went to his paper route and Alf and Reba and I looked at books and we hardly talked all afternoon. Reba's mother made cocoa and we all sipped hot cocoa and looked out the window at the falling snow.

That was a cold winter, for sure. Not long after the baby died, Papa was working out of town for a few weeks and our pipes froze up. Nothing seemed to be thawing them that Mother and I could think to do. She stood looking out the window, then put on her coat and went across the street to the Hill family. They were a black family, the only ones in the neighborhood, and they did some kind of construction work that Mother thought would be helpful. She came back with two men who brought some equipment and were busy outside of the house where the pipes entered the house. Then they came inside to work. It was way below zero out and the cold blew in whenever the door was opened. Those men worked for a long time and got the pipes unfrozen, and everything working again. We were so grateful. I am glad Mother wasn't afraid to ask that black family for help. Mother and Mrs. Hill became friends after that. Later that week we heard the temperature had been thirty-nine below zero on the day the pipes froze.

Good news. Bjarne got a good corner for selling his papers. In fact, he says it is one of the best in town. He says he angled himself in, whatever that means. I think he got the good spot because he knows and likes everyone and knows how to get along. He's tall and sturdy too, so his angling has something to do with friendly tough-guy stuff, I expect. He has skis now and is just crazy about skiing up at Chester Bowl. He's going to learn to ski jump, but I'm not to tell Mother or Father.

I have skates of my own, and so does Alf. Mine are meant to last a few seasons, as they are large in the toe and I have to stuff newspapers all balled up into each toe. Since the skates are of a stiff leather, it doesn't matter that much, having an extra inch. We skate at the Franklin School rink, and not Central Field, where we used to skate before we moved. Our house is on a steep hill over in Little Jerusalem; that's what they call this neighborhood. We're good at moving and I don't mind it much. We know lots of people now and everyone helps, so it's pretty easy to do. Still, I have much farther to go when I want to visit Jean Gronseth, who lives in Kenwood and is probably my best friend, next to Dagny Oie. Jean and I were in the same class at Grant since the beginning, though I didn't get to know her well until the end of my first year at Grant.

Mother likes that she's still fairly close to the Duluth Scandinav office from the new location. She is always busy with her writing or some collaboration with another writer or musician. People are always coming and going at our house. Papa says Mother's friends are too high-toney for him, but he gets along with them all anyway, especially the musicians. Last weekend Mother and another lady from the paper went to a convention in Minneapolis. She said she wouldn't have gone except that her cousin Anton was going to be in St. Paul on business at the same time as her convention. She wants him to come to Duluth with his family so we can all meet. He has a daughter nearly my age named Jenny, and another daughter whose name I can't recall, and they live in the cowboy state of Texas.

Mother loves conventions. She and Papa went to the Sons of Norway convention when it was held in nearby Cloquet; just Mother goes when it's held in Minneapolis or Glendive. Papa is the one who never misses the Trondelag meetings downtown at Norway Hall. Those are once a month and he wears a white shirt to those. All the people from the Trondheim part of Norway go to Trondelag.

Our entire family goes to Norway Hall at Christmas. You go up very steep stairs to a big open room with wooden floors where large chairs are set against the walls. Some of the chairs are quite fancy and formal in appearance, with extra high backs. There is a tall Christmas tree in the center of the room and us kids hold hands and circle around the tree singing Christmas songs, mostly in Norwegian. There is a formal program as well, with more music. Freda Nervick plays the guitar and Axel Larsen plays piano. After the music, Santa Claus comes to give each child a brown bag with pieces of curly, colorful hard candy. Mother said Santa Claus is really Mrs. Stacklie and she does look a bit sad because her red Santa suit is faded and nearly threadbare, though she does fill it up pretty well. Bjarne says she's five feet tall and five feet wide. Papa gave Bjarne a look when he said that, and assured me that when the depression was over, Santa's suit would be bright red again. I never did care for that hard candy, except for the red ones.

Speaking of candy, Nils is coming to America. Solveig is getting back to being like her old self again and writes a letter to Nils every week, but he is already on his way. I remember him from Norway as being tall and handsome, and he often had candy in his pocket for me.

Chapter 6

IT'S A MYSTERY how time passes. I suppose it has to do with being too busy to actually notice. Anyway, I now attend Central High School and wear stockings and dresses to school. I hear my parents speak of what hard times everyone is having, but I'm certainly not having them. Now that we live on Eighth Avenue, between Twelfth and Thirteenth Streets, I see Jean all the time as she is just two blocks up the hill. Jean is taking dance lessons and after a lesson, we head to her garage and she shows me all the new steps she has learned. We practice the new tap dance steps, the Lindy Hop, and the latest is the Charleston. That one's a challenge, but we're getting quite good and our feet really fly. Our Grant Schools days seem decades ago, rather than just a few years past, when we put on summer shows for the neighborhood kids in Jean's garage. Back then we sang and danced and read poetry, charging the neighborhood kids one penny to see our shows. Now we dream of dancing in the movies.

I practically live at Jean's. Her mother is a homebody who is always washing clothes or cooking, and her dad is a traveling salesman who sells shoes. He makes sure Jean and her mother have the best quality shoes, but her mother cuts slits in her own, first thing when she takes them out of the new shoe box. Apparently this is to make them more comfortable for her bunions.

Jean's mother is not fat, but she is large. I have noticed that people who enjoy cooking and do a lot of it tend to be that way. It's probably inevitable. My Aunt Rose fits into that category. Well, every few days Mrs. Gronseth will say she's feeling a bit weak, and then she heads to the kitchen and boils up a huge batch of potatoes. More often than not, Jean's bag lunches consist of sandwiches filled with mashed potatoes and slices of roast beef. Half the time she trades for one of my homemade sandwiches with only a simple Karo Syrup spread. One can get sick of the same thing for lunch day after day, so this works out well for us, and I get to eat meat that way. At home it's usually fish, fish, and more fish.

Jean and I both love singing. At the first of each month we walk to Fossom's Drugstore on Fourth Street and buy a booklet that has all the words to the popular songs, which we know from the radio. We learn every verse from that booklet and copy out the words into our private notebooks. I have also started to write poetry, something my mother does not know I am doing, and which I have no intention of telling her. It's love poetry, of course, since we are at the boy-crazy age. Every day is nearly too exciting to endure. We tell each other every little wild thing we think. Well, nearly all.

Last week we nearly froze walking home from school. We stopped to warm up at the drugstore, and then made our way to Johannson's Bakery on Tenth Street. Mr. Johannson had some day-old kringers for us, our favorites. His bakery is in the lower part of his house and you walk down a stairwell from the outside and enter the warmest and

The Poet's Daughter

whitest place ever, and when the temperature outside is below zero, it is where you want to be, believe me. You warm up quickly from the brick oven and he doesn't mind if you hang around and watch him take the bread out of the oven on a flat wooden board he slips under the loaves. The flour goes flying and there's a rush of extra heat if you stand close enough. He always dresses in white and his red hair is half white with flour, and when he slaps his hands together the flour flies through the air like flour rain. The whole room smells of bread and sweet rolls. Besides the kringers, we like the everyday sweet rolls, even though they're kind of plain. Papa likes Johannson's rye bread with his cheese, but usually we just eat Mother's white bread at home.

When we leave Johannson's, Jean tells me that she has met someone she really likes. His name is Rags. She rolls her eyes as she tells me this before leaving me at my house. She still has two more blocks to go and a wind has come up. I'm glad I'm home. What a cold day.

I have met a dreamboat. His name is Steve and he plays the violin. He waits for me after class and we talk most every day. He thinks I'm fine just the way I am, even with my chipped tooth. I am at school after the Friday night orchestra concert, where I paid special attention to the violin section. Steve is the first violin and had a solo in the opening number, which he performed to perfection, of course. Tonight we are going on a date which will be our first date, and I am wearing my best clothes, including my mother's good wool coat. Steve had to go upstairs to put his violin away and so I am just waiting here by myself. I have been here about two minutes. Here he comes.

It is a short way for us to walk down to Superior Street, where we are going to take the bus to the end of Park Point. We are both wearing gloves and he holds my hand the entire way down the street. As we walk down the steep hill, I understand that line in the song about walking on air.

We waited a short time before we climbed onto the Park Point bus and that was long enough, because it was a cold night. The entire bus was empty except for us. We sat in the back facing the lake side. There was fresh snow on the ground and the street lights made gold shadows at each street corner. We passed the little houses of Park Point, where they say people were always sweeping out sand in the summertime and snow in winter. We thought it must be wonderful to live on Park Point in the summer, because you could step out your back door and be on the beach and have a nice fire in the evenings using driftwood.

Steve asked me if I thought it would be like Norway, living so close to the beach. The beach I remembered was not a long one, but it had fine sand very pleasant to a bare foot. I told him how my mother would row us children to a beach we called Starfish Beach. We had to laugh at that because Lake Superior has no starfish at all, though you sometimes find shells, such as clam shells. We talked about walking barefoot in the sand next summer. We both thought we were talking about summer just to warm ourselves up, because it was about fifteen degrees below zero out.

We talked nonstop all the way to the end of Park Point, the last stop, of course. The ride seemed long while we were moving along, as if we had all the time in the world, yet here we were already with the bus at a complete stop.

The Poet's Daughter

Steve went to the front of the bus to talk to the driver and told him we wanted to take the return trip back to Superior Street. Apparently you have to pay again if you want to go back. Steve dug around in his billfold and had just enough money for the return trip. Again, we were the only riders all the way back to Superior Street. When we got to the bridge, Steve put his arm around my shoulder and that's how we rode the last perfect blocks to Superior Street.

We transferred to the bus that went to my house and he walked me to my door, then left and walked all the way down the hill to his house, which was further east than Eighth Avenue.

The next week, Steve stopped at my locker and handed me a poem he had written:

I met a girl named Lil,
Boy is she a thrill,
She's blond with dark eyelashes,
Oh boy when she dashes
Into the arms of a tall dark fellow,
Jello!

Chapter 7

LIFE AS I KNEW IT came to a complete stop. My mother was in the hospital. She wasn't dying, but she was not well, though no one would explain what was going on. Mrs. Bjerkan said it was something to do with her interior being female, that's how she put it. We had to live with this vague explanation, and an assurance that her condition was not life-threatening. Father was calm about it, and so I followed his lead.

I was in charge of the house and did all the cooking. It was a good thing I had taken a home economics class from Mrs. Sebo when I was at Washington Junior High. I knew how to make white sauce, and everything I cooked was either smothered or simmered in white sauce. I made creamed fish and creamed potatoes and creamed carrots and creamed peas. Although everything was in a white sauce, no one complained.

I had only one year left at Central but I didn't go back that last year, and everyone assumed I should stay home because of Mother. She was in the hospital for six months before she came home, and then she was only home for a month before she went back to the hospital for three more months.

The Poet's Daughter

We now bought our bread from Johannson on a regular basis, and I was in charge of shopping. I could buy bread from Johannson, or I could go half a block up the street to Mabel's store, on the corner of Thirteenth Street and Eighth Avenue. Mabel's store was kind of a meeting place, and I liked Mabel and she liked me. I helped her fill the small brown mystery bags, filling them with stale candy and maybe a balloon or some surprise for the kids. Yesterday when I went to buy a can of beans, she was leaning on the counter telling me she had the fat feeling again. She would have the fat feeling at least once a week, and I knew what she meant even though it didn't make sense, because she was skinny as a string bean.

I liked hanging around the store to see who came and went. There was an old guy who always pinched the bread before he bought a loaf, and Mabel called him "bread squeezer." If she spotted him coming along Thirteenth Street, she'd say, "Here comes bread squeezer," and we'd have to gulp back our laughs. The man who delivered the bread was Ray, and I think Mabel was rather fond of him. He delivered Zinsmaster white bread and Hartman's raisin rye.

Oh, some of the people who came to the store were real oddballs, though most were ordinary folk. There was one lazy guy who came in for milk and to pick up the laundry his old mother did for him once a week. That was Tommy Toot. Mabel said he could afford to have his shirts washed at the commercial laundry, but he was cheap as well as lazy. His mother, Mrs. Toot, lived down in the valley of the crick behind Haldorsen's house, just across the street from my house. She had no running water in her house and had to carry it by pail from the small crick, heating the water on her wood stove. It was surely no easy task to wash those shirts. Mabel said Mrs. Toot ironed them using an iron from the old country, which she heated on the wood-burning stove. She would bring his shirts to Mabel's store, all folded and neat and white from being hung out in the sun. Tommy was too lazy to even walk down to her house to pick up his shirts. We figured he must have taken the dirty laundry down to the house, but we still felt disdain for him.

Mrs. Toot's house was a one-room unpainted wooden house that looked like something from a children's story. Last summer Papa sent me down the steep bank to her house by the river with a letter that had come to us for her. The inside of Mrs. Toot's house was immaculate, with wide plank floor boards and lace curtains in the windows. A row of freshly made jelly in little jars sat sparkling on a wooden table the time I was there. I could smell something that smelled of cloves, simmering on the stove. I remember everything in that house so clearly, even though I was there for only a minute or two. I can still picture the sun shining on a vase of buttercups on her little table. The house was unpainted, inside and out. She was sweet and always wore long dark skirts and a scarf on her head. We rarely saw Mrs. Toot, except for summers when she came around selling pie plant, her name for rhubarb. I hope Mother will be home by the time Mrs. Toot comes around with pie plant in the spring.

I have been making a little money babysitting. Most of the families I have babysat for have been really nice and I have enjoyed the children. There is one family I won't babysit for any longer, though. The kids are genuine rascals, and I would probably like them if I hadn't been

The Poet's Daughter

their babysitter. I expect that family goes through babysitters rather quickly.

There are four children in the family, three boys and one girl. The oldest told me he liked to perform tricks, but the one he wanted to do was very complicated and he asked if I would help. Foolish me, I said yes. He asked for a glass of water, which I gave him. He then proceeded to balance the glass on a tall thick board which he began to raise toward the ceiling. He raised it all the way to the ceiling so that the glass was against the ceiling itself. Then he said he needed to get something to finish the trick and asked me to hold the board while he went to fetch it. It happened so quickly that before I knew it, I was holding up a full glass of water against the ceiling with a tall board while the children all ran outside. I heard them laughing as they ran off. There I was, alone, wondering if I could lower it without spilling the water. Of course I couldn't, and the water went all over, including on my head, but luckily the glass didn't break. Their mother came home with the children standing behind in the yard, looking sheepish. I had just finished mopping up the water and their mother thought I was so ambitious that I had decided to wash the kitchen floor. After that, when their mother called me to babysit, I always had "another engagement."

I always had time to babysit Solveig and Nils's children. Esther and Sis were two years apart and always fun. They lived on Thirteenth Street, just around the corner from us, so I saw them often. I liked to play with them in their backyard under the apple tree, or take them for walks up to a corner where a woman had ducks, and they thought that was lots of fun and quacked all the way back home, pretending to be ducks. Esther wouldn't drink her milk at lunch unless I put a drop of vanilla in her glass. She was quite particular. Sis had her own way of prancing around the kitchen table like a little ballerina. They were wonderful little ones. Sometimes Nils played the violin when I was visiting. It reminded me of Steve, and I wondered how he was. I no longer saw him now that I had stopped going to school.

Chapter 8

THERE WAS SOMEONE ELSE I was getting to like. I first noticed him at Mabel's store. He always wore a formal hat. Mabel said he had been in the hospital during last fall's typhoid epidemic. Several people had died of typhoid while he was in the hospital, but he survived and his doctor told him to shave his head so his hair could be saved and that's why he was always wearing a hat. His name was Karl.

Yes, his name was Karl Haldorsen and he lived directly across the street from our house on Eighth Avenue. His father was Ludwig Haldorsen, who worked as a painter. The Haldorsen house always had people coming and going, and around the time Karl was recovering and wearing the hat, was when I was first asked to help cook for the family. Ludwig's wife had died many years previous, and the oldest daughter, Marie, lived in Michigan, so it was a household of men. There was a brother, Leif, but he was older and had his own place, yet came for dinner fairly often. Of course I prepared everything in white sauce, my specialty, but they would have other foods for me to cook that I was unfamiliar with. Ludwig taught me how to make a good fish stew, how to fry fish, how to roast a chicken, and the best way to roast beef. They had a rather fancy stove with an isinglass door, a warming oven, and a reservoir for hot water.

The Haldorsen house had a piano, and Ludwig played the string bass. One of their regular visitors played violin, and another, a different stringed instrument. A guitar hung on the wall next to the piano. This was a house of music and good cooking, card playing, and warmth. I sometimes felt like a fly on the wall, cooking for them and listening to their stories. Peeling potatoes while listening to a string quartet was something new for me and I loved it. They played what I thought of as concert music, and also old-time songs like "Old Black Joe," which Ludwig liked to sing. "She'll Be Coming Round the Mountain" was another favorite, and "The Red River Valley," and then some of the old country songs, like "Nickolena," which I already knew.

Karl had a lot of friends, and they were always planning some new adventure now that he was out of the hospital and on the mend. He seemed to be the organizer. As far as I could tell, a number of his friends were on the same Duluth hockey team, and I often overheard their hockey talk or plans for hunting or fishing. There was Roy Pedersen and Hi Abelson, and a number of others whose names I didn't yet know. When I finished my work, Karl had recently taken to walking me home, which I thought was quite silly, as I only lived across the street.

It wasn't long before I looked forward to my walk across the street with Karl. He had started to look at me as if to study me when I was cooking, and I had certainly noticed the intense look in his hazel eyes as he held my coat for me when we were ready to take the miniscule walk from his house to mine.

The Poet's Daughter

Mabel mentioned that I was spending more time at her store, especially at times when I expected Karl to stop by. I confided that, yes, I was hoping to see Karl. He often came for canned goods around four o'clock on Fridays, and on this particular Friday, Karl came into the store with his hat off. This was quite an occasion. I had never before seen him without his hat and knew the story of how he shaved his head completely bald after his typhoid episode. But here he was, with hair! It wasn't very long, but it was a soft brown and he looked good.

One fine sunny day not long after the hat came off, Karl invited me to go for a ride with him in his new car. The car was a shiny black, with a rumble seat in back. Most surprising was the radio. I had never heard of a car having a radio before. Riding along the boulevard with Karl was like being in a parade accompanied by music. We drove over to Chester Bowl and parked beside the warming house so we could watch the skaters on the pond.

Not being limited to the time frame of a short walk from his house to mine, we talked a lot that afternoon. He told about his younger days when his father worked at the warming house at Chester Bowl, and how he would pull Karl on a sled all the way to Chester, where he would start the fire in the large wood-burning stove and keep it going from late afternoon and into the evening for the skaters and ski jumpers. Karl had been too young for skating and skiing, but he remembered the smell of the stove and melting snow, and the sound of the skaters clomping around on the wooden floor of the warming house. He could remember trying to stay awake on the return sled ride home so he wouldn't fall off, and how he was small enough to stretch out on the sled and wonder at all the stars in the winter sky. His father had told him that his mother was up with the stars in the sky. I thought Karl must have trusted me and liked me a lot, to tell me such a personal memory.

I told him about how much my brother, Bjarne, loved ski jumping, though he hadn't much time for it this last year. Bjarne and Papa were now working as painters in Hotel Duluth, which was considered a good job with better working conditions than when they both were at the fish packing warehouse. Bjarne hasn't been able to rid himself of his cough since his year working in that cold place. Both Bjarne and Alf only know Karl to wave at him with their comings and goings, being such close neighbors. Alf doesn't like ski jumping, but likes to skates on weekends. Mostly he is busy with his school friends. My skates are now too small for me so I don't skate at all. Karl is a good listener. I think I am as well, though sometimes I am too busy doing nothing but looking at Karl, and then I don't really listen. Time stands still, like in a song Jean and I used to sing.

For some reason I haven't been able to tell him about my mother and her poetry. She has had poems in many magazines and newspapers. I don't know how to talk about poetry, or about my mother and her illness. Karl seems to be reading my mind and says he wants to meet my mother. He already knows my papa. They got acquainted one day when he came to his house to ask about the delivery schedule of the ice man. I told Karl about the tomato my father bought in Chicago when we first arrived in America, and how we had all thought it was an apple, having never seen a tomato before. It didn't seem funny at the time, like it does now. One of my favorite childhood memories was watching papa peel an apple with his pocket knife, making one long continuous curl of peeling. Karl said he'd give that a try, next time he had an apple.

No one was jumping off the ski jumps that day, but we talked about coming up another day when they were jumping. Still, it was fun doing nothing but talking with Karl and watching the skaters. Maybe I'll get skates again and we can join them. I have been saving my money for a good coat, and one for Alf, who is growing out of his old one. In all likelihood, skates are not practical this year.

As we drive back home, I feel more at ease with Karl and no longer think the age difference between us is anything I need be concerned about. Still, it surprises me when I am alone and think about Karl being ten years older.

By the time the winter snow melted, so did my heart. Now Karl and I go fishing together. His demonstrations of fly fishing technique have taught me a lot more than how to cast. He wants me to see every one of his favorite fishing rivers, and there are many on his list. Our routine is to pack a lunch and leave early on a Saturday morning, the day I look forward to all week. Waking up on the morning of a fishing trip with Karl is glorious. It is the best time ever to be alive.

This Saturday we are going all the way up to the Baptism River, the river which he speaks of with genuine reverence. It is one of the larger and wilder rivers, and flows into Lake Superior. To get there you drive along the north shore of Lake Superior, where the road is close enough that you can watch the waves and the shoreline. Today the water is a deep blue and the sky a lighter blue, but still quite bright. Every now and then I spot a fishing boat or a large ship heading to or from Duluth. Across the lake, the shore of Wisconsin is visible and looks like a dark low outline of land. Sometimes you can't see Wisconsin at all, and the lake is just a great expanse of water as far as you can see. Last Saturday both the lake and sky were gray, so that the horizon line blended both grays together and if you saw a ship, it looked like it was sailing in the sky.

When we reach the Baptism River, Karl tells me to watch for a little turnoff where we'll park. Of course he spots it before I do, and we drive in a short ways. It's really hardly a road at all. We get out and I put a scarf around my neck and step into my hip boots. Karl gets on his waders and slips on his creel. He's wearing his fishing hat with mosquito netting on top, ready to be pulled down, if needed. With fishing pole in hand, I follow Karl's red plaid shirt into the woods and up some hills, listening to the sound of the river nearby as we walk along. We pass some yellow violets and a single tiny Lady Slipper under an old birch. The nearby river sounds loud enough to be going over a falls until we get to the top of the hill, where it levels out and the river comes into plain view. The spring runoff is at its peak, Karl says, and we should find it calmer soon, and we do, after a short walk along a flat area.

We come to an open pond with yellow cow slips growing on our side, and a turtle sunning atop a rock on the far side. At the base of a large boulder, Karl stashes our beer bottle, settling it into place with a few rocks. I wait while Karl stands with his hands on his hips, surveying the river. After some consideration, the plan is to go further up river to a smaller pond, and we scramble awkwardly in our boots, or at least I do. Karl takes large, careful steps. I'm to cast near the high end of the pond and he'll take the lower

The Poet's Daughter

section and work his way down to the bigger pond, and I'm to do the same, taking my time, working each section according to how good the fishing is. He recommends staying as long as possible at the opening to the pond by some big rocks, which he points out.

He's off and I make my way to my fishing spot and step carefully into the water. In rubber hip boots, the strong suction of water against my legs is always surprising. I go no deeper than my calves and find a level spot where there are a lot of small rocks, and I set my balance against the one larger rock. Here I go! My line lands just where I want it on the first cast, and the pull of the river keeps it steady. I've come a long way from my first attempts at fly fishing, when I snagged a tree branch every other time. How good it is standing here in the river waiting for a bite. I can hear Karl downstream whistling to himself, or maybe he's whistling to the fish.

It's always been like this. Timeless. Even from my first try at fly fishing. I think it must be in my Norwegian bones. I never think of the time, except for that one time when it clouded over quickly and the temperature dropped. Today it's warm. I already have one good-sized rainbow trout and one small one, but it's big enough to keep. I've almost caught up with Karl and spot him as I turn the corner of the river. Yoo-hoo! I call out. He waves and reels in.

He has the exact same catch as mine, though his smaller one is nearly as large as my large trout. We make our way down to where Karl submerged the beer, now nicely chilled by the cold stream. We find a cozy spot, and I have a cigarette and Karl lights a cigar, and we enjoy the cold refreshing beer, and we have a little romance, not necessarily in that order. It's a perfect day in Minnesota.

Doc Woods and Hilda are in the rumble seat and Karl and I are up front, just sitting here on Skyline Parkway and looking at the lake. Doc Woods took care of Karl when he had typhoid, not all that long ago, which seems surprising now. Hilda is the first to spot the paddleboat, the Montauk, coming into view down on the lake and nearing the docking point. I told Karl how my father used to work on the Montauk, and he said, "Let's try to get down there before it takes off." So we were off, straight down the hill to where the Montauk was docked. Karl parked the car and we rushed along and got on the Montauk just in the nick of time. As it pulled out onto the lake we found nice comfortable green deck chairs, all together, and Karl ordered drinks, even though I was only eighteen. I must have looked older, or they were just looking the other way that day. Anyway, someone brought me a rum and Coca Cola. There was dancing on the boat and beautiful lights all around that seemed brighter as it got dark. Karl said that when the boat was three miles from shore, they would turn over the tables for gambling. We didn't gamble, but it was like being on vacation, being on that boat with Karl. The sound of our voices out on the water was like being in an echoey bubble until the sounds floated away as we moved along and the lights of the city came on all over the hill. What a pretty sight to behold. I'm glad Karl took right off in time to get us on the boat. Doc Woods and Hilda seem happy, too.

It's Friday night and Karl has bought artist's oil paints and an assortment of brushes. He has been talking about painting a picture of a lake or a river for the last two weeks, and we are at Mabel's store discussing appropriate scenic locations, of which there are so many that it's hard to settle on a place. "Let's try Chester Bowl," he suggests. There's a pond where he used to swim as a child in Lower Chester, and he thinks we'll both like it. It has the pond, the trees and twisting roots and waterfalls above, he says. Just as we are discussing when to leave in the morning, bread squeezer comes in and pinches half the loaves before taking his loaf of Zinsmaster white bread to Mabel at the cash register. She tells him he just made it, as she's closing up in five minutes. We all call it a day.

Karl knocks on my door earlier than I was expecting him on Saturday morning, before breakfast even. "Hope you haven't eaten yet," he says. He's planning breakfast by the river and the car is all loaded up. Luckily, I hadn't even started cooking my oatmeal.

The drive to Chester Bowl is a short one, and we have even walked there a few times. There are two picnic tables beside the river, just above the bridge, and we choose the one that's half in the sun. Karl starts a fire in the grill and sets about frying bacon. He has a mason jar with eggs, already broken and seasoned, ready to scramble, and a thermos of coffee and two blue metal mugs with matching plates. His camping plates, he calls them.

Soon it all smells wonderful, and as always happens when you eat outdoors, breakfast is delicious; the bacon crispy just as I like it and the eggs done to perfection. "Don't turn around," he says. "There's a bear twenty feet behind the car, coming this way." Then he laughs, kisses my cheek and says "just fooling." I poke him in the chest for teasing me like that, but I love it.

We rinse the dishes in the river and pack the breakfast stuff away in a box. I carry the two blank canvases and Karl takes the fishing creel with paint brushes sticking out its top. Walking under the bridge toward Lower Chester, the day beckons with possibility. Are we two artists beginning a new journey? Karl is named after his uncle, Karl Haldorsen, a full-time artist who lives in Norway. Ludwig has a painting by this brother above the piano, a landscape, and a still life of daffodils and hyacinths in clay pots hangs beside the dining room table.

We meander down the path, past patches of thimbleberry and wild raspberry, walking with care as the tree roots wind and curve out from the cedars and cross the path every which way. The birds sound cheerful this morning, and a chipmunk runs down a log, vanishing under some roots. Karl is whistling and the river is gurgling and splashing over boulders.

We arrive at the pond. I can imagine Karl and his friends swimming here in the olden days. The water is clear and the sunlight strikes through to a sandy bottom. I love the tall pines and already see which one I want to paint. There are lots of good places to sit, and we find just the right spot where we can put the paints on a flat rock between us. Karl squirts out dollops of the primary colors, plus white and black, so that we each have our own paint, a row on each side of the large palette we are sharing. The little bottle of paint thinner is stashed on the ground, like a beer bottle, and we each have our own paint rag.

We sit there looking at the scene before us, choosing just what to include in our paintings. I start first and mix some colors together to get the blue of the water. I sketch

The Poet's Daughter

in the shape of the pond first, and then add some blue to my mixture and do some sky. Karl watches me and follows my lead. I mix up red and black with a dash of yellow and make some long tree trunks, with the main one being the tallest, the one I spotted when we first arrived.

Karl works on rocks and has mixed a nice grey. It's hard to get just the right green but that is okay, because with my trying different colors together I get a mixture of greens and that's pretty much what the pine greens seem to be made of. I notice that if I don't add much thinner, the bristles of the brush make nice pine needle patterns.

Time goes by and the shadows move from place to place and soon the sun is on my special tree. I use some light colors and touch the tops of the bigger branches to get that sunlight effect. Karl's painting is getting a bit messy. He can't seem to keep the color where he wants it, and I'm afraid he's looking downcast. I've never seen him sad before. Shaking his head, he tells me how he sees how beautiful the pond is before him, and he wants to show that on his painting, but he just can't do it. It's obvious that I'm the artist and he does not seem to take after his uncle, the great Norwegian painter, after all. "Well," I say, and can't think of anything else to say. He laughs and accepts the situation, saying he could take lessons, but he thinks it's just not for him. "But you, my dear," he says and blows me a kiss across the palette.

We clean our brushes and pack up, fitting our wet oil paintings into a carrying device his dad loaned him, and we make our way up river, past the many rushing falls and under the bridge and back to the car. I know that I have been introduced to an art that I will do again.

Konnie Ellis

Mother is well and this time it looks like she won't be going back to the hospital. It's good to have her home. She is at her writing desk at the moment, and the aroma of bread baking in the oven fills the house again. She likes Karl. He notices things I don't, like how she was having trouble eating when he joined us for coffee and cookies one day. Her false teeth had a jagged section and eating caused her pain. She thought it happened while she was in the hospital. Karl took the dentures to the dentist, insisting they be fixed quickly, and got them right back to her within a day. Now she thinks he's nearly royalty. Needless to say, she is happy about my upcoming marriage to Karl. Papa likes him too, and says he is smart and practical, with a solid painting job for a businessman named Wannebo.

We have to wait a while because Karl insists we own all of our own furniture by the time we marry. In addition to twin beds, bedside tables and a dresser, we will need a dining room table, chairs, and a couch. He says twin beds with matching bedside tables are the latest style, and I have noticed this to be true in the movies we have seen lately. All of our furniture will be mahogany. He insists on it because it is a good hard wood, and very beautiful. I have pointed out that furniture with rounded corners is the nicest, because you won't be bumped by a sharp corner. We are now in agreement on that. We are not in agreement about the deer head. He has an enormous antlered head from when he studied taxidermy out in his garage, and he thinks it will look sensational in our living room. This is our only argument, and I'm pretty sure I'll win out. I could not face a dead animal's head looking down on us in our new home.

The Poet's Daughter

I have a planning notebook and have been collecting recipes. I have copied some from magazines, like the waffle recipe where you beat the whites and yolks separately for really fluffy waffles. I have Aunt Rose's anise kringler recipe, which may be just as good as Johannson's. Mrs. Bjerkan has given me some of her tips on baking chicken, and on numerous occasions Mrs. Gronseth has told me the best potatoes to use for mashed potatoes. My mother doesn't use recipes. I have been looking over her shoulder when she makes bread, like this morning. When she makes cookies she will say to use about this much flour and so much milk. I have to guess while I watch her mix up a batch. All of her cookies are old-country cookies and very tasty with a cup of coffee. Of course, I have the repertoire I learned from Ludwig, such as fish stew and roast. I wrote down the recipe for white sauce, just because I use it a lot and wanted to include it to make my book complete, even though I could make it in my sleep. Thank you, Mrs. Sebo, dear seventh grade teacher, for that one.

I am also collecting photos of living rooms and drapery material and general decorating tips. Solveig has magazines I love to browse through. She and Nils like Karl, too. And everyone likes Nils. He could have been an actor because he can make anyone laugh. He does imitations of famous people, like actors, and of ordinary people we all know, like Fur Coat Carlson who lives over on the corner. It's even easy to tell if he's doing Fur Coat Carlson or Farmer-Labor Carlson. Papa says if he hears Nils in the next room mimicking someone, he would almost swear that person was really there, that's how good he is.

My friend Jean married before me. That guy, Rags, is her husband. I can't say he's my favorite person, but she certainly seems happy. I wish I had been able to finish twelfth grade, as she did. Maybe I could have managed and still taken over the house with Mother in the hospital. Or maybe not. I guess I'll never know.

I'd better get ready. Karl and I are going up to Island Lake to watch the fish jump.

Chapter 9

IT'S OFFICIAL. We are man and wife. The marriage at City Hall was just right. I wore my new suit and Karl wore his best suit, the one with the vest. I saved up for my suit, paying a dollar a month to Wahl's Department store. Karl's suit came from Floan and Leveroos Company on Lake Avenue, probably costing ten times what mine cost, but I thought we both looked snazzy. Mother met us there and Juni and Alice were our witnesses. We drove to The Flame restaurant where we were all planning to have a nice dinner, but they were closed for renovations, again. We were so happy it didn't matter. We ate at a nearby place and it was great fun.

Karl had said we could have either a wedding, or we could marry at City Hall and have a honeymoon out West, and see Yellowstone National Park and the great mountains of Montana and Wyoming. I chose the West. Driving down Superior Street, I was feeling elegant in my Empress Eugenia hat, ready for our great adventure. Karl's shiny black car was packed with everything we would need for picnics, fishing, and car repair, as well as clothing, which probably included everything I owned. I turned on the radio and as we drove out of Duluth, and believe it or not, the music on the radio was the Wedding March.

Konnie Ellis

My diary of our honeymoon trip out West was mostly bits and pieces written while sitting in the car, or at the end of each day.

September 4 – 11, 1937

Budget: $125.40

MINNESOTA

Stayed at Fargo. Nice people there agreed to keep our wedding clothes for us.

Hotel $3.60
Tips $.15
Bracelet $.26
Supper $1.33
Root Beer $.10
Candy $.10

DAKOTA

Just saw a runaway horse.
Picked cactus.
Just passed a spot where there had been a cloudburst. Eighteen inches.
Saw a flock of sheep.
Just passed a girl on a horse in cowboy clothes herding cows near Rosebud.
Saw potholes full of ducks.
Met a man at a detour who said "if we had a drink for every time it rains in Dakota, we'll all be Christians."
Karl said jackrabbits travel in herds and eat all the grass of the hills.

The Poet's Daughter

Karl and I got out and ran down hills and shot the revolver and played cowboy and picked agates.

Overnight at Dickenson.

Cabin $1.40
Groceries $ .61
Dinner $.94
Film $.67

MONTANA

Saw first snow on mountains at 10:00 am on Tuesday.
Saw zoo at Red Lodge.
Stayed at Billings.

Cabin $1.30
Groceries $.85
Grease job, etc. for car $1.78
Melons $.10

WYOMING

Just entered Wyoming.
Now on top of a big mountain. All the others seem to be below us.
Still going up. The sky is blue, very few clouds.
Just took a picture of a lake way below.
Snow across from us.
Is it ever cold up here.
10,630 feet and still going up.
10,924 on top.
Dry grass and three buzzards up here.

Just passed Gardiner.

Stopped on top of a mountain even higher,
4 lakes below.
Still cold.
Road switches back and forth 6 times.
Just went down to one of the little lakes to take a picture.
Climbed back, pretty winded.
Saw another marmot, right close.

Stopped at Long Lake and watched fish from the bridge.
Perfectly clear water. Washed our hands.
Dinner at Island Lake, 9,000 feet up.
Shopped and had beer in Cook.

YELLOWSTONE

Entered Yellowstone at 2:00 p.m.
Saw an antelope and now a moose on the hill.
Went to Tower Falls – no cabin there, back to Mammoth springs.
Just fed a grizzly bear.

Cabin $1.25
Park Fee $3.00
Groceries $1.00

7:30 a.m.
Left Mammoth Terrace.
Saw swans and ducks at Swan Lake.
Stopped to fish and saw 2 coyotes.
Saw another one pounce on something and eat it.
Karl snuck up to take a picture but it left.

Now we're washing the car in a brook.
Fished in the river and took a picture of a moose cow and calf, close up.

The Poet's Daughter

Saw another moose in William Park.
Saw 2 black bear and got a close up picture of one.
Saw another moose.

Passed hot springs at Obsidian.
Stopped at more geysers.
Stopped at Roaring Mountain.
It's cold again.
More bears. A big one and 3 cubs feeding at the car ahead of us.
More hot springs.
Stopped at Frying Pan Spring, sounds like frying eggs here.
More smelly springs. Sulfur!
Passed Minute Man Geyser.

Saw a New Mexico license plate, rose and aqua, the prettiest we've seen so far.
Now it's raining, and here's another bear, a brown one.
It's trying to eat Karl's windshield wiper, which is going because of the rain.
Saw more geysers. They rumble down in the ground.
One is erupting.

Still raining when we get to Old Faithful.
Bought groceries and got Cabin 434.
Ate and went for a walk and watched Old Faithful erupt.
A couple told us where to fish so we went fishing.
Stood in warm water and threw our lines into nearby icy water.
Came back and saw a bear sitting on top of a tall garbage can.

Cabin $1.25
Groceries $.90
Film $1.30

Souvenir $ .15

Next Day:

Left Old Faithful at 7:40 am.
Saw 3 elk near Continental Divide.
Stopped at Thumb, Yellowstone Lake and Abyss Pool.
More geysers and more bears.
Beautiful Teton Mountains.
Just took 2 pictures of a little bear.

Made our way down a road between trees and stopped to fish.
A sign said "Limit 5 fish."
We are 1 short of the limit.

Stopped at Dragon's Mouth.
Just saw Artist's Point and took a picture.
16 buffalo across the canyon and more on this side.

Leaving park at 2:00 p.m.
Saw a herd of antelope at Gardiner.

MONTANA

Still mountains.
Saw Devil's Slide.
Stopped at Livingston for gas and beer.
Stayed at Yellowstone Camp and walked to town, to the Cave.

Cabin $1.50
Dinner $1.00
Beer and nuts $.40
Melons $ .10

The Poet's Daughter

Slot machine $ .10

Next day:

Left camp at 6:45 a.m.
Sun was coming up over the mountains.
Passed Old Baldy.
Passed two passenger trains.
Listening to KGHL Billings.
Nice cabins in the shade on east side of Big Timber.

Crossing Bighorn River where the hills are getting smaller.
Lots of ducks.
Opened all the windows but still too hot.
Lunch at Goodman Café at Forsyth.
Stayed at Barnum Tourist Cabins
Walked downtown for dinner at Log Cabin.

Cabin $1.75
Candy and beer $.30
Groceries $1.00

Driving at 3:30 a.m.
Stopped at a fair with a rodeo.
Left Miles City at 6:20 a.m.
Still driving along the Yellowstone.
Picked up a kid and gave him a ride to beach.

Had malted milk.
Bought Karl a sweater.
Crossing Little Missouri.
Cowboys wearing cowboy boots.

Badlands.
Took a picture of Painted Canyon.

Bought gas, and a sword for Gerry.
Stopped at Glen Ulm for candy.
Roads under construction here. Pretty bad.
Listened to KGHL Billings.
Time to change the clock.

Stayed in Bismarck.
Bought groceries, cleaned up and went downtown.
Had coffee and sweet rolls.

Cabin $1.00
Rodeo in Goodman $.20
Jacket $.98
Sweater $3.04
Ribbon and groceries $.30

Next day:

Left Bismarck at 7:50 a.m.
No more hills now, just prairie.
Crossed the Red River.
Tired.

Next day:

Back to Minnesota at 12:10 pm.
Good old Minnesota!
Got a cabin at Fargo.
Picked up our wedding clothes we'd left with the owner.

Last Day:

Lunch at Detroit Lakes.
We finally saw a live jackrabbit, 15 miles east of Frazer.
Karl got full of stickers chasing him.

The Poet's Daughter

Coming in to Duluth and beautiful Lake Superior.

Gas Total: $26.52

Solveig and Lilly Buan in Duluth, Minnesota.

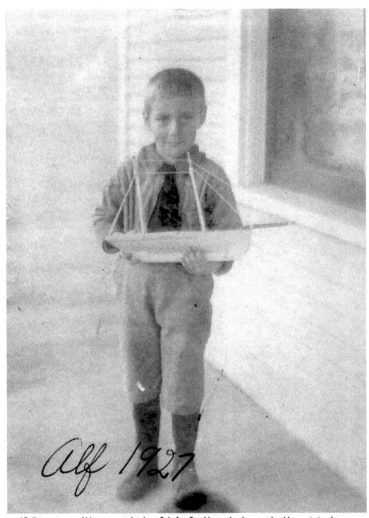

Alf Buan with model of his father's boat, the Melana.

1925. Norman Svarte, Lilly Buan, Bjarne Buan, and Alf Buan by Buan home at 1211 North Eighth Avenue East in Duluth, Minnesota eating bananas.

Lilly Haldorsen in front of Ludwig Haldorsen's house on 8th Avenue in Duluth.

Lilly Haldorsen at Lax Lake in her hunting outfit.

Lilly and Karl Haldorsen at a cabin on the North Shore of Lake Superior.

Bertha and Haldor Buan in the kitchen of their 13th Street home in Duluth, Minnesota.

Haldor Buan, Karl and Lilly Haldorsen on a summer day in Minnesota.

Lilly Buan Haldorsen and mural she painted in her Duluth, Minnesota bedroom depicting her birthplace of Hylla, Nord-Trondelag, Norway.

Chapter 10

WE ARE BACK IN DULUTH and find the apartment we were to move into had been sold while we were enjoying ourselves at Yellowstone, so we had to find something else, and quickly. Our last-minute find was not in the location we would have chosen, but then we didn't have many choices, so it'll have to do. It is the upstairs apartment in a house on Fifth Avenue, a block and a half above Fourth Street, and it is roomy enough. The furniture store is delivering all of our new furniture this afternoon, so I have been sweeping and thinking about where to direct the movers with the various pieces of furniture. I hope the couch will make it up the stairs without getting stuck. With all the moving my family has done, I've seen a few problems.

I think I am in love with my furniture. It must be some reflection of the love I feel for Karl, or of being young and in love and still spinning with the thrill of mountains and the great yellow plains with antelope racing along the road. Oh, just everything. I hope this feeling lasts forever.

Nothing has been damaged by the movers and all is in place. The couch is by the big windows that overlook the lake, and the two easy chairs are on either side of the big coal-burning stove. The dining room table is in the middle of the dining room, surrounded by these beautiful chairs. I keep running my dust cloth over their edges. The dresser is a divine dark wood with reddish tints. I have opened every dresser drawer several times because they glide so smoothly, unlike my old dresser at home where you couldn't even open the bottom drawer unless you gave it a kick. Our matching beds are perfect, with the large round mirror on the wall between them. The brown and beige satin bedspreads were the right choice, and I think the arrangement looks like a picture in a magazine, especially with the side tables in place with their matching lamps.

Jean and Rags were over for dinner again, and afterwards Karl put the big quilt on the table with the board on top and we played ping pong. It's a good game for Rags because he doesn't have to move much with his wooden leg and he's pretty good at it. Karl is the best, though Jean and I can hold our own. I know that the next morning Mrs. Olson from down stairs will say "I heard Step-and-a-Half upstairs playing ping pong last night." She always called Rags that: "Step-and-a-Half." She's nosy but nice enough. I only see her when I'm coming or going.

We have a lot of friends who are going together and not yet married, so they like to come to our apartment for dinner and ping pong. We always have something simple like spaghetti, or beans and franks, and maybe one large bottle of beer for a group of four. Often we play cards. Dagny and Sandy are here a lot, and Evelyn and Earl. Dagny and I go to movies together twice a week, at least. We want to see everything. Dagny and I have known each other forever, it seems. She reminded me this week that our mothers were confirmed together in Norway. I had

The Poet's Daughter

forgotten that. I hardly ever think of Norway, and sometimes it doesn't seem that I actually lived there until I was six years old.

On many of our weekday nights, Karl and I read. There is a small library at the drugstore on Fourth Street and that's where we get our books. We set ourselves up with coffee in the living room, and Karl sits on one side of the coal-burning stove and puts his feet on the stove and reads his Westerns, while I sit on the other side in my chair with my feet up and read mysteries. I just finished an Agathe Christie, and have started the first in a series called the Jalna books. It's all about a family in Canada called the Whiteoaks. We also have a good radio and listen to the big bands from Chicago's Aragon Ballroom, or the Trianon. We especially like Wayne King and Glen Miller. The quality of the music from the radio is excellent, unless there's a snow storm.

It's early spring and the smelt are running on Park Point. Karl went up to get his nets and pails from his dad's garage after work yesterday, so we're just about ready to head to the beach. I have the outdoor cooking gear, flashlight and stuff in a box, ready to go. It's a clear night and fairly warm, just right for smelting, so we're ready to leave as soon as Dagny and Sandy get here.

By the time Karl has everything in the car, I hear Sandy's laugh in the hallway, so I put on my jacket and we're off. The bridge is up when we get to Park Point, but the ship is already halfway through the canal, so our wait for the bridge to come down is a short one. If the ship is still out in the lake, it can take a while for them to get through, even though they move fast when you actually see them enter the canal.

Karl and Sandy have both agreed where we'll park, just at the turn. We all love that part of the beach, and the sandbars are perfect for smelting. We get a good spot and Dagny and I spread our blanket and set out the cooking gear. We turn the box upside down and put a dish cloth on top for a mini table. While the guys unroll the nets and get into their hip boots, we walk the beach for wood. There's plenty of driftwood and we gather enough to last the evening. Dagny and I can make a fire as well as anyone, and ours is soon going, one of many fires along the beach. Sandy hands us each a glass of beer and we settle back to watch the smelting ritual begin.

The sky is rosy and the last of the afternoon sun makes the pink sand of the beach golden. I love this time of day at Park Point. Karl and Sandy take the long net to the shore, and then with one at each end they lift their poles so the net is slightly above the surface of the water. They start the slow walk out into the lake. It is absolutely silent except for the sound of waves lapping against the shore. Sandy is a talker, but Karl shushes him if he makes a sound. They don't want to surprise and scare off the fish.

They take the net out to the farthest point of the sand bar, where they look like small dark figures in the lake. We watch them turn to lower the net and see Karl nod before they start walking toward shore. They take their time coming in, keeping the poles just skimming the bottom of the lake. As they near shore, Dagny and I settle our beer glasses into the sand, get the pails and flashlights, still turned off, and walk as quietly as we can to the water's edge.

The Poet's Daughter

This is the moment of truth. They arrive at the shore, and in one quick swoop tilt and lift the net out of the water and settle it on the sand. We turn the flashlights onto the net. It's full of smelt, jumping and shining in the last light of day on the last night of their lives. We scoop them into our metal pails, where they'll sit until we fry them over at Esther and Al's when all the fishing is done.

We take the net out three more times. I go out with Karl, and then Dagny and Sandy take a turn, and finally, Karl and Sandy do the last run. Karl and Sandy's first try of the day was the largest catch, and the last had just a few fish in the net. By then, of course, it was dark and all the fires could be seen for miles down the beach. The moon was shining over the lake, making for a very romantic scene, even though there were a lot of fish involved.

After fishing and the nets are rolled up, we wash off the fish slime in the lake and stroll along the sand, greeting the smelters at nearby fires to see how they've been doing. Someone Sandy knows got hardly any, so he brings them half a pail of ours. They give us their leftover chocolate cake and we gobble it up to the last crumb with some almost-warm coffee still in our thermos. Then Sandy gets his ukulele from the car and we sing some of our favorite songs. A teenage girl and her boyfriend who are walking along the beach stop and sing along to "Blue Moon," one of our favorites. She has the prettiest voice and makes all of us sound almost professional. How good it is singing around the fire, now burnt down to these last glowing embers.

Al and Esther should be home by now. They live across the street from our smelting place, so we fold up the blankets and walk over with a pail of smelt, ready for the frying routine. In the Johnsons' kitchen we get down to business, and set up our stations and spread out newspaper. First, Sandy cuts off heads and tails. Next on the assembly line, Al and Karl clean the fish. I rinse off the fish and dip them in flour and place them on a long wooden tray. Esther and Dagny do the frying, and we keep it up until we have enough smelt for a feast. Most everyone feasts. I only eat one, as I don't really like smelt. And that's the end of smelting until next spring.

We're at the Lion's Den, and Karl is taking a late afternoon nap. I just woke up. We had a long jaunt on our snowshoes, and my legs feel wobbly from all that odd sort of walking. You have to turn your feet out a bit, and so muscles you don't usually use get used a lot. Maybe it's how you feel after riding a horse, though I've never tried that. I wanted to take my snowshoes off for a break when we were out by a grove of birch trees and Karl just said, "Go ahead, but you'll sink." Did I ever! I went in up to well above my knees. I suppose I had to prove it to myself, or I would never have known how well those snowshoes keep you up.

The Lion's Den is pretty much an old shack made of logs, and is actually half of a cabin, done in the old-time style. It's partly built into the hillside with a cupboard for food that stays cold, like an indoor root cellar. The cabin has bunks, a table, and the wood-burning stove, and that's about it. It was built by a postman who lived there with his family, the Dillys. They had a son, David Dilly. Karl and I both liked the name David. In case we have a son someday, we could name him David. I think they moved to town, as

The Poet's Daughter

no one has lived here for some time. It's near the old CCC camp by the railroad overpass, and that's how I know we're close when we drive up here. We'll have chili for supper when Karl wakes from his nap. Tomorrow we're going hunting.

The next morning the sun is out and it has stopped snowing, and it's cold, but not too bad. I slept well, finally, after the wolves stopped howling. I'm taking my gun, the 4-10, but I really just want to get outside and I don't really feeling like shooting. I know it's not partridge season and that's about all I have ever shot.

We drive down the road to a spot Karl knows and says we'll walk in from there; Four-mile Lake isn't that far past the old gravel pit. After walking a while, I decide I'd rather go back to the cabin and read my movie magazine. I assure Karl that I'll be fine, as all I have to do is follow the road, and anyway, I have my gun. He has enough confidence in me to know I'll get back on my own okay and says he'll see me later. I watch him head into the woods toward the lake before I leave.

I pass our car in no time and start down the old dirt road. I keep going and going and the woods are quiet and thick with snow. It is a lot further than I had thought. It didn't seem very far when we drove out, but now I'm not so sure. Eventually I see a hill and am quite certain the cabin is over the hill. But no, it's not. There is another hill, and another hill, and it's beginning to cloud over. I am not panicking, but I am definitely anxious. I need to get the idea of last night's wolves out of my head. Finally, one more hill and there it is. I trudge into the woods to the cabin and step inside.

It's so comfortable and cozy when I get the stove going. And I'm glad I thought to take a movie magazine along. Still, it was taking me a while to get over that feeling of being nearly lost and like I didn't even know where the cabin was. I've had my share of close calls since I met Karl, no doubt about that. There was that bull moose at the river when I was alone, fishing the calmer part of a river when Karl was by the falls. I made it to the car and just stayed there until Karl came back. I had thought the moose would chase me, and it may well have. I pretended it wasn't even there and didn't look back when I crossed the river that day. Then, of course, there was blueberry picking in July, and I thought the noise behind me was Karl until I turned around. The bear just kept eating berries while I high-tailed it out of there, signaling to Karl about what was in the bushes.

Just as I was in a reverie and near to dozing off, someone knocked on the cabin door, rattling the hinges. Who could it be out here in the middle of nowhere?

It's John Bradley, one of Karl's fishing buddies, coming in and stomping his snowy boots. He's brought fudge, the newspaper, and some rolls. "Thought you and Karl could use some of this," he said. "I knew you two were up here."

I made coffee and we sat and visited a bit, and then he was on his way. I ate a big piece of fudge as I watched him walk down the path to the road. The fudge was excellent. Nice and creamy. What a strange day. Thankfully, the rest of the day was normal. Karl returned about when I expected and we drove back to Duluth.

The Poet's Daughter

After that I didn't see John Bradley for a few years, until we met him at a dance. He said he had just married, and his wife liked the outdoors, that she liked hunting and fishing just like I did, and that she one-upped him because she could tie a fish fly knot. Then he added, "And she looks exactly like you." I didn't know what to say to that, but I was glad he was happy.

Chapter 11

KARL IS UP ON THE ROOF. I make myself speak clearly and in a calm voice: "Karl, turn around slowly. David is almost to the top rung of the ladder." David is eighteen months old. With one smooth movement, Karl lifts David to the roof with him. While Karl climbs down the ladder with David, I am shaking so that I hear my teeth clicking together. "There we go," Karl says, calm as a cucumber, though I know he is not as he sets David down, still holding his hand. I had turned toward the crick for just a moment, and that's all it took. He was up the ladder. My brief inattention had nearly caused a catastrophe when all I had done was consider where to plant a lilac bush, yet I was shaken to my core.

Our house was going up as Ludwig's house was coming down. Karl's dad had given us the property, and he was going to live with us. The old house at the back of the lot was nearly completely down, and our new house at the front of the lot was half built. The digging of the foundation took the longest, even with the help of several friends. The lot is thick with red clay and the digging was a messy business. They couldn't work when it rained, but had two full weeks with only one rainy day, so luck was with us there.

The Poet's Daughter

I have barely calmed down by the time David and I get back to the apartment. I fix David's lunch and put him down for a nap. I don't know what's the matter with me, being so nervous and unlike myself. Well, I do know. It's my mother. Her stroke was so unexpected, as she's still relatively young. I think of fifty-one as still fairly young. Solveig has been more helpful to her than I have been, but Solveig tells me she has the time, as her girls are in school and David is at that age that requires constant attention. Something I certainly agree with after the ladder incident.

Solveig is stopping by in the morning after the girls are in school, and I'll have David all set to go. We'll do Mother's wash and make a pot of stew for their supper. She's getting around with a cane, but it's a struggle, and hard to see her so very slowed down. There was no way to talk her into getting a wheelchair, though we all tried. She is stubborn and independent, like the rest of us. Each day she learns to do more for herself.

At Mother's house, David was happy playing with his blocks on the kitchen floor while Solveig and I peeled potatoes and cut up vegetables for the stew. Then he was so involved with what he was building that he didn't want to go upstairs. Usually he liked stairs, but he hated these particular stairs and would say, *No, no. No blue. No, no, no*. The stairwell was blue and he just would cry if he had to go up those stairs. Of course, Mother had to stay upstairs because of the bathroom being next to her bedroom. David was usually quiet and good and liked to stay with one project at a time, so I let him stay with his blocks. Solveig and I took coffee and rolls up to Mother, where we sorted clothes and sat visiting and darning Papa's socks.

I went down to check on David and he had given up on the blocks. Mother kept the eggs on a low shelf, and he had found them and broken an entire dozen onto the floor and was busy mixing the sticky mess into the dirt of two overturned pots of geraniums. I called Solveig to come and help me. How had we not heard the commotion?

Back home while David was napping, it came to mind that he was afraid of his grandmother, now that she walked so haltingly and held her left hand in that lifeless manner. Then there was the clunking sound of the cane. That may be the real problem with his not wanting to go up the stairs, and it was a problem, because Solveig and I went to Mother's every morning.

That evening Alf stopped by after dinner. He had big news. He had bought a house on Thirteenth Street that would be just right for Mother and Papa, and he would stay there with them. He said it was a small house, but everything was on one level, and had a porch where Papa could sit and look at the boats on Lake Superior, and there was a small garage and a backyard. Alf was so excited, and I was as well. The house would be half a block from our new house on Eighth Avenue, and the stair problem would be solved as well. Alf had been saving his money since he started working at the newspaper office and I greatly admired him.

Our new house was finished on the outside and the roof was on. Karl hired two competing companies to finish the interior, one for the front of the house and one for the back of the house, and he said they would check up on one another to see who was doing the best job. He said the woodwork was going to be perfect, as he had seen the work of the carpenter doing the molding. The kitchen will have a counter measured to be just right for my height. The downstairs will have a bathroom, two bedrooms and a nice living room with an entry hall. The upstairs will be divided into two bedrooms and three storage areas, plus a hallway with a window halfway up the stairs that overlooks the backyard. Ludwig will have the upstairs.

It wasn't long before I was choosing drapes for the living room and when they were up, the room had a lovely finished look, like something out of one of the magazines I loved to cut pictures from. The only two items on our wish list that would not work were a clothes shoot, and a fireplace. But other than those two, I thought the house was perfect.

Soon, moving day arrived and all of our friends helped move furniture into place. David's room was painted blue and he looked over the room and told me where he was going to keep his blocks. He walked from room to room to see where everything was, then settled down under the living room table and sat there like a thoughtful little man.

Ludwig was seldom in the house and was busy building a playhouse for David. Karl's duck boat was out in the backyard, and David liked to sit in it. One day, shortly after we had moved in, Solveig stopped by when I was hanging clothes on the line and David was in the boat. She asked David what he was doing, and he said, "I'm sitting here in the frog." Was he waiting in a frog or in the fog? Maybe he was waiting for his dad to take him fishing. Karl had already taken him fishing a number of times, even though he was barely two years old. Karl took him everywhere, and he liked riding in the car.

Ludwig was good about watching David when Solveig and I went to Mother's. She was doing very well in the new house and had started cooking again. A friend of hers came in once a week to give her a bath and a massage, and a routine was falling into place for chores. Solveig and I used our old names for one another as we went about our domestic work, and I called Mother *Ma*, and they both called me *Li*, as when I was young, and Mother and I called Solveig *Sol*. It was a connection only we three had when we were together.

Mother was trying to write but was having some trouble and has asked Papa to look for a typewriter. Her desk was set up in the living room, and since the house was small, nothing was too far from anything else. Papa had hung pictures, at Mother's direction, on most every wall space available. They had many beautiful oil paintings of ships at sea, done by their friend George Roll from Iowa. Every time he came to Duluth he brought another painting, and they were all good. He was a professional artist who specialized in seascapes. The house was starting to look like a small art museum.

Mother had so many friends, including those she left behind in Norway and still corresponded with. I brought the mail to her when she was in the hospital and wondered about all those people who wrote to her. There were always letters from both men and women. I had a feeling she had a lot of admirers, because she was so pretty and interesting and conversant in so many subjects. And then she was a good listener and a marvelous writer besides, so it would be natural that she would be an excellent correspondent.

She has boxes of letters in the back bedroom, and it seems she has all the postcards she ever received taped to the glass of her big cupboard. Soon I had to leave for home, leaving Solveig to finish up the ironing of Mother's house dresses.

David had watched our house being built, as well as the playhouse Ludwig built for him, and he wanted to do that too, like a real carpenter. When I returned from Mother's, David was pounding nails into the basement stairs. He had pounded probably two dozen nails into the bottom two stairs. Ludwig had given him the hammer and nails, and said, "Isn't he something?" proud as a grandfather could be. Oh my. I was learning that Ludwig was the most patient man in the world, but not always the most practical. He removed the nails calmly, satisfied that his young grandson was certainly a genius carpenter-to-be. He had wanted to wait to show Karl, but I said it would be safer just to tell him about it when he got home from work.

Karl's painting business has been doing well. He has two people working for him and has had billing stationery printed up that says Haldorsen Painting and Decorating, as well as some little posters to hang up on the job with a picture of a painter that says "Wet Paint, Karl Haldorsen – Painting Contractor, Stewart's Quality Paint Products." I have started to do some of the accounting for him, and I take messages from customers when they call the house. Ludwig and Karl have begun a white picket fence around the backyard to keep David safe when the guys drive in to pick up paint or ladders from the garage. We still have the old garage Ludwig built, with an underground level for working on cars. It's painted white to match the house. I think my flowers are going to look beautiful against the new white picket fence. I might try roses.

Konnie Ellis

Wouldn't you know, but we are now a family of four. Little Konnie was born on September fifth, the day after our anniversary. Her formal name is Konstance Marie Haldorsen, after Karl's mother, who died when he was six years old. Karl bought me a pink-gold watch and a fur coat and one perfect red rose. I couldn't be happier. Konnie looked like a round moon when she was born, full-faced and yellow with jaundice, and topped with soft reddish hair, but she was healthy and perfect.

The day I came home from the hospital, Bjarne and Kay came driving in behind us. They had little Janice with them and everyone huddled around to admire Konnie. David touched her hand and remarked at how small her fingers were. Janice leaned in and brought her face very close to Konnie's cheek, wondering at her newness. I am glad that Janice and Konnie are among us now. When Bjarne and Kay would visit and David was the only child, I felt bad to know they must be thinking of their son, who didn't live, and would have been David's age. That baby was born too soon and his lungs were not ready for the world.

Now the babies are born into the war years. Another ration book for Konnie means a new pair of shoes for David, as Konnie only needs booties. Last winter Alf trained at Camp Hale in Vail, Colorado, with a troupe of Norwegian Americans who were to be with the ski patrol in Norway. As events changed in Europe, their regiment ended up as part of the 101st Infantry. Alf drove a jeep delivering ammunition to the front lines, something he never told Mother in his letters. The letters aren't amounting to much lately, but we're all so glad to get them.

The Poet's Daughter

The government blacks out a great deal of information, apparently to keep it out of the hands of spies.

David is helping Mother with her scrapbook of articles about the war. They cut out every story about the war from the Morning Herald, the Duluth News Tribune, and the Duluth Scandinav, and carefully paste them into books. They are on their second scrapbook.

Karl has one bad eye, and that has kept him out of the army. So many of our friends are overseas now. Dagny's husband, Sandy, has flat feet, so he's still here, thank heavens. Dagny is expecting her baby in a few weeks. I hope it's a girl because then she and Konnie can be playmates.

My, but David is growing up. He has a robin in his bedroom with a broken wing. Two months ago it was a sparrow. He used part of two matchsticks and some string and made a little brace for the bird's crooked leg. He didn't seem surprised when the bird mended and flew away. He thinks the robin will take longer to heal, but seems sure that it'll be ready to go by the time fall arrives. Here he comes now. "Hi, Davey. I suppose you have more bugs and worms there for Robin." "Yup," he says, heading straight to his room and the robin in the cardboard box.

I have been to very few movies so far this year. Last year I was going over my diary and figured I had seen seventy-two movies during the year, about as many as the year before David was born. Then we lived so close to downtown that I could easily walk down for a matinee, and then Karl and Dagny and Sandy and I would go to another movie in the evening. I was crazy about the movies and movie stars, and the cinema cost only twenty cents, or a quarter for something special, so it was cheap fun. Sometimes we saw double features on the weekends.

Last year Mrs. Bjerkan would stay with Kathy, and Ludwig would stay with David, and Dagny and I went to a lot of matinees together. Now, with Carol and Konnie still babies, we're homebodies for much of the time. But we all get together, even though they live in Kenwood and I'm down here on Eighth Avenue. David and Kathy are close in age, and Konnie and Carol are three weeks apart. What fun we have. I should feel guilty with the war going on, but it's best to keep your spirits up. Everyone has a victory garden, and we get the tastiest carrots and beans. It doesn't take much space.

Dagny and Sandy have an enormous garden and access to eggs and dairy products, with her parents right there at the bottom of the hill with the dairy and chicken coop. They also have an apple orchard. I have a bag of apples to take home from their tree today tucked under the baby buggy. I'm going to make an apple pie tonight. Karl does love pie. He always prefers pie to cake for his birthday. He'll be away for a while with a job in Illinois, painting the big oil tanks, so the pie is kind of a going-away pie. I hope he won't be gone for too long.

His backup will fill in as Block Warden while he's away. Karl is good at being the Block Warden, the one who makes sure all lights are out when they give the "lights out" alarm. Duluth being an international port city and having an air force base, we have many nights of "lights out." Karl puts on his helmet and heads right out as soon as he hears the alarm. He knocks on any door where he sees the

The Poet's Daughter

slightest light and has them turn it off, as even a closet or hall light has to be off. The city has to appear completely black from any enemy plane that might fly over. Karl also makes rounds to make sure each house has their pail of sand well filled, apparently to put out a fire if need be. Usually David is asleep when the alarm sounds and sleeps through it all, but if he's awake and sees his dad put on the helmet, he has a very serious look for one so young.

We're fortunate that Karl is usually home and occupied working for Zenith in the shipyards, where they paint the P-41 torpedo boats. I am so worried for Alf over in Europe. And for Bjarne as well, because I know what's coming for him and it is not the war. Kay called to tell me he has to go to the Nopeming TB Sanatorium and she and Janice won't be able to see him at all. Not only that, but she said she has started to knit a baby layette, her subtle way of telling me she and Bjarne are expecting another baby. She's both thrilled about the baby to come and scared for Bjarne's health. These are the things I ponder while I'm doing my own knitting. I'm working on soakers, which are thick double-knit diapers we use since rubber pants aren't available. All rubber is needed for the war. Thank heavens Konnie is nearly potty trained, and she's early in that regard. One thing at a time, it seems, with the little ones. I thought Konnie would never learn to crawl forward. She crawled in one direction only, and that was backwards, but with surprising speed. Then she simply stood up and walked, and perfectly normally, I was happy to see. She likes to follow David around and calls him "Dade."

There's a letter from Karl today. I'm always happy to find his handwriting on an envelope in the mailbox. I like to pour a cup of coffee and sit at the kitchen table to read his letters. It feels like a ceremony.

Wednesday evening

Dear Lil,

Sure was glad to hear from you. I really looked for that letter. It's so darned lonesome down here. I said before that I didn't like this town. Well, I think even less of it now. We work, eat, lock our doors and read until bedtime. We don't dare go out nights unless you are 4 or 5 together. There's at least 20 people who get slugged every night. And the food here is the poorest.

We're staying in a tourist camp about 4 miles from the center of town. Say, did anyone drain the radiator on my car? Tell Sandy I'll be home soon for hunting.

I sure miss you and the kids. If I am not home by the time this letter arrives, please write. Sure enjoy getting a letter from you.

Tell David I haven't been able to get to a store. They close before we get downtown.

This painter who works with us was robbed. They grabbed him right in the main part of town and hit him on the head with a blackjack. I carry my knife open in my pocket all the time. Just in case.

Say hello to everyone. I'll be seeing you soon.

Yours, Karl.

Still the same.

Box 642, Route 1

It wasn't long after that letter arrived that Karl returned. I saw him coming down the sidewalk and told the kids. Konnie called out to her brother: "Dade come, Daddy comes," and she ran to the front door, jumping up and down. And here he is!

More homecomings. D Day is here at last, and Alf is home. My parents are thrilled that the horror of the war has ended and their youngest son is safely home. Many in our neighborhood and town will never return to those who received the dreaded telegram in a black envelope. I wonder how their families must feel, seeing everyone else celebrating wildly, and pictures in the newspapers filled with scenes of victory parades with confetti flying and lovers reunited.

Alf had his share of close calls, only a few he's told me about. When he was in France, he and his troupe were stuck in the basement of an old house while the Germans were outside shooting and bombing. They didn't know from minute to minute if the house they were in would be next. This went on for two days and they were without food or water, all holed up in one small damp basement room, just trying to survive and keep their spirits up. That's when one of the guys pushed open a small door in the corner of the room, which turned out to be a small wine cellar. There were enough bottles so that each guy could have two, so the uncorking began. No matter what came next, life for a time did not seem so bad. When the wine was gone, the bombing had stopped. They worked their way through the dust and rubble, hoping the house wouldn't collapse from their movement. They opened a door to the outside and sun. All of their jeeps had been bombed to smithereens, but the streets were empty. These were the jeeps they had been using to deliver ammunition to the front. The Germans were gone, and soon the quiet of daylight changed to the sound of Americans talking. They were going to survive. The nightmare had ended.

Mother wrote a great deal of poetry about war and about peace and about sacrifice during the war years. I know she has been reading Alf some of the poems she has written while he has been gone, and there are a lot. Now her poem, My Christmas Boat, has been translated into English and set to music by Carel Oscar Ellefson. They worked hard on getting it all just right. She has been so busy in her little house on Thirteenth Street, and the new piano has been getting a good workout. People are coming and going every day. I like that I can see her house from my house, and from the front yard I can see Solveig's house as well.

The *Three Leaf Clover* is Mother's latest work. She and two other writers collaborated on the booklet, with each poet writing on the same subject on the same page. Mother has the middle section. I can understand some of it, but I have to sound it out in order to understand much of it. The book is over fifty pages long, with as many subjects as pages, so you can imagine what a lot of work that involved. The booklet is red with a flower design on the front. That one is published by The Fuhr Company. I am now looking

The Poet's Daughter

over my very own copy. I have a copy of many of Mother's poems, mainly from magazines and newspapers, but I also have a copy of her green book of verse with the Norwegian title, *Dikte* by Bertha Buan. Mother has used Bertha, rather than the Norwegian Berta, ever since we came to Duluth. I have never asked her about that. But then Bjarne goes by Barney, or some just call him Bee, like the initial. I really don't see what's so hard about the "j" in Bjarne.

I can hear Ludwig sawing outside. He's making a slide for David and Konnie and they can hardly wait for him to finish. Konnie has collected a pile of the curls from the planer that she keeps in a box. David is still playing with a truck in the backyard. Oh, no. Konnie is not in her sandbox.

"David, where's Konnie?"

"She went in the house."

I find her in the basement standing next to the coal-burning stove, just as I hear Karl come in the back door. "Karl, you'd better come look," I call up the stairs.

Konnie has melted every last crayon of her new large box of crayons on and around the door of the coal-burning furnace, hot enough to melt the crayons. Every color in the rainbow, plus the extra colors, like silver and gold, have dripped over and hardened on the front of the furnace. The door is especially ablaze with color. I'm speechless and shake my head. I head upstairs where Karl is changing his shoes, and leave Karl to deal with it.

When he comes up the stairs, he says he gave her an old camping spoon and a dull knife to scrape it all off. He said he explained to her that it wasn't safe to do that because it could start a fire, and she would have to scrape it all off. "She just said, 'okay,' and started scraping when I handed her the spoon. She's going to be an artist," he said.

She was in the basement until supper time, removing the melted crayons. When she came upstairs she acted like nothing unusual had happened, and we just went on with the day.

A few days later, Konnie was driving us crazy. She kept repeating everything David said. When he said *I'm going out*, she'd say *I'm going out*. Then he would say *Don't copy me*, and she would say *Don't copy me*. Then he'd say, *Mom, she's doing it again*, and she would parrot and say *Mom, she's doing it again*. So I'd say, *Stop doing that Konnie*, and she'd say *Stop doing that Konnie*. Exasperated, I'd say *I mean it, you stop that*. Finally she said *Okay*. Then two minutes later in the living room I'd hear David call out *She's doing it again*, and then Konnie's echo: *She's doing it again*. I had to get really mad. She never did it around her dad. I gave her the new crayons I had hidden away to keep her quiet and busy.

Chapter 12

MY LIFE IS MOVING like the Baptism River. There are ordinary gurgling and bubbling along days, then some years leap like waterfalls from one year to the next, and you're too busy to notice how fast they have gone. I'm sitting on my favorite big rock here at Lax Lake, looking out over the water. It's as calm as the big pool of the Baptism River, though of course much larger, and I have a rare moment of contemplation. Kurt is taking a nap on the blanket beside my rock, and Konnie and David are working on a lean-to next to the cabin. David is doing the construction and Konnie is decorating with moss and wild flowers. Karl is up at the lodge talking over the wolf situation with Rudy Wax Lax. He is concerned about how close the wolves sounded last night.

The peace will be gone for the rest of the week as soon as the Oies arrive. They'll be staying in Cabin No. 7, the largest; what with Kathy, Carol, Sandra, and baby Stevie, they can just manage in that one. We have the green cabin by the rock, as usual. I think it has the best screened-in porch. Oh, do we have fun! The kids get along and keep busy all day.

Rudy's dad is already working on the sauna for tonight. I like to watch the children in their bathing suits walk in a line toward the sauna. Of course Kurt and Stevie are yet too young, and Sandra as well, but David and Kathy and Konnie and Carol all love it. Konnie says she likes how it smells. David and Kathy are in charge of throwing water on the fire. Usually Karl will go over when they've been in long enough and send them all scurrying to the lake. He stays to watch over them.

When they get to the cabin, David and Konnie shiver until they're into their pajamas and then we have a pillow fight, with the kids on one side of the wall that separates the bedrooms, and Karl and I on the other side. We throw pillows over the top of the wall, which is open, and after that, instant sleep for Kurt and Konnie. And I'm sure it's the same for the youngest Oies. David and Kathy are the official babysitters when the grownups head to the lodge.

When I am back in Duluth thinking about the lodge, I imagine it as a large pine lodge. But in actuality it is small, with room for just a few tables, the candy counter with rows of canned goods behind, a refrigerator, and a lot of wolf skins on the walls, plus a few deer heads and mounted wide-mouth bass.

Nighttime at the lodge is a time for relaxation and a time away from chores and children. Everyone has a tale they can't wait to tell, and we have our beer and snacks and each story becomes an amazing saga. Soon enough, Sandy runs back to his cabin to get the ukulele, and the singing begins. The wolves will be complaining about the noise. Yet when we all return to our cabins, tired and exhausted, all is quiet, and when Karl puts out the kerosene lantern, the dark of night is the dark of ancient times.

The Poet's Daughter

And so it goes. We have been coming to Lax Lake Resort for several years now and know where the Swallowtails congregate, what the smooth black mud path to the beach feels like on bare feet, and what the sound of the waves against the dock foretells of upcoming weather. I like an occasional rainy morning when I can sit on the screened-in porch with a cup of coffee and watch the rain falling on the lake. It makes the softest sound.

Rudy and Ebba Wax Lax live on the lake side of the lodge with their children, including baby Mabel, and their scruffy dog Topsy, who appears out of nowhere with that curious look, expressive even though you can never see his eyes for the white mop of fur covering them. He might be a poodle, hidden beneath all that untamed fur of burrs and bits of forest.

To prepare for a trip to Lax Lake, Konnie heads to our Duluth backyard with the scissors and fills a paper bag full of fresh grass for Tommy, the pet deer who lives behind the lodge. David packs his bow and arrows. Kurt takes his tiny cars. Karl puts everything in boxes and I make sure we have everything we need.

Each visit to Lax Lake is pretty much the same. First we pick up our keys from the lodge and park behind our cabin. Karl gets the boat from the main dock and brings it to the dock in front of our cabin. David gets the water at the pump, and Konnie goes along because she likes to watch him swing the filled pail over his head, amazed that the water stays in the pail. David and Karl go to the ice house for ice, if old John Wax Lax has not yet put ice in the ice box, but usually it's already there. Then I take Kurt and Konnie to feed Tommy the deer. They laugh at Tommy's wet nose when they feed him. Next order of business is swimming. Usually there are two swims a day, late morning and again mid-afternoon when the bathing suits are still wet and cold. And if it's a sauna day, there's another swim at twilight after the sauna.

I'm up heating water on the stove and hear Karl whispering: "Konnie, do you want to go fishing?" She is up and dressed in no time. David isn't ready to get up and Kurt is sound asleep. This is her special time with her dad. The sun is up, but just barely, and the lake is still. I watch as the five-horsepower motor starts up and they head directly to their fishing point. In the middle of the lake, Karl lets Konnie steer the rest of the way, until they get to the big rock marking their point. I know the routine. They'll get their poles ready and the red and white bobbers will sit on the surface of the water, ready for action. Karl will light a cigar. Time is timeless over the lake as the sound of quiet surrounds them. They catch their fish and head back in time for breakfast.

After breakfast, I take Kurt to look at the ice house. Old John Wax Lax is shoveling sawdust, and digs away enough so Kurt can see the ice. Kurt touches it and laughs, but is too young to realize how amazing it is that sawdust can keep the ice frozen. It was cut from the lake as it is each winter, a hard job. We walk to the lodge and I buy Kurt a box of Junior Mints. Konnie bought hers earlier, along with a Little Lulu comic. She's out in the boat anchored in the reeds, her favorite spot to read comics. That's as far as we let her row. David can row all the way across the lake. He is busy making arrows out of willow and carving designs on the green bark with his pocket knife. He keeps his eyes on his carving as he tells me about the crayfish he found in

The Poet's Daughter

a can down by the big dock, wondering if they're like lobster and can we eat them. We never have, I tell him.

Chapter 13

IT'S ANOTHER WINTER Saturday night in Duluth and we're getting ready to go out. So what should I wear tonight? I think the new dress with the crackly taffeta skirt, the blue one, and the matching necklace and earrings with dangly black circles. I hum to myself as I fasten the earrings. Karl stops buttoning his white shirt just to look at me. He likes me to look fine and have the others admire me, and I do admit I have my Ginger Rogers side. I expect that dancing at the Highland Supper Club is as close as I will ever come to dancing on the big screen.

By the time we leave, Kurt is already asleep and David and Konnie are working on a puzzle. Ludwig is reading the paper. It's stopped snowing and there's only about an inch of new snow on the ground. What a winter it's been, though; cold with several blizzards and the snow banks are high, making it hard to see what's coming at the corners. When we drive into the parking lot at the Highland, we pull in next to Sandy and Dagny's blue Buick. Fred and Esther Nervick arrive just as we're getting out, so we wave and take our time so we can go in together.

Bissa and Al Sorenson are already there and we join them. The band has set up, the usual group with piano, accordion, and violin. They all sing too, and are really good

The Poet's Daughter

and know the latest popular songs and the old-time favorites. We women check out one another's outfits. Well, I'm sure the men do as well, but more surreptitiously. Esther is wearing a black dress with green trim, very chic, and Dagny is in red, which shows off her dark hair. Bissa likes softer pastel colors, and tonight it's a pale peach.

We are all famished and get our dinner orders in right away, as we always eat later than we're accustomed to up here, only nibbling at bits when we feed the children before we leave. Usually everyone has either steak or shrimp, with baked potato and a little salad. And of course we all have a drink, and that gets the stories going, and probably we all get a little louder than we would otherwise.

As soon as our plates are cleared, we're ready to dance, and wouldn't you know, Karl's favorite starts up, "The Tennessee Waltz." I like that one too. A slow waltz is my favorite, and I think it's the most elegant of the dances. I like to waltz with Karl, and he enjoys it if one of his favorites is being played, but he prefers a fast dance. As the evening goes on, the band adds a few polkas and schottisches. Everyone dances with everyone else, and a little harmless flirting goes on and we all catch up on the latest news from the past week.

On the way home I feel totally relaxed and danced out. It's started snowing again and Karl drives slowly through all the white. At the Rice Lake crossroad, two deer stand at the edge of the road, staring at us with their glowing eyes before they dash off into the pines instead of crossing the road.

My life has become more complicated. During the school year, it's PTA, and for First Lutheran Church there are large dinners to plan, both in the fall and at Christmas, requiring much time and work. How many tables do we need and how many meatballs should we order from Eric Rehbein to feed two hundred people, and how many people will we need to set up, to cook, to clean up afterwards? Who is going to make the rommegrot this year? I enjoy it, though, and seem to have a knack for organization. I like the bustle of the crowd and the sound of all the voices at a big dinner, with silverware clinking and the smell of food and coffee filling the dining hall, and then the satisfaction of a good turnout of people having a fine time.

Last year I had my appendix out shortly before the big Christmas dinner, and Karl told me about the call he took from someone at church, who could not accept the fact that I was in the hospital. "But we need her!" the woman had exclaimed, as though I could just hop right out of a hospital bed and rush over to the First Lutheran Church. They carried on, of course. No one is indispensable, though we may sometimes think we are.

This year I joined the Hunter's Park Garden Club and have made some new friends. I think people who like to garden and grow flowers are a lively and enthusiastic group. We take turns hosting the club and we all share ideas. You only need make a dessert and have coffee when it's your turn, and I've been inspired by some of the yards I've seen so far. My prettiest flower bed is the one by the white picket fence, on the driveway side of the backyard. It has seven rose bushes, and when I was hostess, they had all just started to bloom. Still, my back garden wasn't a

The Poet's Daughter

complete success. When I planted spring seeds I hadn't considered height, so the taller plants ended up in front of the shorter flowers. Gardening is a learning experience; we all share our mistakes and our successes.

A flower show is coming up in September and it will be my first time to enter an arrangement. Cris Klein has been most helpful with suggestions and has loaned me books on ikebana, the Japanese style of flower arranging. Cris was one of the few women in the group I had known before I joined the garden club. Karl and I first met Cris and Bill Klein at a dance at Hotel Duluth. Cris's husband is the bone doctor in town, and one of the people in the group Karl hunts with each fall. They stay at Buntrock's cabin at Lake Kabetogama, and the women come along for partridge season, but not for duck or deer hunting. Not all of the wives like to actually do any shooting, but Cris and I both shoot partridge. Mostly we just love being out in the woods, doing something as simple as walking down a dirt road on a beautiful fall day, like we did last year.

Cris had been taking modern dance lessons, and it was an unusual experience to see her set down her gun and prance along the road to show me what she had recently learned in modern dance class. Her only musical accompaniment was the rustling of the bright fall leaves and a few startled birds. She leaped up into the air, landing on heavy hiking boots that stirred up the dust. Cris threw her arms above her head and swayed to and fro, leaping this way and that, before sashaying down the dirt road with exaggerated hip movements. She ended her performance by tiptoeing on her boots like a ballerina made of wood, followed by a low bow. I tried my version of her modern dance, and she joined in, but we were just too funny, and I'm glad no cars came down the road. Cris is out to explore everything and is always into something new. She is a grand friend.

Today Cris and I are at the end of Park Point with our collecting bags. We are hunting for tall reeds and grasses for our arrangements for the flower show. The poison ivy has turned red, making it easier to avoid. There is a lot of driftwood at this far end of the Point, and our hands are full of interesting twisty pieces, possible focal point pieces for our arrangements. She spots some grasses with interesting seed heads and cuts a big bunch. I like the spiky grasses with the sharp tips, but add some of the seed heads to my collection as well. By the time we get to the very end, our bags are overflowing. We lean against the old Minnesota Point canal where you can see right across to Wisconsin Point, and pour ourselves a nice hot cup of coffee from the red thermos. Delicious! The lake is deep blue today with a few white caps, but nothing serious. The breeze is pleasant.

I won a second place ribbon for my arrangement in the flower show and I am pleased. Cris got a first in the category she entered, and a number of the other women from our club won ribbons as well. Looking at the great variety of floral arrangements made for a wonderful afternoon of viewing and flower sniffing and inspiration. I'm going to enter the next flower show when it comes around. Flower arranging is definitely my cup of tea.

Chapter 14

ANOTHER WATERFALL OF YEARS speeds along. David is in medical school and Konnie has one more year of college, where she is specializing in art and English. Kurt is in high school, Karl has been drinking too much, and my mother is dying. I am sitting next to Mother as she sleeps, here in her little home on Thirteenth Street where she and Pa have lived so many years. I don't remember when I started just calling them Ma and Pa, but sometimes I do. It seems to fit. The kids say Grannie and Grandpa.

I have been reading the articles in Ma's scrapbooks while she dozes. Two scrapbooks are all about World War II, the ones David helped with. The third scrapbook is filled with her poems, cut from dozens of magazines and newspapers. I page through, noting some from the North American Press, the Viking, the Chicago-Minneapolis Posten, the Duluth Skandinav, and the Washington Posten. There are also several from a paper in Norway called Jule Vesterheim. One article notes how she has written prologues for conventions and festivals and speeches for visiting dignitaries. It goes on about how well known she is. I was just re-reading the section about when Crown Prince Olaf and Crown Princess Martha were her guests in Duluth, but in the middle of the article, Ma awoke. I read part of the article to her. "Yes, I remember," she said, then asked when Dr. Pedersen was coming.

He stopped by each day after lunch and gave her a pill that helped her relax and fall asleep. Roy told me it was a sugar pill, but it did the trick. He told me what to expect as the week went on. She was leaving us day by day, he said. She could no longer see and had kept her eyes closed since Tuesday. She is over an angry period she went through last week, when she threw her pills against the wall and was not at all herself. That lasted just a day, but Solveig and I hadn't known what to do, and I know I was shaking when I went home at the end of the day.

She has stopped eating. Solveig and I take turns staying with her, and Pa is always here. Bjarne stops by when he can. She asks when Alf is coming. We tell her he'll be here after supper. He is on his way by train from Spokane, but won't be here today. She sleeps most of the day and through the night.

I sent Konnie up to see her after school. When she came back she looked as white as a ghost. We talked, and she said: "Grannie asked me to put blue flowers on her grave, and to remember to visit Norway."

It is Memorial Day and the sun is shining. Ma seems peaceful and has taken a sip of water. There is a buzzing above her head and she moves as if to bat something away. She uses the word for spider, moving her arm toward the ceiling, but it's a mosquito. You used the spider word but I'm sure you meant mosquito, I tell her. She laughs and lets her arm fall back. After that she falls asleep. Pa comes to sit beside her with me. Then he stands up and abruptly walks to the kitchen. I am so startled that I follow him, and pour us each a cup of coffee. "She'll die at quarter to five," he says. It is now nearly four thirty. I go to sit beside her.

At exactly quarter to five she inhales, and then she is gone. Her face relaxed, and her hand, curled up tight since her stroke, is now open with her fingers at ease. Pa comes in. We both cry. He wipes his tears and says, "She was the prettiest girl I ever saw."

She was buried at Sunrise Cemetery, and when I stepped into the house after the funeral, I knew that my life as I had always known it to be was over. I had no idea what was ahead.

Solveig and I have been sorting through Mother's papers for weeks now. Today I have been cutting her poems out of the duplicate magazines, and Solveig is working on the letters. We have kept most of the other magazines intact and have two boxes full of those. One box is full of letters and there's a shoebox full of nothing but postcards over on the couch. The biggest box contains notebooks and single sheets of poems, and we really don't know what to do with them.

"Here's a letter from Cousin Anton," Solveig says. All of his letters to Mother are in Norwegian, even though he spent all of his adult years in Texas. Solveig reads in Norwegian, translating the parts I don't understand. Most of the letter is about planning and building the Foshay Tower in Minneapolis, and how he believes it will come to be an outstanding symbol and beacon for the city of Minneapolis. He explains in detail about the manner in which it was built, and has included little drawings with measurements, using engineering terms neither Solveig nor I understand. The last paragraph of the letter is about a beach on the Lofoten Islands where Hegge was built. We can't figure out what or who Hegge could be.

"It's funny how you don't know much about the life of someone so close to you," Solveig says, folding up the letter. "We'll never know what Hegge meant."

"No, I guess not. Oh well, not much we can do," I say, half to myself.

In the same soulful manner, Solveig says, "I can't even understand my own life."

Then we laugh and call it a day. When I get home, Karl is mowing the lawn in the backyard. I watch him for a while, thinking how he hardly knew his own mother. I took my own mother for granted. Papa too. But that's what you do. I decide to mix up a batch of brownies.

Before long, David finished medical school. He was the first to marry. Claudine was Jewish, and David converted to Judaism. Their first two children, Barak and Gideon, were born in Duluth and then they moved to New York where Ruthie, Rifka, Naomi, and Zevi were born. I heard next to nothing from them for several years, but I eventually got to know all of the children and liked each and every one of them. The food is another story, though. I fear I will never develop an appreciation for gefilte fish. Perhaps there was just too much fish in my early years.

The Poet's Daughter

Konnie married a musician and they had two sons. Since they stayed in Minnesota until the boys were ready for school, I got to know Lane and Erik, as they came to visit quite often. Then they were off to Colorado, where I made many journeys for visits and climbed the mountains, trailing after the boys to see old gold mines, and picnicking in fields of wild flowers. There was always an adventure in Colorado, whether it was to some unusual movie at the Telluride Film Festival, or a scary ride over the Million Dollar Highway to the historic town of Silverton.

Kurt was last to marry. His choice was Kathy, from an Irish background. They had a son, Bobby, and a daughter, Colleen, and the family remained in Minnesota, living near the woods not far from Duluth, up near Twig.

I was looking at photographs of the children and grandchildren one day after lunch when the phone rang. It was Lucille Magie. She had signed up for a painting class at the new Central High School, an evening class for adults, and wanted to know if I would like to join her. Well, I thought, why not? I certainly have the time. I choose to try watercolors. Both classes started the following night, and she would pick me up.

I bought everything on the list of materials, and Thursday night I was off to my first class, taught by an old classmate of Konnie's from UMD. The new Central High School is on top of the city where the view of Lake Superior is wonderful but the wind nearly blows you off your feet, so holding onto our art supplies, the wide notebooks in particular, was a challenge. We clutched our supplies and headed into the wind to our respective classrooms.

My teacher got us right to work, and we set about taping our paper to the table with masking tape. Next we wet the blank white expanse of paper with a wide brush dipped in plain water. Then we dipped our brushes in blue and, following our teacher's easy brush movement, dragged the brush across the watercolor paper. He said let the brush do the work; let the water on the paper do its magic. I was enthralled. We added gray and pink on a sandy rocky beach. We added black, gray and brown driftwood, a few small dark trees, and a gull sitting on a rock. We learned how to wipe paint off a brush to just the right point of dryness and add a bit of dark green to make the bristles on a pine, using the bristles of the paint brush. Let the brush do the work, we were learning, and I loved it. I could not believe when the announcement came that class had finished for the evening, and it was time to pack up. My watercolor was mostly dry by the time we left the building, but Lucille had to struggle against the wind with her canvas, wet with oil paint.

That was some beginning. Karl reminded me of our painting trip to Chester Bowl from yesteryear, and I was amazed at how many years had passed before I had started painting again.

Chapter 15

KARL DRANK AND I PAINTED. The more he drank, the more I painted. I know he tried to quit. He really did. After all our years of parties, dances, picnics, lake excursions, duck dinners, and celebrations with our rather hard-drinking friends, Karl was the one who ended up with a problem with alcohol. Some of our friends were helpful when he tried to quit; others simply tempted him and made it more difficult. Of course, his very good business went downhill.

I had trouble sleeping and took to painting in the middle of the night. This was my escape, my release. I painted mountains, I painted lakes, and I painted boats, little cabins with grass roofs. I painted cows, horses, sheep beside Norwegian barns, and children picking strawberries. I might paint three paintings in one evening, going to bed exhausted in the middle of the night.

Waking in the morning, I would look over my midnight paintings, sometimes astonished at how well they turned out; other times, they were all disasters. I reminded myself what our teacher said, that you might do one hundred paintings and only one would be perfect. And was that so bad? He didn't think so, and I was inclined to agree.

People began to buy my paintings. On the one hand, that surprised me; on the other, I knew I had a knack for painting.

New discovery: Karl had taken out a second mortgage and was unable to make the payments. I stood at the kitchen window looking out at the birch in the backyard. The tree we had taken back from Lax Lake as a tiny sprout was now a big, healthy birch tree. Some things went well at the same time others failed.

I went to work. For a short time I worked at St. Luke Hospital's coffee shop. I liked the people I worked with and I liked getting a check, though it was small indeed. Next I worked at the Green Stamp Redemption Center on Superior Street. After collecting Green Stamps for years, here I was working in the Green Stamp store, something I would never have foreseen when I was pasting in stamps as a young woman. What I didn't like was waiting for a bus in the cold of winter, but other than that, it was a pleasant job, consisting of waiting on customers and counting out their books of stamps, keeping knick-knacks dusted and everything in its proper place.

I was promoted to assistant manager and worked at a desk doing accounting and ordering, which I soon found to be boring as I never saw anyone. I asked to be put back on the floor again, where the time passed more quickly. I liked being with the customers, talking to them about the Revere ware with the fine copper bottoms, the latest waffle makers, or a crib for babies. They always had a story to tell, and the transactions were fun, as the store was not an ordinary place at all.

The Poet's Daughter

The manager and I got on well, especially after the blizzard. It was one of those storms that come on quietly and quickly. Snow was nothing new in January, and we watched this one start up just before lunch. By mid-afternoon we had no customers, and we sent the stock boy and other women home. Within half an hour the parked cars were covered in snow and the door of the store was frozen shut. After a few calls to headquarters, Verna was ready to close up. We had finished the books, as I was still assistant manager at the time, and we readied the store and I went to call Karl, but the phone was out of service. We had a genuine blizzard on our hands and turned on the radio for an update. We could get one station. Buses had stopped running; schools had closed early, as had all government offices. Downtown businesses were all closing up, like we were. Verna tried the phone again and was able to get through to Hotel Duluth to see if they had rooms where we could stay the night, as we would only have a few blocks to walk. They had just filled up and said every other place in town was also full. We were too late.

"Good heavens, we're stuck here," she moaned. "We've got to get some food."

We bundled up, wrapping our scarves over our faces, put our combined weight against the door and stepped outside. The wind nearly knocked us over. It was a complete whiteout. We leaned against each other and made our way two stores down, to a market that sold foreign foods. A light was still on in the back and we were able to open the door. The owner was just about to turn out the lights and was going to Hotel Duluth, where he planned to sleep on a chair in the lobby. Before he closed up, we were able to buy two cans of refried beans and were on our way again into the storm. I could hardly hear Verna for the howling of the wind.

Verna stopped halfway to our store. She said, "We need some booze." She knew of a small store that sold liquor a few stores up Lake Avenue. We managed to cross Superior Street, and walking like two bulls with heads tucked down and low, and arm in arm, we made it up to the liquor store. With one small bottle of brandy in hand, we struggled back to the Green Stamp store. It probably took us ten minutes to cover the half-block of distance back to our door. The storm whistled and blew behind us as we stepped safely inside with our supplies.

We both knew what the store's stock consisted of and we made our plan. We would open a couple of boxes of blankets, and two boxes of baby crib mattresses. Just as we were coming upstairs with our blankets, the phone began to ring. It was Karl, very glad to hear my voice. Apparently people could now call in on our line but we couldn't call out. He said the hillside was a mess and cars were stuck as far as he could see. The news on the radio was to stay put and off the roads. Many were without electricity, and it was so bad the plows couldn't do much, if anything.

We were thankful to have heat, and made up our beds. We didn't know if it was dark from the storm or from the early setting of the sun, but it was probably both. Verna went hunting for a package with an automatic can opener and found a shiny red one. We set up a card table and chairs, used some dishes Verna kept in the back, and had our blizzard dinner, which was not too bad and seemed to get better as we sipped our brandy in paper cups. The radio came in clearly for a time, reporting that medical

The Poet's Daughter

emergencies were being taken care of by snowmobile, a new form of snow transportation that year. The announcer told of a woman who called the police wanting a snowmobile to pick up some cigarettes for her, as she had run out. Verna and I couldn't stop laughing over that one. I remember falling asleep to the sound of the wind rattling the doors and windows, and static on the radio. The baby mattress was quite comfortable, and I was glad I was a short person.

The next day was calm and quiet and the sky was blue, and there was snow, snow and more snow everywhere. We breakfasted on refried beans and longed for a cup of coffee. It wasn't until afternoon that a plow went down Superior Street and a crew was out on the sidewalks. Duluth knows how to plow itself out; that's a fact of life here in the northland. Before long, Verna's ex-husband picked us both up and delivered us to our respective homes. Karl had shoveled the sidewalk and our dog Pepi was just coming out to do his business when I got out of the car and climbed over a snow bank to the house. Pepi wagged his entire body at me in welcome. First thing, I had a cup of coffee. Karl had made spaghetti sauce and the aromas in the house were inviting.

That was my last year at the Green Stamp store. The folks at headquarters closed the store after nine years and reopened in another town. Rumor had it that if they remained open for ten years, they would have had to give their employees a pension. So there was no pension in my future, but I was able to pay off the second mortgage on the house and have new cement steps added to the front of the house in the spring after the storm.

I keep meeting interesting people at my bus stop on Thirteenth Street, usually when I am on my way to the library. I still like to walk downtown in good weather, but I am grateful for the bus in the winter. One day a few minutes before the downtown bus arrived, a tall lady in a long black coat, wearing an elegant hat, arrived at the bus stop from up the street. "Well, say now, do you want to be a Christmas elf? Aren't you the lady who is such an artist? You do all that crafty art and such?" she said in a right friendly manner. I told her I liked to paint, and I made dolls and elves and quilts.

"You must come and be a Christmas elf! Help make ornaments for six rooms of Christmas trees, for six different countries, down at The Depot museum. Now, how about it?" she asked, expecting an immediate reply. Well, I became a Christmas elf, and for one day a week, for the next six weeks, made ornaments for Christmas trees at The Depot with the Hansen sisters. The lady in the black coat was Hazel Hansen, and her sisters were Evelyn and Middie, and they all lived together in a charming house, neat as a pin, up at the corner of Skyline Parkway and Eighth Avenue.

After our elving, I joined the Hansen sisters for many an outing. They were great organizers and before long we went to plays and concerts together, took excursions by bus around Minnesota and Wisconsin, and tried our hand at gambling at the new downtown casino, in the old Sears building that used to be the Wards. We had lunches at my house and at theirs.

For a few weeks, I took a job with the Hansens counting people. Yes, we were to count the number of people riding busses, starting at rush hour and ending each noon. The Hansen sisters were such professional women, and in their retirement kept very busy. So we counted, or tried to count as best we could, the number of people getting on at each bus stop, and then the number getting off the bus. It was mind-boggling, to say the least, yet fun in an odd sort of way. Sometimes I thought it the perfect job for a crazy person, though I know that term is not politically correct, yet you know what I mean. Every family has one, or possibly more; you never knew. My sanity was saved by the shortness of the survey weeks. And I did discover the routes of busses I had always wondered about.

Now Hazel has commissioned me to paint a very large scene of Norway for their living room. I've switched from watercolor to acrylic, much easier in a lot of ways. For one thing, you needn't use glass in your frames, making lugging paintings around a lot easier. And the density of colors seems to fit my subjects, like this large summer scene I'm working on. It's after midnight, and I'm not far from finishing the painting. There are a lot of green hills and a meadow beside a lake, a barn-red house, birch trees, and high mountains on a blue-sky day. Something was missing until I added a woman in a red dress with long hair, walking along the path by the lake. I think she might be me.

Chapter 16

IF MY LIFE IS LIKE A RIVER, just how does a flood fit in? The water is roaring down Eighth Avenue and great chunks of asphalt are tipped every which way along the sides of the street. The crick in the back sounds like Gooseberry Falls, and the rain keeps coming, and the wind is blowing the trees every which way. Karl is up at Lake Kabetogama camping and probably doesn't even know what's going on here in Duluth. You can't get a radio to come in out there where they camp, so of course they would have no reason to bring one along.

It is just Pepi and me here on the couch. He's mostly dried off, but I rub him with the towel. Poor thing. I don't know why it took me so long to check the basement, but by the time I did there was a good two feet of water down there. While the storm outside was loud and howling, the water in the basement seeped in as quiet as a snake. The water was up to the second basement step and I saw cardboard boxes floating and throw rugs everywhere. Just as I was taking note of a round green throw rug that looked like a lily pad, Pepi came swimming around the corner from the furnace room. I waded in and picked up one sorry, soaked and terrified dog, and brought him upstairs. I wrapped him up and toweled him off and sat with him by the radiator. He was shaking, and so was I.

The Poet's Daughter

When I looked out the window to check on the storm out front again, I saw Mr. Perpich standing in his doorway across the street. I opened the front door and yelled over that my basement was flooded and what should I do? He said just stay out of there or you could get electrocuted. Good thing I hadn't asked earlier.

Will it ever end? Rain and more rain. It's the lightning that is the worst. I decide to climb into bed. The whole house feels like it's shaking with each thunder clap, so I pull the sheet and blanket up over my head and listen to the storm. I've unplugged the radio, the coffee maker, the TV, and the living room lamps. Every hour I make myself go down the basement stairs to see how high it's risen. It's only 5:30 in the evening and the water level has gone up one step since I rescued Pepi. Each time I check the stairs, I reward myself with an Oreo cookie.

At some point I must have fallen asleep, because I awoke and the rain had stopped and the sun was shining. How could I have slept? But after my nap I thought it was morning, yet it was only 7:30 in the evening of the same day. I rubbed my eyes and looked outside. What a disaster! Eighth Avenue was broken up into great chunks of street with a deep crevice in the middle. What I could see of Thirteenth Street was even worse, and red mud was everywhere, and I remembered that tomorrow was my father's 81st birthday and everyone was to come here to celebrate. Yes, there is the potato salad in the refrigerator, along with the chocolate cake. The roast is out of the freezer and thawing for baking. Now what? The telephone lines are down and out.

Pepi wags her tail, wanting to go out. Do we dare? I let her out the back door into the soggy backyard. She seems to know it's best to take care of business and get right back inside. It looks like the back third of the yard has washed over the steep hill into the crick, including Karl's garden, which had been doing so well.

Back inside, Pepi followed me everywhere before deciding to settle down in her usual spot by the radiator, even though there was no heat coming on, as it is August. When I open the front door I see that all the driveways along the avenue have washed away, except for ours. That I can't explain, but Karl probably will be able to. Yet he won't be home until the day after tomorrow, unless he gets word of this flood.

I see Judy and Solveig up on Thirteenth Street. And Pa's there too. I wave and step out to the sidewalk. "What are we going to do about your birthday, Pa?" I shout across the broken-up road. Judy's stepdad catches up to them as they near Eighth Avenue and says, "We'll all get there tomorrow, don't worry. We'll figure something out. We'll be there at two o'clock."

They turn back, since they can't cross the avalanche of a crevice in the street. A lot of people are out surveying the damage and no one can go very far. We all wave and the whole neighborhood seems inappropriately jolly, considering all the damage. I suppose we're all just glad to be alive and see that others are okay as well.

Before I climbed into bed for the night, I heard the buzz of electricity turn back on. The refrigerator hadn't been off long enough to do harm, and now I knew I could bake the roast in the morning. I was exhausted, but there was peacefulness in the house and I knew I could sleep. I decided to think about the flooded basement and the birthday party tomorrow.

Everything is ready for the party, even though I don't actually believe anyone can make it over here. The plates and silverware, the napkins, cups and saucers are all on the table. The candles are in the cake. I feel like I'm preparing a party for ghosts.

It's two o'clock, so I stand at the front door. The sun is out and I feel a bit giddy. Oh, there they are! Solveig and Pa and Judy and Dick Greene and Bob Rhine. And Ed and Sis, how in the world did they get this far? I watch as they navigate up the avenue to a place that seems like a possible crossing place. It looks like the slabs of asphalt have collided to make a tentative bridge. Actually I can hardly bear to watch, but I do, and they all make it across. Then Bjarne and Kay come along behind, waving madly. They must have found a drivable road and a place to park.

I can still hardly believe it, but the party is going to take place. Everyone adds something tasty to the kitchen counter lineup of food items before taking a turn surveying the damage in the basement, which has drained itself, leaving a layer of mud on the formerly bright red carpet and soggy debris scattered about. Next we file out to the backyard. The guys go close to the edge of what's left of the yard, next to the steep hill to the crick.

"Well, look at that. Karl's garden, all gone."

"Look at all those carrots down there!"

"Let's go get them," Bjarne says.

The men hustled right over to the garage to hunt for rope and found just what they needed: a sturdy length of rope, and a pail. Bjarne and Dick tied rope around their waists, and Pa anchored it to the metal pole where the raspberries used to be, using a good knot. They lowered themselves down, taking big leaps like mountaineers, straight on down to the carrots. Ed had on his good clothes and didn't want to get muddy, so he stayed at the top, where he and Bob helped pull the guys up with their pail full of the orange loot. I must say, they had a pretty good time doing it and didn't mind the audience cheering them on. I was mighty anxious, though, as the crick was still roaring and the hill was slick with mud. They got back up okay, but of course they were a muddy mess with all that awful wet red clay. But so what, the carrots were beauties! The guys left their muddy shoes on the porch to dry. Kay and I made coleslaw, adding a few of the precious carrots. Judy stuck a few of the smaller carrots into the cake, next to the candles. Sis got the coffee started, and the party went on.

Chapter 17

I'M SITTING ON THE BED in my old childhood hometown, looking out at the fjord. We're staying at Peter Austad's house on the hill. Peter is Nils's brother. Solveig is clipping her toenails. She wonders aloud what to do with the clippings. Throw them out the window into the fjord, I suggest. She opens the window and throws them like she's tossing crumbs to the gulls, and well-satisfied with the gesture, starts laughing. We have been laughing a lot this week. Any silly thing will set us off. Maybe we feel like kids again, with the easy feeling of freedom to do whatever occurs to us. It really is amazing for all four of us to be here in our tiny village on the fjord. Me and Solveig, and Bjarne and Alf. I don't know how many pictures Solveig has taken of Austad's store, which is still a general store, but it's considerable. I've done a lot of sketching.

Bjarne has gone for a walk to look for an old friend he has inquired about, and has some vague instructions about where the guy lives, less than a mile up the hill, he said. He seemed to think it was near where he used to ski.

Alf has lived in Fauske up in northern Norway for some years now, and he and Aashild came down to join us. Aashild has kept to herself and has been good about leaving us to reminisce, and to explore our childhood haunts. This morning Alf and I found the rocks where we used to play. As kids, we had pretended the rocks were horses, or big boats to sail away on, and so we remembered them as huge boulders. When we found them, they were just puny little rocks, not boulders at all. Still, they were our rocks, and they were still there.

Yesterday I rinsed out my tan trousers in the fjord down by the dock and hung them on the line. Of course they were stiff as a board when I took them down. I had forgotten about the salt of the sea. I also forgot about the tide. When we walked to the shore on the day we arrived, I wondered where our beach had gone. The tides that ruled our hours of youthful play had been quite forgotten in our years of living in Duluth.

There is nothing quite like memory lane when you revisit your birthplace when it is a faraway country. We often sit in silence with our private thoughts. Solveig likes to sit on the bench over by Austad's store, where I'm sure she is thinking of her youth, and of Nils, now gone. I'm glad for Solveig's earlier trip to Norway with her daughter, Elizabeth, whom we all called Sis. Sis had joked about how she was going to find a husband in Norway, but met her husband-to-be, Ed Salveson, back in Duluth on the very day of their return back home. They married, and all of those handsome children soon followed: David, Jerry, Ron, Diane, and Jeannie. Solveig knitted incredibly beautiful Norwegian sweaters, hats and mittens for them all, and for the rest of her grandchildren, and mine as well.

Sis died too soon, of breast cancer. As did her sister, Esther, leaving her husband and Judy, Bobby and Mike all alone. A scary culprit, cancer.

The Poet's Daughter

Alf and Aashild lost Cynthia when she was twenty-one and had just begun a modeling career. She died in a car accident. Her brother, Bill, is a great comfort to them, and is a car nut like Alf. He had his car shipped to northern Norway when they moved to Fauske.

Bjarne has been taking a lot of walks. His wife Kay died recently. Their son Lee died in Viet Nam, but their daughter Kathy still lives in Minnesota, and Janice is in Florida.

The grim reaper has certainly had his way in our families. Pa died, but he was an old man when he passed away. Just last night we were all sitting around drinking coffee, remembering the year before he died, and how he would go missing. One of us would make the calls and organize the search party, each of us taking a different part of the city where he had been out lost previously. Bjarne found him the last time, after dark, walking fast as he always did, looking for a store that no longer existed. He wanted to buy some chewing tobacco. Snoose, he called it. Bjarne drove to Solveig's house with Pa and we had a sort of party to celebrate finding him. Pa said, "Well, there's no fool like an old fool," and was glad to see us all and be safely home. I don't think he ever got his snoose, though.

I'm sitting above the old family homestead, sketching and thinking all these thoughts. I try to picture Pa walking down this road I'm next to, which is still a dirt road. Pa walked like a sailor, as if trying to steady himself at sea, but he walked so fast, even up into his late 80s, that you had to really hustle to keep up with him. Looking down on the fjord, I can almost see his boat sailing in, coming home. He showed me his captain's papers once. He was proud that he was so young when he received them and said he was one of the youngest ever to receive them. He rarely bragged, but with him, it didn't seem like showing off but rather just being matter of fact. Oh, what a fine father I had. I close my sketchbook and head back down the hill.

No one else is back yet. It's the perfect time for me to take the dried flowers out of my suitcase, the ones I saved from Mother's funeral. Pa made a couple of trips back to Norway after her death, but she had never been able to fulfill her desire for a return trip to the homeland. I slip the envelope of flowers into my sweater pocket and walk down to the shore. Austad's dock will be just the right place for my little ceremony. I walk to the very end and toss the dried flowers into the fjord and watch the pink and blue petals float and bob along with the waves. This is my way of having something of Mother back home in Norway, finally.

I've been home for a month now. It took a long time to get used to the time change, but morning seems like morning again and the robins are chirping in English. In Norway, Solveig had insisted the birds were chirping in Norwegian. Maybe they were. There goes that squirrel with the skinny tail, running along the telephone line above the street. I worry about that one. It doesn't seem to have a normal sense of balance without the bushy tail. Well, I don't worry too much, since I prefer the chipmunks.

Karl is snoring. He sleeps on his back and snores. I don't know how anyone can sleep on their back, but it makes his snores louder, I'm sure of that. I close the bedroom door and settle back with a cup of coffee and a sugar lump and a slice of still-warm coffee cake. The show I'm watching in the living room is a surgery show that

The Poet's Daughter

shows actual operations. This one is a hip replacement, the exact surgery Karl had last week. I'm sure he wouldn't want to see it. I know I wouldn't, if I had just gone through it. Too bloody, and so invasive. I'm going to make myself watch it to the end so I know about it.

Just as the surgery ends, I hear Karl moaning and I look in on him. He's awake and trying to move his walker nearer the bed. I slide it to him and offer to help. "No, no, I'm fine," he insists, pulling himself up. The bathroom is close. It's good having a bedroom and bathroom on the first floor.

I heat up a bowl of soup for Karl when I hear him working his way to the living room. The TV is still on and the surgeons are talking to the patient who just had the operation. Karl says he would like to have seen the hip operation. Well, maybe they'll repeat it sometime, I say, surprised he'd want to see it. "I could watch it on TV, but wouldn't want to go through that again," he tells me. Still, I can already see he's maneuvering around better in just one week than before the operation.

Leif comes to visit and brings a ham. I bring them both coffee and coffee cake. I wash the baking dishes and listen to their conversation about their dad. Ludwig has been living with their sister Marie in Flint, Michigan, and he's not doing so well. Marie is to call if there are any changes they need to know about. "She feeds him too much cake," Leif says. Karl agrees. Then they're quiet, probably thinking of Marie's cakes. She is a gifted baker. Butter, butter and more butter. When she came to visit during the war years, she used up my month's supply of butter in two days. I decide to have another piece of coffee cake.

Karl is asleep again when Bjarne stops by after lunch. He has three Ciscoes for Karl and hands them to me. "I know, stinky smoked fish," he laughs. I went for a drive up the shore and stopped at Kendalls. He tells how he looked in on the attached dance hall just to see if it was still there, and said it looked just the same. No sawdust on the floors, though. "I may have heard the ghosts of those musicians we used to hear," he tells me. "They were pretty good, some of them. All those polkas and schottisches. They could play the slow ones too, though." He has to rush off. He has a Toastmaster's meeting. As he drives up the hill, my mind is filled with the lilt of that old song, "The Tennessee Waltz." I hum myself around the kitchen, happy to see Bjarne. He does really well. He has so much energy that I forget he's living with one lung.

Chapter 18

ANOTHER BLIZZARD, another lifetime snowed away. Karl is gone. He died on the day the Twins won the World Series, and he was buried the day before the blizzard buried Duluth. Konnie and Bob have returned to Colorado, and I wander the rooms of the house by myself. The puzzle we all worked on is still laid out on the dining room table. I'm not quite ready to slide it into the box and break up all those pieces.

It was a good last year with Karl, as he was his old self. Well, he was his old self in a decrepit body, but then it's the spirit inside where we really reside, isn't it? In my dreams I'm always sixteen years old and it's always summertime. Look at it now. Still snowing. Two, three, and another car down on Twelfth Street, and let's see, four cars buried on the avenue, covered with snow like giant marshmallows, each car at a different angle. And it's cold besides. Even so, it is beautiful. White as newly fallen snow, as they say.

We went up to Beaver Bay before the storm moved in. Watching the marigolds float on Lake Superior, moving outward toward the deep; that was when it ended. We all stood there, bundled up in winter clothes listening to the waves lap against that old boat. I don't know how I knew to go there, where Karl had spent so much time as a child. Some instinct, I guess. Karl had always spoken so fondly of the Mattsens, and of how Mrs. Mattsen fed her family on fish stew and homemade bread, and what fun it was exploring the cove and hills of Beaver Bay when he was a kid. He said that was the place that still seemed normal, after his mother died. All those Mattsens were fishermen back then.

Before we left to go back to Duluth, we took some pictures of the flowers floating in the lake and a photo of the original log cabin, now on the historic registry. I peeked in the windows at the long table still inside. All the fish stew eaters now gone. Karl gone, just bits of golden flowers from his funeral bobbing in the waves of Lake Superior.

I keep forgetting to eat. This morning I was thinking of all the times Karl brought me breakfast in bed. It was just coffee, toast and a sugar lump, along with the paper. When we were first married he noticed that I was a bit cranky in the mornings until I had breakfast, so that's when he started that. He kept it up for many years. I guess I took it for granted after a while.

It's already lunch time. I had set out a package of frozen chili that Karl made a month ago. I'll have that and crackers. I know I need to make myself eat. Maybe his chili will give me one of those dreams. Twice now, I've woken in the middle of the night from a dream I don't remember, but I hear something in the kitchen. Then I see a shadow and I know it's Karl. Isn't that the darndest thing? It's nothing you would mention to anyone, but still. I'm not scared when it happens, I just turn over and go to sleep, like it's natural and I feel okay.

The Poet's Daughter

I'm glad I've been sleeping. Last week I saw Dr. Arvold for my annual checkup. I'm doing well, he says, but to call him if I have any concerns. He is a doctor who really cares about his patients. Also, he's Norwegian, and so we have that in common. I'm lucky to have such a smart and nice doctor.

Kurt says I should move into assisted living. Konnie says I should stay in my house as long as I can. I decide not to think about it and get out my paints instead. It took a while to find the old photo I wanted, of the boathouse at Beaver Bay. This may be one of my best paintings. Although I only started two days ago, it's coming along just the way I want, with the rustic boards of the boathouse a nice authentic brown and grey, and the waves of Lake Superior a perfect blue. Waves are always a challenge, but I've got it right this time. I only have the rocks of the beach to work on.

Good timing. I've cleaned my brushes when the phone rings. Bjarne wants me to go gambling with him, just to Hinckley this time, not to Las Vegas. I tell him I'll think about it. The time I went to Las Vegas with Bjarne was after Kay had died, and Kathy came along. Back then we used coins and there was a handle to pull down. No buttons to push, like with some of the newer machines. We always played a few coins over in the corner Kay had liked, the place she called "Amen Corner." I call Bjarne back. Sure, I'll go, I tell him.

That winter I told a lot of people, yes, I'd love to, when invited to lunch or a play or a movie. I liked to keep busy. I was seventy-three, but I didn't feel the least bit old. Many of my friends from the early years were already gone, as I was the youngest of them all, and just sixteen when I met Karl. Nowadays I often wish that Roy Pedersen would stop by for a visit, but he was gone. Jean Gronseth lives in California and we have been out of touch for years. I think about the Oies and the day they moved to Minneapolis. There sure were a lot tears when they backed out of our driveway on moving day. Evelyn has been a great help this year. Her laugh can chase away anyone's blues. And then, what about Steve? Was he still alive?

This winter was becoming endless and I longed for warm weather. I need to get outside. Would we ever have lilacs again? Considering the amount of snow still on the ground, spring is going to feel like a real miracle this year. Surely it is each year, but this year it feels different, my need for spring nearly desperate.

I've written a poem about the old fog horn. I always loved its deep bass sound. Tourists complained about it because it would wake them up, but I found it a comfort at any time of day or night. The new fog horn has a higher note and is pleasant enough. Still, I miss the old one.

Spring in Duluth

> To some a robin on the wing
> may be a certain sign of spring
> or should a crocus
> raise its head
> above its cold and snowy bed
> yet the sound we wait so long to hear
> a welcome nuisance to the ear

The Poet's Daughter

the moaning fog horn
that's the thing
that lets us know
at last it's spring.

The water is trickling down the sidewalks and I hear the rushing of water in the crick, gushing along over the boulders. Our tiny bubbling crick has a roar this year after the big snow storm. The melting has been going on for weeks, and there are just a few spots of snow left in the shade. The yard has that smell of earth, tired of snow but not quite awake. It's still too soggy to go out and clean up after Pepi's winter leavings.

When I get the mail, the front yard has a hint of green in the grass that it didn't have yesterday. There's a letter from Colorado. That's always fun. I'll read it while I have my second cup of coffee.

Dear Mom,

How's everything in Duluth? My daffodils are starting to come up and we're supposed to have 12 inches of snow tonight. I'll cover them with something. I was in a rush this morning and didn't bring boots or a hat, so since Bob has to come downtown and deliver two articles to two different places today, so I told him to bring my boots and hat.

We saw an unusual flying machine on Saturday when we took a drive and stopped for lunch near a small airport. The flying machine looked like a home-made helicopter or a machine from one of those old movies of people who tried to fly with various contraptions but could never actually fly, or never for more than a foot. Anyway, this one had a motor and an odd propeller and rudder, and a lawn chair for a seat – one of those with the woven green plastic strips. There was no top or covering to the thing at all so he was just completely out in the open.

He wound something up by hand, started the motor and moved forward very slowly down the runway and then came back very slowly again, before starting to speed up fast enough to lift off the ground. He took off and flew in a circle, flying about three blocks before he landed. It was weird seeing him up there. He looked so serious the whole time sitting in that lawn chair. He had a rope for a seatbelt, and a funny helmet with a propeller on top.

I read such a good book. Called "My Antonia" by Willa Cather. You might like it. It takes place in Nebraska at the beginning of the century.

How is Bjarne?

Love,
Konnie

P.S. I am finishing this after reading your letter. I loved the drawing of Hazel at the party, and description. Must have been fun.

We had planned on going to a concert in Colorado Springs last night but it was snowing too

The Poet's Daughter

much so we didn't go. (Bob just skied down to the 7-11 for milk.)

That was a good letter. I might look for the book she mentioned at the library. Maybe I'll walk downtown in the morning. I need white thread, new needles, and something else that I wrote on my list. I could stop at Woolworth's and then go on over to the library, and take the bus home. There's a rumor going around that Woolworth's might close. I sure hope it doesn't.

I've always loved walking downtown. Alf and I walked downtown so many times as kids. We walked to the canal to watch the Leif Erickson boat that sailed all the way from Bergen, Norway, to Duluth, back in 1927. That was a thrill, seeing such a fancy boat all decked out with colorful shields, and a dragon's head at the front and tail at the back. The boat was green with a square sail of red and white stripes. It didn't really look like the *Malena*, but Alf and I thought of Papa's boat back in the Trondheim fjord as it sailed in. We had to sit on the edge of the canal to see because there were so many people there. Everyone was waving at the boat as it passed through the canal, and we waved too.

Today is a sunny day just like then, but I still need a coat. One of the best things about living on the hillside is seeing Lake Superior every day, and of course when you walk downtown, you're walking down to the lake. If you drive straight down Eighth Avenue, it looks like you're going to drive right into the lake. It must be the steep hill that creates that effect.

This is my old memory lane walk. One block down and I'm passing Grant School, where we all went to school—even Karl went here—and then our children went to Grant. Those good old PTA days are over. I loved the carnivals the kids had; not in my time, but for David, Konnie and Kurt. They had movies in the gymnasium, and Halloween events with cake walks. Oh what a big deal it was to win a cake at the cake walk! And there was the white elephant table with fancy junk, and a fishing table where the kids used bamboo poles. The lines went over a large standing chalkboard with someone on the other side to tie a surprise to the clothes pin that served as a fishing hook. I was a fortune teller at one of the school carnivals, and a good one, because I knew so many of the people who came to have their fortunes told. I knew what they wanted. Of course it was mostly the same. Love and health and money, pretty much in that order.

I always turn at this corner so I can walk past Johannson's bakery over at the corner of Seventh Avenue, long closed by now. I always glance at the old doorway where you had to walk down some steps to get inside. What I wouldn't do for one of Johannson's kringers!

Daydreaming my way along, I pass two houses where we used to live, plus one empty lot where there was a house where we lived for a short time. I walk by two former grocery stores, now apartment buildings. Even the old fire station is now an apartment building. I miss the corner stores. They were everywhere in the olden days and so handy. You didn't need to drive or walk far at all.

Here at Sixth Avenue I have to wait for traffic to lighten, and then I cross just above Storey Taxidermy. Through the years, all the kids I knew, plus my own, loved

The Poet's Daughter

looking in the windows here at the stuffed bear, pheasants, deer, and fish. It was a wonder seeing all those animals looking alive, yet totally dead and unmoving.

When I get to Fourth Street I walk west, so I can pass by Rehbein's old grocery store where I used to buy meat. I can picture Rehbein back at the meat counter, a stocky guy in a white apron, always pleasant and aiming to please with just the right cut of meat. Next is the drugstore, where we bought books for twenty-five cents apiece when we were first married. Across the street is Bridgeman's, still there. Next time I'll stop in for chocolate malt.

One block above Superior Street I see the first dandelion of the year, bright yellow and cheerful as ever. A good and happy sign. And on to downtown. I pass the old Green Stamp store for old times' sake, and pick up my notions at Woolworth's before heading over to the library. After all that, I'm right on time for catching the Kenwood bus back home.

The phone was ringing the minute I stepped inside. I put down my books and packages and hurried to answer.

It was that caller again; the one who doesn't say anything, but just breathes into the phone for a while and then hangs up. This has been going on for over two weeks. It gives me the creeps.

Chapter 19

I THINK I'VE FIGURED OUT who the breathing caller is; at least, I'm about ninety-nine percent sure. For one thing, the call always comes at the same time, about four o'clock in the afternoon. I've been keeping an eye on Drake, the next-door neighbor on this side of the avenue. He gets home just before four each day, and it's about five minutes later that the ghost call arrives. That has happened for the past three days. When the call comes this afternoon, which I assume it will, I have a plan. I'm going to pick up the call, listen, then pretend I have a phone connection to the police or the phone company. We'll see what happens.

In the meantime, I plan to make bread and cook up a batch of jelly. By the time the bread is in the oven, I see Drake coming into his driveway. As expected, the phone rings in five minutes. I pick it up. The usual deep breathing.

That's when I say: "Yes, this is the one. Track this one."

He hangs up.

Success! I never receive another call. I've outfoxed him, at least this time. I am still worried, though, even though it's been a month without those awful calls. Kurt has installed a deadbolt lock on the back door, so he's worried for me too.

Drake used to be a normal sort of person, but something has happened to him. Karl had told me that his mother ended up in Moose Lake.

The next incident occurred when I had a coffee party and showed the women around the backyard. I wanted them to see my roses. Drake came out to his backyard and called over at me, "Foreigner. Foreigner. Go back to where you came from." I felt terrible. What could I do?

After that I only worked in the yard when his car was gone, so I knew that he was away. Even then, I didn't feel wholly comfortable in my own backyard. I didn't know that the worst was yet to come.

He would wave at me and pretend to be nice. Then he started playing a record called "Lili Marlene," by a singer with a smoky German voice. He played it loud with the screen doors and windows open so the whole neighborhood could hear, but I was the closest house. Every day he played that song when he was home.

What am I going to do this time? Well, the woman who lived directly across the avenue from me was a distant relative to Drake, and they spoke occasionally. I decided to tell her that Drake has been so nice as to be playing my very favorite song lately, "Lili Marlene." Apparently she told Drake, for that was the end of the music!

Before long, Drake became ill and died. I tried to remember him from when he was a good neighbor, back when Karl was alive, yet I am just a tiny bit ashamed to say that I didn't shed any tears at his passing.

Chapter 20

TODAY I'M WAITING for my ride to the annual birthday party. Three of us have the same birthday, June 23rd, and the other four have birthdays close enough. Today it's at Francis Ink's house, and she's sending someone to pick me up. It'll be the usual group today: Martha Hammer, Josephine Contardo, Rose Chida, Cris Klein, May Banzoff, and of course, Francis Ink and myself. Oh my gosh! Francis has sent a white limo to pick me up. Here's the driver coming up my walk in a uniform. Well, if that isn't something. I wish Karl could see this.

    I sure felt special being driven to Francis Ink's in that white limousine. It seemed that I should be waving to people along the way, but there was no one to wave to. It turned out each of us had the white limo experience that day. Leave it to Francis to think of something like that. She always added the extra unexpected touch to whatever she did. Her yard, for instance. Not only was it beautiful and perfect, but she used cocoa mulch around her flower beds so that after a rain, walking up the walk to her front door, the waft of chocolate was delectable. As were her lunches. Even though we had a tasty, yet ordinary tuna salad on lettuce leaves, it was served on exquisite plates. She had quite a collection. Today we had chocolate cake for dessert, and each of our dessert plates came with an old-fashioned

Christmas tree candle holder attached, candle in place and lit with flair.

Although it was a delightful birthday lunch, it did bring to mind some of those who had died, and I think it was Cris who was trying to remember the month Roy Pedersen died, so that evening I got out my Bible to check the date for her. I have run out of space to put the names of the dead. I suppose that's a natural occurrence, when you get into your 70s.

I got out my box of favorite photos, with the idea of finding one of Roy and the old gang. I did find the one I had in mind, as well as many of others, some gone and others still around. I have been blessed with an abundance of friends, that's for sure. Maybe making friends is what I'm best at.

Some time after Karl died, my grandson Lane came to stay with me. He had broken up with a girlfriend and needed a new start. We hit it off just fine, and it was great having a good snow shoveler in the house. He found a job and we settled into our routines. We went grocery shopping once a week in the evenings, when the store was quiet. Shopping with Lane was kind of an adventure, rather than just a chore. He had a good sense of humor and was thoughtful and didn't mind driving me wherever I needed to go. But Lane moved on, as young people are apt to do, and married Julie Ahasay, a delightful person and a busy actor and director who taught at St. Scholastica.

I felt quite independent and capable, unlike how I felt those first months after Karl had died. Without this new strength within me, I don't know how I would have handled Bjarne's death, followed not long after by Solveig's demise. Here I stand at the front door, as I have so many times in the past, looking up to Thirteenth Street, to Solveig's house, now occupied by another family. They have already expanded the front porch and added a deck with three white flower boxes filled with red geraniums. Solveig would have approved. I wonder if the apple tree in her backyard is still producing a good crop. Those were good pie apples. Now she doesn't have to go up and down those incredibly steep steps from her front door to the street. I don't know how she managed all those years, even navigating the stairs by herself two days before she died in the hospital.

I have Solveig's plant that I took from her back hallway. It's doing great. I call it the "Solveig" plant. I'd better water that one, and all the African violets, as they seem to be in a midst of a blooming spree. They like my kitchen window sills. Karl never liked African violets. He said he was always moving them when he painted in the east end, or just about anywhere. He didn't like stripes either. Said they were too hard to match up for wallpaper.

I'm just babbling to myself. I'd better fix some lunch and get busy looking over my wardrobe. I need to figure out what to pack for Las Vegas next week. Either Kathy talked me into going, or I talked her into going. Without Bjarne, I just think we need a trip to Las Vegas. We were laughing our tears away last week, talking about Bjarne's last Las Vegas trip. He got home to Duluth in the middle of a snowstorm, and although a cab got him to his house way up there on Chambersburg, he had to make his way through snow nearly up to his waist, getting from the road to his front door.

I'll heat up this fruit soup for lunch.

It's Saturday and I have a roast in the oven for Kurt's birthday. Thank heavens Kurt and his family eat what I cook. They are the only ones who do, though Kurt is rather fussy. As a child there were about five foods he would eat. Potatoes, hamburger, tomato soup, spaghetti with nothing on it, and his vegetable was corn on the cob, though he didn't actually eat it but liked to suck off the butter. Konnie liked everything except fish and meat, which she would hide in a drawer in the kitchen table just below her usual place setting. Sometimes she ate chicken, but she picked it apart, rejecting nearly all of it and ended up eating just one tiny piece. David said she needed a dissecting kit to eat chicken. David liked most everything. But that was back then.

When David was in pre-med at UMD he took a parasitology course and whenever I prepared fish, he would insist on taking the raw fish to the basement to examine under the microscope. He always called Konnie to come look, and she insisted she saw tiny white wiggling things when she looked at the slide under the microscope. Oh course, I didn't eat fish anyway. I'd had an overabundance of fish as a child, but everyone else ate theirs, except for Konnie.

Now David and Claudine can eat nothing I make, because they keep a kosher kitchen. Konnie and Bob are vegetarians, and so are Lane and Julie. Erik and his wife, Lynn, are vegans.

The Poet's Daughter

Alas, cooking and sharing one's heritage through food is something I've always loved to do. At Christmas I am the one who always made the old traditional foods no one else would bother with, such as blod polse, and krub with gjetost gravy. I still make all the traditional cookies, like fattigmann, and Berliner kranser, and spritz. Ludwig used to make kjot roll and chokecherry wine for use at Christmas. It's ironic how Konnie was the one who liked to help Ludwig make kjot roll. He would buy expensive cuts of meat suitable for the sausage, and they cut up onion and the various meats, and the roll would be wrapped and tied with string and put into the ceramic jug in brine for three days before it was boiled for Christmas. I used to cook lutefisk, but no longer. That's one traditional food I didn't enjoy preparing. It's just plain too smelly.

Everyone loved my duck dinners in the fall. Each person would have a whole mallard, which I baked slowly with apple and onion inside each bird. We would have wild rice, cranberries, and cornbread to go with, and usually ended up eating late, so the kids would eat first or take their plates up to bed to eat while they listened to their radio programs. The Drs. Klein and Pedersen were nearly always on call, so if one or the other had to leave, I would turn the heat down low and we would eat when they were back and ready. Those delays seemed inevitable, but the mallards cooked slowly were the best, they all said. I ate everything except the duck. I never cared for wild game, except for partridge, if it's made into a stew.

Here comes Kurt and his family. I'd better mash the potatoes.

Chapter 21

I CANNOT GET USED to writing 2000 on my checks. I also can hardly believe I'm still around. The year 2000 sounds like a science fiction date, but here it is and here I am. There's no explaining why I've been busier than ever. I had a table at the First Lutheran Bazaar again, demonstrating quilting, and displaying the little gnomes I like to make. Konnie knitted some little red hats for some of them, and I used felt for the others.

After that bazaar it was the Rosemaling arts and crafts show, where I had quite a large table in an excellent location and sold my dolls and gnomes and several paintings, plus two quilts. One quilt was made of squares with appliquéd and embroidered dancers in Scandinavian costume. Those are a lot of work. The other quilt I sold was a small baby quilt with ducks in each corner. It's a long day sitting at a table, but the people are friendly, and I like the atmosphere. They usually have music, and sometimes Arna Rennan and friends play Norwegian music I'd like to dance to, but I just tap my toes. They're really good.

So 2000 is here and I was so busy I didn't have much time to think about it. Well, now I've finished my bookkeeping for the month. It's always a relief to have everything balance in the checkbook. It drives me crazy when I'm a few cents off, but then I hear even the bankers aren't exact. One person who worked at a bank told me he just had to close his checking account from time to time and open a new one to keep everything in good order. This month I'm not even a penny off.

That must be Allison knocking at the door. Good timing, because I just finished my work and the coffee pot is full. That doorbell hasn't worked for the last fifty years. I met Allison Aune at the bus stop on Thirteenth Street when she commented on my vota, my Norwegian mittens. I was wearing the mittens Solveig made in the traditional Norwegian double-knit style with the snowflake design. They last forever and are so warm. Well, Allison is such a calm person, yet she is most industrious and accomplished. She is working on a Ph.D. and has little children, plus she paints and travels to Norway and Sweden. She lives down on Twelfth Street. Did you ever notice that the word Twelfth has the word "elf" within it?

"Come in, come in. Velkommen." The house becomes alive with the little ones as soon as they take off their coats. There is Leif, and Linnea, and they are so cute and curious about everything. I get out the box of empty thread spools and they get busy making stuff and stacking spools as high as they'll go. I use my Farmer's Rose cups for our coffee, and we have coffee bread to go with. Leif wants to know if he can look in the drawers in the kitchen, and I tell him which ones he can look into and which ones he should leave alone. Linnea is still busy with the thread spools. Allison shows me her latest greeting cards, which are portraits of the children in Norwegian sweaters with complicated designs circling the cards. Her husband does the printing. Each one is a unique work of art like nothing I have seen before. Allison tells me she is going to Norway soon, even though she is expecting another child. She has enough energy for twenty people. We have such a good visit and laugh a lot, that when she and the children bundle up and leave, I feel they have left behind a swirl of good feeling. I have another cup of coffee, with a sugar lump this time, and sit at the kitchen table to unwind. A squirrel makes a mad dash across the backyard.

This is turning into a good week for entertaining young people. I'm going to be showing Clara and her friend Isabelle how to embroider. We can do a few of the first steps, like the chain stitch, and make some daisies. Maybe we'll try some French knots. I'll have to see how it goes. Clara is Solveig's great granddaughter, and Sue will be over with them after lunch. Sue is busy sewing for a ballet.

Here they come. Clara is wearing a bright knit cap with a long braid, and Isabelle is in a red coat. I think she's a little older than Clara. "Oh, hello, hello. Come in, come in."

We all have milk and cookies before we get started, and Isabelle says her nickname is Izzy. They look around the house and admire the doll furniture I've been working on this week, and they like the dolls I made last month, all sitting in a pile on the bed in the back bedroom like they're having a party. I immediately decide the embroidery lessons aren't for today. We'll make doll furniture instead. Fortunately, I already have some of the pieces cut out for chairs and couches. That's the hard and slow part, as you have to cut through thick poster board with a razor sharp cutter, something they're too young to handle.

The Poet's Daughter

I dump a bagful of material in the middle of the living room floor and they have fun going through the material to choose the colors and textures they want for their furniture. Both Clara and Izzy get right to their miniature furniture making, having both decided to make easy chairs. Clara is doing hers in blues, and Izzy is using an orange and red print. I spread newspaper and the girls trace the cardboard pieces and cut out their material. I pour the glue in a bowl and show them how much to spread on the cardboard before settling the material over the pieces. We smooth the material over the shapes and over the edges, and I can see we're going to have some very nice little chairs here. It's a little tricky to put the pieces together, but the girls take to furniture making with ease, and by the time Sue comes back to pick up the girls, two perfect little chairs are sitting by the radiator drying. I find two old cigar boxes for transporting their chairs so they can finish drying at home.

Alf is not doing well and we all know he is nearing the end. But where is he? Sitting in a lawn chair in my backyard smoking a cigar! And why shouldn't he, at this point, as Aashild is gone. He has been staying with me for a few weeks now, long enough for me to know what he likes. He prefers a grapefruit at breakfast, and oatmeal, with coffee, of course. He likes his music, and we play tapes that he recorded from the radio when he lived in Norway. We even hear Elvis songs sung in Norwegian. I like to hear the announcers speak in Norwegian between the musical numbers, because it's almost like being in Norway. Alf is so very weak now and sleeps a lot. He's best in the mornings, and it's wonderful when the weather is warm and sunny and he can sit out for a time. We reminisce and look through the old albums. Kathy visits often.

The time arrives for his son, Bill, to take him home. Alf spends his remaining days with Bill and Kitty, in the apartment attached to their beautiful home on the river in Oregon, where he smokes his last cigar.

Susan arrives in Duluth. Susan was Konnie's best friend when they were kids growing up, and now she is my best friend. We both love going to rummage sales and estate sales and we hardly miss a one. She says her car cannot pass a garage sale sign without automatically turning in. Sometimes we drive up the shore for a sale, if the weather is nice. Since Susan moved to Duluth, I have been accumulating a lot of knick-knacks, and we are getting into the habit of having our own rummage sales with all this stuff. Sometimes Kathy Carr joins us for a sale. Other times, just Kathy and I have a sale over at her house in Superior. Susan lives up behind UMD in that area full of sugar maples which are so gorgeous in the fall.

Susan is an extrovert, no doubt about that, and she likes to have fun. When she calls me in the morning, she'll say: "This is your social secretary calling. The plans for the day are as follows...." So there's always something fun to do.

When Konnie flies in from Colorado, which she does often, the three of us have an event, which is simply an excuse for dressing up and having a lot to eat and our full share of wine, or some fancy drink with a cherry and an umbrella. Usually we will have a poetry evening at my house where we take turns reading our poetry or poems others have written, listening to music, partaking in lovely and creatively presented food, all in all making for some totally jolly, silly and delightful evenings.

Our most ambitious event was a play about the early history of Norway, in the time of trolls and Norsk gods, which I did research for ahead of time at the library and made a painting of the characters we would portray. Bob and Lane joined us for this, and we all wore costumes. Bob was Odin; Lane was Thor; Susan was Loki; Konnie was Freya; and I was Bryn Hilda, sporting long braids of pale blond yarn. We had music, a theater curtain for entrances from the kitchen to the living room, and a video camera was set up to record the entire event, including the after-performance commentary by our New York City critic, Bob, transformed from Odin to critic. His commentary ended with: "I'm signing off, not from New York City, the town that never sleeps, but from Duluth, Minnesota, the town that never wakes up."

Chapter 22

THERE'S LANE IN THE DRIVEWAY. I can always hear his car when he pulls in because it has a kind of purring sound when it stops. He's going to mow the lawn. Sometimes Kurt mows, other times it's Lane.

"Hi, Grandma. I have a surprise for you," he tells me and gives me a hug.

He has a chunk of Jarlsberg cheese for me and I think that's the surprise, but that's not it. He has discovered where Steve lives and has his phone number and address for me. I'm amazed. But then, Lane is such a good genealogist and researcher that I shouldn't be. Yet he did a search about six months ago and nothing turned up, partly because Steve's last name is so common, and then his official name is George, and not Steve. I had thought the search was over, or that Steve was dead, since he's my age and not many of us live into our 90s.

I looked at that piece of paper with Steve's phone number and address every day for a week. I almost called one day and even started to dial, but then I chickened out. What if he is deaf? What if he is bedridden, or has Alzheimer's and hasn't the foggiest notion of who I am?

The Poet's Daughter

I hate to make phone calls, especially long distance. But today I'm going to make myself call. I need to find out. I dial the numbers and pause quite a while before dialing the last number, and I'm almost holding my breath.

"Hello."

"Steve? This is Lilly, from Duluth."

"Lilly! My gosh. How are you? What a surprise."

We must have talked for an hour. He sounded just like he used to and we caught up on what had been happening in our lives. He and his wife lived in California and had a son and a daughter. Their son died at a very young age. His wife died a few years back, and he now lives with his daughter and they both like to travel but haven't done much traveling the last few years, though they did get down to Las Vegas recently for a little gambling. He likes to play the organ, which he does every day, and he sings in a choir. One of his favorite hobbies is wood carving. He likes to swim and has a swimming pool in his backyard.

I told Steve about my life, and by the time he took down my number and we finished our conversation, I was in a state of amazement. I just stood there in the kitchen by the phone. Steve. Just the same as ever. I got out an old yearbook and cut out his picture. I had almost forgotten how handsome he was.

That was the beginning of five years of delightful phone calls, birthday cards, and postcard exchanges. I liked to send him old postcards of places we both remembered from the olden days. We had many pleasurable conversations about the past in Duluth, as well as what we were currently doing. We did sometimes speak of getting together, in Duluth or in Las Vegas, but I think we both mostly wanted to remember the other as we had been, back when we were both teenagers. It made us feel young again. When you reach your 90s, there aren't that many people who remember the same things that you do. It was an unexpected bonus to my life, which I treasure. The day his daughter called to tell me he had died during heart surgery was a sad day. May you rest in peace, dear Steve.

Chapter 23

IT'S NOT IN THE CARDS for me to spend my golden years in Norway, returning to my roots as some do, but now I have my home village and fjord right here in my bedroom. I have finally finished the mural on the largest wall of the bedroom, complete with mountains, green hills, and all the little houses of a Norwegian village. I painted a church with a white steeple, a sail boat out in the fjord, a boat house and a wooden dock. On the dock stands a girl looking at the young man she just picnicked with. He is tying up the boat by the boat house. The sky is either a sunset or a sunrise, and I call it whichever I choose, depending on the time of day. When I awake in the morning, the mural is the first thing I see, and then the sun is rising, of course.

  I'm ninety-nine years old and it's a cold day a week before Christmas. I've finished wrapping presents and my Christmas bread turned out fine, but the fattigmann were too hard, so last night I made them into crumbs and used them in a pudding. The living room is decorated and I have three trees: a tiny artificial one, a wooden Scandinavian style tree hung with straw ornaments and tiny elves, and a real tree that Kurt brought which sits on a table; and though short, it looks just right and it smells pleasantly piney. My two Father Christmas statues are by the front door to welcome everyone, and Bob hung the wreath with apples and pears outside from the flag holder. The mistletoe ball is above the kitchen door. The upstairs is ready for David and Elaine, who will be flying in on Tuesday. It's been many years now since Claudine died of brain cancer. That was so sad. I'm glad David found Elaine in his later years. It seems the oddest thing that they are both so crazy about rodeos. I don't think they've missed a year of the Cheyenne rodeo for quite some time now. It's surprising how things work out.

The snow is not up to the top of the backyard gnome's red hat, like it is some years, thank heavens, but who knows what will come before the week is out? I'm amazed that the old birch tree is still alive, just like me. It sits above the crick at the back of the yard and despite having lost bark near its base, it thrives. That year of the last heavy snows, two deer slept at the foot of the birch every night of December and must have chewed off the bark. Karl dug up the birch as a sapling from the woods up by Lax Lake, and I planted it back there. That summer day is fresh in my mind and I can almost feel the breeze from the day I dug the hole and stuck it in. I took the sheets off the clothes line shortly afterwards, they had dried so quickly in the wind.

And so it goes. Christmas has come and gone in a whirl of lights and fun, plus one trip from the plumber, but no snow storms. Elaine and David called to say they are safely back home and ready for their next night of Hanukah. Konnie undid the tree and took all the trimmings up to the Christmas room until next year, God be willing.

Today I feel as if I'm in a tower, like Enger Tower, only higher, and I'm looking down over Duluth and Park Point and Lake Superior, and it's all there, my whole life, from way back to the days of the Incline right up to today, and it's all jumbled together, people and places and music and dancing. You might say it was like a dream. Isn't that what they say in the song, "Life is but a dream?"

I can picture Karl and me out on the Montauk when they turned the tables over for gambling and the night lights came on across the city, and then in the blink of an eye the kids are putting on their jackets to leave for school, and my dad walks down the hill for a visit. Is that Ludwig closing the back door, bringing some smelly fish from Kendalls? Am I choosing a dress to wear to a dance? The blue one, or the black? Or I am unpacking from a trip to Norway? Is that Bjarne heading off to Chester Bowl with his skis, while at the same time I am snipping roses for a flower show? Now Bjerkan's old phone number comes to mind: Hemlock 4688. Must be quiet now, shhh, Mother is writing a poem. This tumbling jumbled history comes and goes, most often when I look through my big box of photographs from different years and places, all next to each other in the same box.

How ever can a human brain contain an orderly view of it all when you're nearly one hundred years old? It is now twenty-six years since Karl died. The years have been good, for the most part, though certainly there have been sad and unexpected events I would not have wished for. But I consider myself fortunate and blessed, all in all.

Enough philosophizing. Kathy is picking me up to go the Black Bear Casino in fifteen minutes. I'd better get a move on.

PART THREE

MEHANA – PALO ALTO, CALIFORNIA

2017

Chapter 1

"Hello."

"Hello. This is Mehana. Great Grandma Lilly?"

"Yes! Hello, Mehana, how are you?"

"I'm fine. How's the snow out there?"

"Oh, I think we have enough. You probably don't have any there in California."

"No. We still have flowers. And hummingbirds."

"Oh my. And how old are you now, aren't you ten years old?"

"No, I'm twelve now."

"Goodness. And I'm ninety-nine, almost one hundred."

"Wow. My dad said you were our oldest relative. That's partly why I'm calling. See, I'm writing this family history project, and I have some questions. Maybe you want to sit down while I ask them?"

The Poet's Daughter

"I'll just get a cup of coffee. Okay. I'm sitting at the kitchen table now. I'm ready."

"Here's the first question: Where were you born?"

The end.

Konnie Ellis

The Poet's Daughter

With thanks to my grandmother, Bertha Buan, and to my mother, Lilly Haldorsen, for the inspiration of their adventurous and remarkable lives. I have had the good fortune of being able to call my mother when in the middle of a chapter and ask for details, such as about the little beach in Norway where their mother rowed her young family. She told of the treasure box they always brought along, the starfish they collected, and what the sand felt like on their bare feet. Time and again she brought me to the various events in her life. Thank you Mom, for living to be 100! Thank you to my son, Lane Ellis, genealogist and keeper of the family history, for answering so many of my questions, and for your excellent cover photo. Thanks too, to Julie Ahasay for the laptop. I have tried to be true to the family stories in spirit, yet have added my share of creative embellishments. It has been a pleasure to enter their worlds and bring the stories of these immigrants to life. I am grateful to all those who have gone before me.

CPSIA information can be obtained
at www.ICGtesting.com
Printed in the USA
BVHW030301080722
641458BV00006B/523